To
KIKI

Second Chances

Heart Series: Book Two

Abigail Lee Justice

Dare to Test Your
Limits
Abigail Lee Justice
XOXO

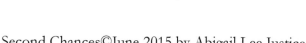

Second Chances©June 2015 by Abigail Lee Justice

Cover design by Robin Ludwig Design Inc.
www.gobookcoverdesign.com

Second Chances

Knowing that happily-ever-afters only happen in fairy tales, Sophie Spencer spends an amazing night with her Prince Charming. Being new to the lifestyle, she allows her hidden fears to take over and does the unthinkable. She screams her safe-word…and runs directly into danger. Will her moment of weakness cause her world to be torn apart again? Or will she overcome her trust issues and fully surrender to her Prince.

Falling in love had been the furthest thing from Kyle Zellar's mind, but when Sophie Spencer fully submits to his dominant demands, his only recourse is to claim her as his. Before he can claim her, he is forced to let her go.

Fighting his inner demons and past issues of childhood abandonment, he knows he must sort out his own life before he can move on with his future.

But will it be too little too late?

~Author's note. This is the second book in The Heart Series, and NOT a stand-alone. You may read them in any order you like, of course, but I would recommend you read Bound By Her Master first.

Acknowledgements

To the very creative and talented wordsmith, Brynna Curry, your calming words during our many phone conversations put my mind at ease night after night after I hung up with you. Without your kind words of encouragements, fine tweaking, and most of all your knowledge of writing and editing, I'm most sure this book would have stayed on my iPad forever without being published. Thank you from the bottom of my heart.

Special thanks goes out to my beta readers, Lisa, Jenn, and slave Tara, without the bantering back and forth, this book would still be locked away in my mind.

To my loving parents, my sons, in-laws, family, friends and especially readers, you all are very near and dear to me. Without all of your guidance and support I wouldn't have become the person I am today. Thank you.

To Orja, when I first read your poem a few years ago, I never dreamed that it would be the final puzzle for reshaping my life. Your words strengthened me. Each day is a new chapter in my amazing journey. Thank you for allowing me to publish "Surrender" in my books.

To my loving husband this book is dedicated to you. Your support these past 30 years together has had its ups and downs, you've always supported me in everything I've ever done and this book was no exception. For sleepless nights, cursing and swearing, crazy computer issues, weekends away from home attending cons and book signings, thank you from the bottom of my slave's heart. SRD: I love you :) PG.

Chapter One

Darkness filled the night, not only in Sophie's mind but within her soul. Ambushed by the feared gang members she had been running from for the past two years, she now lay motionless in Lexi's car, blood oozing from her best friends chest.

Hearing sirens in the distance, Sophie stirred, at that moment she realized she was FUCKED.

Screaming her safe-word was the only thing she could have done to end the best sexual experience she had had in a really long time. *Crash!*

Running on pure fear and adrenalin, she had called her best friend, Lexi, to rescue her from Kyle's home. Feeling trapped, Sophie ran back to the only place she felt safe, her apartment, but they never reached the safety of her home. She tried to sit up, but a blast of pain was too overwhelming, causing darkness to shadow over her world once again.

She came to when someone pressed their finger against her neck. A male voice spoke bringing Sophie out of the darkness.

"Miss, I'm Officer Ferguson with the Baltimore City Police. You've been shot. I need you to stay calm while I assess your injuries. We're waiting on EMTs to arrive. Can you tell me your name?"

She struggled to say her name, "Sophie Spencer."

"Ok, that's great. Now, can you tell me your friend's name?"

Trying to sit up to look over her shoulder, worry and fear hit Sophie as she recalled who was sitting in the seat next to her. Seeing Lexi's lifeless body slumped in the driver's seat brought reality back into focus. "Lexi Blackston."

"My partner, Officer Drake, is assessing her injuries."

Realizing what had happened to them; she tried to turn towards Lexi. Officer Ferguson placed his hand on her shoulder, telling her to "just stay calm."

Not wanting to move a great deal, Sophie turned her head and saw that her friend hadn't moved at all. Tears began to streaming down her checks as the EMTs approached the police officers.

Why is it so hard to take in a deep breath? Fuck this really hurts. She watched as her friend lay perfectly still while the EMTs worked on her. One of the EMTs made his way over to the passenger side of the car. He asked if she was allergic to any medications or if she had any serious medical problems. Sophie tried to take another deep breath, but instead she started to gasp. Struggling to talk, she said, "I'm allergic to penicillin and have had a slight issue with taking morphine."

"Try not to excite yourself, Sophie, while I get your vitals."

He placed a mask over her nose and mouth. She hoped the oxygen would help her breathe better, but as the pain hit her again, so did a wave of nausea. She felt like she was going to puke. Still trying to sit up, a firm hand settled on her left shoulder pressing just hard enough to keep her from moving.

Sophie looked back over at her friend as the EMT placed an IV in her neck. Watching the EMTs work on Lexi as fast as they could, told Sophie her friend must be in bad shape, especially if they had to place a line in her neck.

Finally, they removed Lexi from the driver's side of the car and placed her on a stretcher. Everything seemed to be happening quickly now. Next thing Sophie knew, she too was being taken from the car and placed on a stretcher. Pain struck her again when they pulled her from the car. Struggling now for air, her chest and right lung burned as if they were on fire.

Sophie heard a familiar male voice in the distance. *Bryce.* She watched as he went over to where one of EMTs was working on Lexi. She heard Bryce tell the EMTs who he was. He gave the EMTs important medical history about Lexi. Then he picked up her hand, placed it to his lips, kissing her fingertips, telling her to hang in there, and she didn't have permission to leave him. She needed to be strong and fight to make it through this.

Listening to the words Bryce spoke to Lexi, she heard the strong dominant man reinforce to her friend that he was by her side and wouldn't leave her. Hearing his terms of endearment broke her heart. She had put her best friend's life in jeopardy. Tears burned Sophie's eyes as they fell onto the side of her face. This was all her fault.

Watching the EMTs pack Lexi up and place her in the back of the ambulance, Sophie realized that Lexi's status was grave. Bryce made his way over to Sophie as she let out a loud scream.

At that very moment, the pain had overwhelmed her entire body. She looked up at the stars and tried to take in a deep breath, which was nearly impossible. Bryce reached for Sophie's hand and told her everything was going to be fine, and that she needed to be strong; he would take care of her until he reached Kyle. Her only job was to let the medical staff do their jobs once she reached the hospital. "No fucking around, or pulling rank over the hospital staff, got it Sophie? You're the patient, not the doctor."

Sophie tried to say something back to Bryce but scorching pain radiated throughout her chest. She had no more air. Frantically, she managed to say, "I pushed the emergency button."

Blood came pouring from her mouth and filled the oxygen mask that covered her face. Sophie screamed once more as they placed her in the back of the ambulance. Darkness took over her once again, as the pain seared her insides.

Sophie felt herself drift once again. The ambulance made its way speedily down the dark road. Trying to fight the darkness, she kept saying repeatedly in her head, *Kyle is the man for me. I just got spooked that's all. I have to survive this and tell him I'm sorry for running away from him.*

Several minutes later, she felt the ambulance jerk to a stop. *We've arrived at the hospital.* Keeping herself as calm as possible, breathing into the oxygen mask, making sure she her lungs filled with enough air. The ambulance doors opened to the bright entrance lights of the Emergency Room.

Chapter Two

She had stood on the opposite side of these doors for the past six years while being a Cardio Thoracic Surgeon, now she was being wheeled in as a patient. As they pushed her down the hall, she pictured her parents being happy and having a cookout in their large spacious yard. Her brother and his family were there, as well as Lexi and Bryce. What made her blink twice was envisioning Kyle cooking on the grill. He stood flipping burgers and hot dogs, looking just as handsome as could be. Everyone joked and laughed just like a family should be when together.

Sophie felt a pair of hands cover the wound in her shoulder with gauze. A familiar face approached the side of Sophie's stretcher. Doctor Sanchez, a trauma surgeon, came into sight.

"Sophie we need to access and stabilize your injuries first, you know the drill, and you've said the same thing to enough patients wheeled into the ER. You need to let the team work on you as swiftly as possible, no ifs, ands, or buts coming from you, understand?"

She nodded her head in acceptance.

"Tell me your pain level on a scale of one to ten. I know you haven't had anything for pain yet, which I think is very brave of you. Stop being a brat, and give yourself over to the team. You know the pain is going to become more than what your body can handle and when it does, you're not going to like our options. Surrender to us fully."

Sophie cleared her throat trying to suck in as much oxygen as she could through the mask. "Eight, but what is worrisome is I can't take a deep fucking breath."

"Ok I see on your chart that you had a reaction to morphine after your car accident. Let's get you some dilaudid for the pain. I'll watch you closely as we get some X-rays of your chest and shoulder, then go from there."

Coming to a halt in ER room 5, Sophie had triaged many patients in this very room over the past few years. She began to worry about Lexi, so without hesitation she said, "Dr. Sanchez, my best friend Lexi Blackston was also brought in just before me. She was shot. Can you get me an update on her condition?"

"Sure. Let's get you assessed first, then your pain meds on board. I'll have Nurse Jackie run over get a quick update while Nurse Carol gets your pain meds."

Nurse Jackie asked Sophie, "Is there anyone I can call to let them know you're here?"

Sophie shook her head no. "Bryce Spann is with my friend who was brought in just before me. Don't get him yet." She suddenly realized she was truly alone for the first time in her life. Her parents were still in hiding in the mountains. Carl, her husband, was dead and he definitely couldn't help her, which left Kyle. He hadn't responded to the emergency trigger on her phone.

Sophie looked around the busy room as staff members came in and out. One nurse took her temp, while another cut off her clothes, an IV tech stuck her in her arm, placing an IV. After being the lead Cardio Thoracic Surgeon at the hospital for the past six years, having her colleagues work on her was a little too much to handle.

The burning sensation in Sophie's arm told her the dilaudid was starting to enter her blood stream. Feeling a warm feeling coursing throughout her body reminded Sophie of how she felt after her car accident two years ago. A numb feeling spread from her right shoulder down to her fingertips, then to her entire body.

A radiology tech came in with a portable bedside X-Ray machine. She took multiple X-rays of Sophie's chest, shoulder, neck and head. When everyone was done with his or her duties in the room, only Carol remained at Sophie's bedside. She knew the sedative Dr. Sanchez ordered was working because she no longer felt the burning pain in her shoulder. Her breathing seemed a little easier too.

Lying flat on her back on the stretcher, Sophie looked up at the ceiling. *What the fuck have I gotten myself into?* She made a vow to herself if she made it through this; she would do just about anything to get Kyle back. She would run back to Kyle with the biggest apology she could come up with.

Slowly, Sophie started to fade out of consciousness from the analgesic coursing through her veins.

Dr. Sanchez entered the room holding several X-ray's in her hand, bringing a stool closer to where Sophie laid. Sophie opened her eyes trying to focus on the films Dr. Sanchez held up in the air, but the anesthetic had fully kicked in.

Her colleague pointed out to her where the bullet entered her right shoulder, missing all of the major veins and arteries, but noted multiple shell fragments sitting in her lungs. They would need to go in surgically to remove the fragments from her shoulder and lungs.

Just as Dr. Sanchez finished explaining what was going to happen, another friend and colleague, Dr. Clancy, entered the cubicle. Fear seized her as she walked towards her stretcher. Dr. Clancy was known for her expert skills in plastic surgery.

"Sophie, I need to talk to you about what I found on your films. Dr. Sanchez and I have already reviewed the films together. The bullet exploded in your shoulder; it tore through multiple layers of tissue and muscle. I'm going to take a graft from your hip and thigh to cover up the damaged muscle, but the most important part of the surgery is to get you to retain the use of your hand. I know you're bandaged up so you're completely immobilized and can't feel anything now, but until I get into your shoulder, I won't necessarily know if I can save the use of your hand." At the same time Sophie heard those words, she felt all of the air being sucked out of her lungs.

Not knowing what to do, Sophie let out a loud scream, "You need to save the function of my hand. That's all I have left in this world is my surgical skills, I need both of my hands to do my job." Sobbing uncontrollably, she now wished she had never run from Kyle's house like a child. How could she be so fucking stupid?

The nurse was instructed to give Sophie another dose of dilaudid in her IV to calm her down. Sophie began to shake. Once the medication hit her veins, she relaxed once more. It was amazing how fast the dilaudid worked. It only took a few minutes for Sophie to settle down completely.

"Sophie, I'm going to do everything in my powers to save the function of your hand, but I needed to be up front with you. It's going to be a long recovery, a lot of physical therapy. You'd end up hating me if I didn't fully tell you all the possible outcomes."

Sophie held back her tears; she bottled up everything inside in heart and put on a brave face. "Gail, I understand fully."

Her friend and college, Dr. Sanchez reached her hand out, placed it onto Sophie's left shoulder, and said, "Sophie, you know we're going to do everything possible to get you back up to full speed. The OR is ready; we need to get you down there ASAP. You sure you don't want us to call your parents for you or even a friend?"

Sophie took a deep breath in, trying to fill her lungs with oxygen. "Can you tell me what the status on my friend Lexi? Did she ever regain consciousness?"

"Yes, she did. She even asked about you, just before Dr. Grant took her back to the OR. Looks like she'll be out of surgery in another hour or so."

Sophie closed her eyes, saying a quick prayer for Lexi to make it out of surgery safely. Blinking back the tears she asked, "Is Bryce Spann, Lexi's boyfriend, out in the waiting room?"

"I think he's making some calls to Lexi's family."

"I need to talk to him. Get him for me please." Dr. Sanchez quietly asked Nurse Carol to go and get Bryce. Both doctors turned back to Sophie, each one reassuring her and making small talk until Bryce entered the room.

"We'll leave the two of you alone for just a few minutes." As they left the room, Bryce took the stool that Dr. Sanchez vacated and scooted it closer to Sophie's bed. She pulled the sheet covering her body with her left arm and tried not to flinch from the pain.

"Bryce, I'm so sorry. I fucked up big time." Not wanting to say anything else because it took everything within Sophie's power not to break down in front of him.

She could see that he was worried. It was written all over his face. She felt the tension between the two of them. Taking Sophie's left hand into his, Bryce slowly caressed the tops of Sophie's knuckles.

Finally, what seemed like an eternity Bryce broke the silence between him and Sophie. "Sophie, I'm not mad at you at all. I just wished you would have stayed put at Kyle's house and talked about what caused you to run like you did. He was devastated when you left. He doesn't know what caused you to safe-word on him and he's confused to say the least. I'm sure the two of you will work things out. Relationships take time to build, especially a power exchange relationship."

Looking directly into Bryce's eyes, Sophie knew he spoke the truth.

"What's most important now is both you and Lexi make a speedy recovery, and in a few years we can look back on this as a memory and not a tragedy."

Feeling overwhelmed with guilt, Sophie quietly asked, "Any word on Lexi yet?"

"No. The OR nurse called just before I came back here with you and said everything was going smoothly. She should be out of surgery in about an hour."

The expression on his face showed a little glimmer of hope. "Oh God Bryce, I fucked up again."

"Yeah you did, Sophie, but people make mistakes."

"I'm so glad to hear that she's going to be all right. I couldn't live with myself if she died." Yep, the second injection of medication was working. Sophie began to struggle to keep her eyes open and her words seemed to be slurred. She dozed off for just a few minutes as Bryce held her hand. Bryce told her to try to sleep until they came to take her back to the operating room. He would stay with her. He wouldn't leave her side. Feeling secure enough to let her guard down, she drifted off.

What seemed like hours had only been a few minutes when an orderly came into her room. She felt Bryce squeeze her hand as the orderly took Sophie's chart and placed it on the stretcher alongside of her head. Sophie slowly opened her eyes and looked around the room, trying to get her bearings. The orderly told Sophie, he was her taxi driver to dream land.

She started to sit up and realized she didn't have the strength to pull herself up. The pain scorched her insides as she tried to shift just slightly. Bryce tried to settle her down as best as he could.

He spoke in a dominant voice. "Lay still until they get you in the operating room. You know the drill. You need to cooperate. That's an order, sub." Bryce had never used the word sub with her, which told her his dominance was bleeding from his pores.

Fear and guilt weighed heavily on Sophie's conscious, not knowing what was going to be the outcome of surgery. She felt her heart beating extremely fast when she thought about her future. *Would she be able to practice medicine, would she be crippled, would she be alone for the rest of her life?* Things just started flashing through her mind. *Would her best friend hate her for putting her life in jeopardy? But the big question was how she was ever going to face Kyle again.* Trying not to hyperventilate, Sophie took deep shallow breaths in, remembering her yoga instructor in college as she tried to reenter her thoughts. Reaching her peak anxiety level before breaking into a thousand pieces, Sophie asked Bryce if she could use his phone to call Kyle.

Bryce hit the preset button for Kyle's number and handed it to Sophie. She took hold of the phone as it started to ring, instantly the phone went directly to Kyle's voice mail. Not wanting to sound disturbed or panicky Sophie began speaking. "Kyle, I'm so sorry for running away tonight. Please forgive me. I know I screwed up big time. I really do need you. I'm scared of not knowing what my future will hold. Please forgive me." Sophie began to breath heavy again.

Exerting herself was the last thing she needed to do, but at this point, she had nothing else left. She had to face reality. She was either going to wake up from surgery a wounded, single injured women, or she would have the man she was falling in love with by her side. Sophie's last words that escaped from her weary voice were: "I love you, Kyle." The pain overwhelming, she had been brave for just as long as her body would let her. As the last word slipped from her tongue, her eyes drifted shut, the cell phone dropped to her side, as she passed out from the exhaustion.

Chapter Three

Sitting in his private Lear jet on the tarmac at Martin State Airport, Kyle waited impatiently for takeoff. He thought back on the events that led him to tonight. Sophie had gracefully submitted to him without any hesitations.

She had fully surrendered to his every will, desire and command. Sophie had expressed her love of him, the Shibari type bondage, everything sexual Kyle had done to her. Plus she had conveyed to him that she couldn't wait for more. The sex was just off the Richter scale; not having been with a woman sexually for the past year had super-charged his male libido. The energy released from her body was spiritually lifting to him.

Thinking about the hot sex, he realized his slip. *Damn no condom had been used between us.* It was the first time he hadn't gloved up. Could he have just started the next generation of little Zellars? God he hoped so.

What could have caused her to safe-word and not want to discuss her feelings with him? Even though he had cautiously gone over the protocol with her, she still ran, she didn't follow protocol. His primal instinct kicked in as she abruptly shut down in front of him. He wanted nothing more than to grab her, tie her down to his bed and never ever let her leave, but he knew he couldn't forcibly hold Sophie under the duress that she was showing. So instead, he let her walk out on him, praying silently that she would find her way back to him soon. Or, he was going to pull out all of his Dom tricks to win her back.

Suddenly, Kyle heard his team entering the plane. He had asked Jake Snyder his head of security to stay home and watch over Sophie while he was out of the country. He needed to find answers to his question of why his father had abandoned him and his family so many years ago.

Billy Jones was one of the first of his security team to come over to Kyle to greet him. Stanley Citrus, the second man on Kyle's team, sauntered over with a half asleep look on his face. "I have half a mind to kick your ass for disrupting my cuddling session with my very pregnant wife."

Kyle just brushed off the negative words.

"She was a little pissed to say the least. What's so important that it couldn't wait until tomorrow morning?"

Having a mental picture in his head of Sophie all round and fat filled with a child in her belly made Kyle smile just a little. "Nice to see you too, Citrus." He handed both Billy and Stanley a folder. They opened the folders finding inside classified documents pertaining to Daniel Zeller aka Matthew Hendricks, otherwise known as Kyle's father. Multiple recent photos, his current passports, and several different overseas bank account sheets lined each of the men's folders.

Master Sergeant appeared from the back of the jet with his folder in his hand. All four men knew each other. They had been on many missions together. Taking Kyle's private jet wasn't something new for any of them; it just made their traveling easier and faster. That was one of the perks of being rich as fuck. Once the men were seated, Kyle knew it was time to update the team why this mission was near and dear to his heart.

Breaking up the silence, Darlene, their normal flight attendant, and a cute little submissive, asked each guy to buckle up and prepare for takeoff. She didn't go through the usual take off procedures, each person had taken multiple flights during their employment by Volkov Security. No need for formalities during this flight either. Plus it was in the middle of the fricking night.

Captain Jackson Terrance came over the PA system informing everyone to prepare for takeoff. Jackson, the eldest of Kyle's cousins was the best pilot he had on his team. Not just because he was family, but also because he was one badass motherfucker. Fear of landing his plane in unfriendly territory was not only challenging, but also exhilarating for the ex-Army pilot.

Both Jackson and Kyle had grown very close as young boys. A horrible car accident claimed the life of both of Jackson's parents. Orphaned after his parents' death, Jackson and his three brothers were raised by Elsie and Horace Zellar, Kyle's grandparents.

All four boys were raised under the same roof. Kyle often confided his darkest fears about his father's mysterious disappearance with Jackson. Jackson did the same with Kyle about the death of his parents. The two would reminisce over how different each of their lives would be if they'd had father figures steering them into manhood.

Being rough and tough boys growing up, Jackson and Kyle were constantly trying to out do each other, especially with women. Pulling pranks on one another wasn't out of the ordinary when all of the Terrance and Zellar clan got together.

Kyle took his phone out one final time, looked at the display. No messages or texts from Sophie. He quietly turned his phone to airplane mode. As many times Kyle had flown in the past with the military and for his personal business ventures, he still hated the feeling of being helpless during a flight. Normally, he would have a stiff drink and chill until his final destination. No, not on this flight, too much was at stake for Kyle.

Trying not to dwell on the reason why Sophie had yelled her safe-word then fled from his house, Kyle had to stay focused on finding his father, but the Dom in him was determined to get to the bottom of her emotional departure.

Kyle's alpha male traits bleed from his soul, when giving out orders. He needed to make sure each guy knew their particular role in finding his estranged father. Drilling each man for the next few hours, trying to eat up flight time to Ceiba, Puerto Rico was the mission at hand.

Kyle remembered during his childhood his father took several business trips a year to Puerto Rico, where he owned several pharmaceutical companies. Carmela, the Zellar's live-in nanny, would always travel with them on trips. Kyle was the oldest, Derek was the middle child and Piper was the baby of the Zellar children; each child had a special bond with Carmela. She lived with them up until his father's disappearance. Kyle often wondered if his father and Carmela were having a fling. He saw Carmela more with his father then his mother.

Many times, Carmela would accompany Mr. Zellar as his personal translator when conducting business in Puerto Rico. Even though Daniel Zellar spoke fluently in Spanish and French. he still managed to have Carmela by his side at all times. Never had Kyle heard his own mother complain about Carmela being so attached to their father, or her children because Carmela was considered part of the family, not an employee.

Remembering the past, reminded Kyle of what his family life had been while growing up as a child. Yes, he was a happy toddler, always in the presence of two loving parents. It was only when Kyle turned six years old his father wasn't in the country for his birthday party. He was suddenly called away to deal with a hostile takeover at one of his pharmaceutical facilities in Puerto Rico. Looking back now, Kyle could pin point his father's attitude changing around his mother.

Kyle looked through his file folder when suddenly he felt his heart skipped a beat, was it being on a flight, getting ready to come face to face with his father after all these years, or was his emotions coming to a head?

Kyle knew the flight was just about to land in Ceiba, Puerto Rico. He excused himself to go use the bathroom facility in the private quarters of the jet. Stepping into the master bedroom, Kyle looked around at the perfectly made king-size bed. He envisioned Sophie curled up under the comforter, snuggling up against her on their way to a private Caribbean Island getaway. *DAMN she would look beautiful all curled up under the comforter.*

Bringing himself back to reality, Kyle had to finish his mission: find his father first, then he would high tail it back to Baltimore and win his girl back into his arms.

Splashing cold water onto his cheeks, feeling the water running down the side of his face, looking into the mirror, he saw the lack of desire shining across his eyes. *I must begin to make a difference in Sophie's life, I need her in my life to make myself complete.*

Over the overhead speaker, he heard the captain say, "prepare for landing."

Walking back to his seat, Kyle looked down to where his watch snugly wrapped around his wrist. He had received the watch from his grandfather for his high school graduation. It was one of the only things he remembered his father wearing on his arm.

It had been exactly five hours since Sophie walked out on him. It was 4:00 a.m. back in Baltimore and 5:00 a.m. in Ceiba, Puerto Rico. Kyle had planned to be in Puerto Rico only a few hours. His motto…get in, get the job done, and have his plane back in the air by lunch. If he needed more time he would reschedule another trip next week sometime after he settled things with Sophie. Everything felt like a blur. One sure thing resonated with him; once his confutation with his father was over he was high tailing it back to Baltimore and getting his girl.

Taking his seat, feeling the airplane slowly starting to descend, Kyle buckled his seat belt. He looked out the small window, the sky was still dark, and the sun hadn't started to rise yet. Everything was still and calm from what he could see. The downtown business area of Puerto Rico hadn't woken up yet, which made his surprise visit to his father's estate even more chilling.

As soon as the plane touched down, the captain announced, "once we're cleared by the Puerto Rican government, everyone will be free to depart the plane; should only take a few minutes." Kyle pulled out his cell phone from his pants pocket and gently turned off the airplane mode. As soon as his phone regenerated, his emergency GPS started beeping like fucking crazy. Several text messages came across the screen from Bryce. Six voice messages.

"What the FUCK!" Kyle shouted.

Bryce: Time: 1:35 a.m.: Kyle, EMERGENCY heading to Sophie's apartment building, EMERGENCY GPS TRIGGERED.

Bryce: Time: 1:48 a.m.: Sophie and Lexi have been shot. Heading to Mount Seton Hospital, doesn't look good, MAN!!! Will update once at hospital.

Bryce: Time: 2:25 a.m.: Sophie heading into surgery, trying to save her arm. She's stable for now. Lexi took a bullet to the chest, in surgery; Doc says it will be hours before we know anything. Get your ASS back here NOW!

Kyle took a deep breath, raked his hands through his hair. Thinking to himself as he listened to his voice mail, suddenly hearing Bryce's voice made him feel queasy.

As soon as he finished listening to the first voice mail, he hit the next one, which happened to be from Jake Snyder his right hand man, telling him that Sophie and Lexi had been ambushed in the parking lot of Sophie's apartment building. He was already viewing the surveillance footage trying to get a jump on who could have done this to the girls.

The final message came up Bryce's number. Kyle hit the listen button on his phone. He heard Sophie's weak, strained voice. "Kyle I'm so sorry for running away tonight, please forgive me. I know…. I screwed up big time. I really do need you. I'm scared of not knowing what my future will hold. Please… forgive me." He heard her take a deep breath, and she then spoke her last four words to him, "I love you, Kyle." Kyle had to blink back the tears that were forming in his eyes, just from hearing her sickly voice.

He had done the same thing that Sophie had done. He ran from the situation with Sophie too. *What had he been thinking, he should have stayed put, gone after Sophie with fire and gusto, but no, he jumped on a plane to track down his missing father. How was that showing his dominance? He couldn't even protect the woman he loved.* If he had stayed put in Baltimore until he had things settled with her, he wouldn't be in putting himself and his team members in possible danger, by tracking down his father.

Pulling himself back to reality, he hit the speed dial for Bryce on his phone.

Kyle's heart began to race while he waited patiently for Bryce to answer his call. Signaling to his team members to give him a minute, Kyle listened to the voice message on Bryce's phone.

That wasn't the response Kyle needed at this moment. Without a second thought, Kyle dialed Jake's number, and

Jake answered on the first ring. Kyle's voice was shaky when he asked Jake to bring him up to speed on everything he knew about Sophie. The two talked back and forth. Kyle was given a full update on exactly what had happened to the two girls. Not wanting to waist anymore time, he informed Jake he was aborting the mission in Puerto Rico and would be back in Baltimore in four hours. Kyle instructed Jake to have a car at the tarmac waiting for him.

He abruptly ended the call, when his cell beeped with an incoming call. Wasting no time, he punched the green phone key, hearing Bryce's voice on the other end of the phone sent shivers up and down Kyle spine, needing to hear what Bryce had to tell him was the most worrisome Kyle had ever felt. Even worse than when his father up and left. Kyle never truly understood, he never feared not ever having a father in his life; he only feared what he would do when he finally came face to face with him. That would have to wait. What was most important to him now was Sophie. He needed to get to her ASAP.

Signaling to his team, everyone circled around Kyle. He informed everyone about the situation back in Baltimore when the Captain interrupted their conversation, he gave the all clear signal over the loud speaker. Kyle never let his emotions show; he had the look of a soldier ready for battle on his face. Kyle always felt it was better to face challenges head on. His current issue about his father was just going to have to wait.

Kyle politely excused himself from the group to go speak directly to his cousin. Kyle knew Jackson would do everything in his power to get then back up in the air. Jackson requested an immediate flight plan change. Originally, the flight plan that had been submitted was for a return flight sometime later on Thursday, but with the new emergency back in Baltimore, it was imperative for Kyle to return immediately. Jackson began speaking into his microphone attached to his head, working out the flight information with Air Traffic Controllers, being refueled, and last minute details.

Kyle made his way back to where everyone else was chatting; he reported that it was only going to be a short while until the plane was re-cleared for their return flight back home. He told them to make any calls or check their emails while they still had service. Knowing that once they were back in the air, all communication methods would be cut off.

Pulling out his own cell phone, Kyle looked for any more texts or emails from his team back in Baltimore. No news was good news as far as Kyle figured; he scrolled through his photos looking for the photo he had taken of Sophie while lounging out at the pond on Sunday. She had the most perfect twinkle in her eyes, making them look like stars. Kyle quickly texted a message to Sophie's cell.

> Kyle: Baby, I'm on my way…hang in there. I'm going to take care of everything. Just don't you dare leave me again. I LOVE YOU SOPHIE. :)

As soon as he sent the text, Jackson walked into the open cabin area and told everyone they would be ready for takeoff in under ten minutes or so. Kyle had a look of desperation on his face when Jackson made his way over to him.

"Look Bro, I'll have you back on the ground in Baltimore in less than three hours. Why don't you take a quick nap, that way when you get to the hospital you'll be able to deal with the situation, without being jet lagged?

Kyle let out a huge sigh. His cousin was right in saying he needed to be on his top game when he saw her for the first time. Nodding his head in acceptance, Kyle shook Jackson's hand. "Thanks man, I appreciate you doing this for me."

"I'll have Stacy turn down the sheets for you, and bring you a glass of Glenkinchie to help ease you into a nice sleep."

Kyle let the team know that he was going to retire in the bedroom for a little while. He knew it would only be a few more hours until he was able to hold his Sophie in his arms. She would need all of his strength while recovering. He owed it to her to be at his best. Kyle took the cup of Scotch and swirled it back and forth in the glass, causing the amber color to splash around in the glass, he gazed at it as if hoping to find an answer within.

Once his girl was all healed, he would take matters in his own hands. Trust, honesty, and integrity were three key points that made up all power exchange relationships. Hell, even vanilla relationships have the same basic principles. He knew exactly what needed to be done, and if they were going to have any type of future, he was going to show his dominant side. Her ass would be red for at least a week if not more, when he was done with her. She knew the rules and chose to break rule number one TRUST. What was even worse, she had failed to communicate her feelings to Kyle.

Chapter Four

Sophie slowly woke up from her fairy tale sleep, feeling as if her body was being held in bondage. This wasn't 'sort of' bondage, it was bondage and it didn't feel like the Shibari Japanese bondage she'd experienced with Kyle.

Wearily, she opened her eyes to find that she was indeed strapped down to a hospital bed. It took a few seconds for her eyes to focus. She searched around the room, finally recognizing the surroundings of a hospital room. No, not just any hospital room, but what looked like the ICU. *DAMN why was she in the ICU?*

Monitors were beeping all around her. Still struggling to free herself from the straps, Sophie called out, "Please will someone help me?"

A redheaded woman sat at the foot of Sophie's bed. Trying to force her eyes to focus on the woman, Sophie began to struggle against her bonds. Not having enough strength to free herself, she began to panic. The nurse came into view; unfortunately, Sophie had no clue who she was. *Why was that? She knew every nurse in the ICU.*

"Now, now, dear, you need to stay calm. Don't twist yourself all around."

Sophie still didn't recognize the nurse. She could barely get her eyes to focus on the woman's badge. "I need to check you, now that you're waking up. I hope that you haven't done too much damage to your surgical sites. You've given all of us a time dealing with your violent reactions."

Where the hell did this crazy nurse come from? Shit I must be trapped in a crazy ass dream.

"Why am I restrained like a prisoner?"

"For safety reasons. We felt it was better to restrain you so that you didn't do more damage to yourself or possibly injure one of the staff members." The big, burly nurse said with a look of pleasure on her face. "I had you restrained."

Feeling ashamed, Sophie didn't know how to react to the nurse's words. She just lay motionless and let the nurse do her job.

Sophie had only been awake for a few minutes when she recognized, Gail, her friend, coming over to her bedside. "Well missy, you gave us all a pretty nice scare."

"I don't know what you mean." Looking more awake, Sophie swallowed several times. Her mouth was so dry; she had no saliva to even wet her lips, it felt as dry as the Sierra Desert.

Tubes were shoved up her nose, in her arm, and coming out of her cooch. Her blood pressure was being monitored, so was her oxygen. None of this was new to Sophie; she saw this kind of stuff every day.

Gail reached over to the side table for a cup which held a sponge on a stick; she began swabbing Sophie's lips with the liquid from the sponge.

Taking a deep breath in, Sophie took her tongue and ran it along her upper lip to move the moisture all around, closing her eyes she willed herself into total submission. She remembered Bryce's final words to her. Let the hospital do what they had to do to her without fighting them. Surrender all possible cares, worries and fears over to someone else.

Her breathing and pulse slowed as she settled herself down. Giving her power over to the medical staff taking care of her, remembering the way Kyle's voice eased her mind with her parent's this was no different; she just had to submit. And so she did.

Fearing what had happened while she was in surgery, Sophie had to ask the burning question that was now on her mind, "Gail, can you tell me if my friend Lexi is ok?" Gail, without any hesitation and giving a little smirk responded, "Lexi most likely will be discharged sometime later today.

She'll recover fully from her gunshot wound. You on the other hand will be stuck with us for a few more days. The big challenge for you is to get you out of the ICU, maybe later today. Aren't you going to ask who's been more demanding on the ICU staff then you?" Gail gave Sophie an evil look.

"Mmm is Kyle here?"

"Oh yes, he's here. Let's just say he hasn't left the hospital in three days.

He's stayed outside of the ICU like a watchdog. He would come back during normal visiting times, stay as long as we let him, and then return to the waiting room.

You must be really important to him; because he had me pull a few strings to have a few nurses take care of you. It's a wonder that I'm still taking care of you, but since I've known Kyle my whole life, that wasn't going to happen."

"Oh, Gail, I'm so sorry to have caused such a ruckus around here." Feeling a little drowsy, she started to nod off again.

Gail placed her hand on the side of Sophie's cheek.

"No need to worry. He'll be glad that you're finally starting to come around. I think I might be able to sneak him back before the next visiting time starts. Just get a few more minutes of rest while the nurses check you over one more time, and I'll send for Kyle.

Kyle paced back and forth. Since early last Thursday morning, he'd returned from Puerto Rico with a different outlook on life. Instead of driving back to his house, Kyle had his driver take him straight to the hospital. The only other option was having his jet land directly at the hospital but he couldn't pull that many strings. Not even money could persuade the higher ups to grant permission for his private jet to make an emergency landing.

Driving everyone just a bit crazy, Kyle continued to pace.

Jake picked up Sophie's parents on Thursday evening after they had been holed up at Kyle's family cabin in the mountains. He had informed Sophie's parents of her injuries. Something he truly didn't want to do, but he felt they both needed to know Sophie's medical condition from him, not anyone else.

Everyone gathered and waited in the family waiting area. Sophie's brother Joseph had flown in while the rest of his family stayed back in Ohio. Laura, Sophie's younger sister, even made the trip up from Florida.

Several members from Carl's family waited in the family waiting area keeping vigil. Family members had their time going back to visit Sophie while she was in the ICU unconscious.

Kyle's family members had made many trips to the hospital to check in on Sophie's condition. His brother brought over several sets of fresh, clean clothes and toiletries for Kyle. Since he had graciously donated to the hospital in the last few years, he was given a room to freshen up, or to take a catnaps, which he never did.

He refused to leave the hospital while Sophie remained in the ICU.

Again, Kyle's money came in handy by hiring three nurses designated to Sophie's care. Using his powers to get extra special care for his Sophie was his number one priority. Even though Gail and Sophie had been friends and colleagues for years, Kyle knew her in a different way.

Gail was a member of his BDSM club, one of the first members. Gail understood the need for Kyle to show his dominance when it came to taking care of Sophie and went out of her way to make sure Sophie had someone at her bedside twenty-four-seven.

Kyle had gotten to know Sophie's parents, Josie and Coston Spencer, on a more personal level while waiting for visitation. Kyle already knew Coston Spencer from Volkov Security, but never had the father/son connection that he had formed in the past few days. Kyle made sure that Sophie's parents were protected when leaving the hospital nightly. They would soon be family and he wasn't going to let anything happen to them.

Seeing Gail go back into the ICU, stirred up Kyle's anticipation. Maybe Sophie was finally making a turn for the good. They had gotten several false hopes during the past few days. Only to be told that Sophie experienced another setback. Kyle sat down in a chair holding his head, patiently waiting for word from Gail that Sophie was ok.

Sophie you need to come out of this, baby. I need you more than you could know. We have so much to look forward too. My life isn't complete without you.

The long wait was taking its toll on Kyle. He had bags under his eyes. He hadn't eaten a whole lot, just barely enough to keep his strength up. Candy had brought food over for everyone waiting.

She knew Kyle would sit vigil over Sophie just as he had done for her when she had been brutally beaten by her ex-DOM last year; Kyle was so pre-occupied he'd forget to eat, but he made sure everyone else did, including Sophie's family. Living off coffee was about the only thing that seemed to keep him going, pure caffeine.

Gail came out of the ICU. She too looked tired, and she hadn't left Sophie for less than four hours at a time, only to get a nap in the doctor's lounge occasionally. Gail strolled over to where Kyle sat. He couldn't read Gail's facial expression; she was a stern dominant and it showed not only in the lifestyle but also in her job. She was damn good at both.

Kyle needed her to be honest and up front with him about Sophie's condition. DOM to DOM.

Kyle met her half way across the room. Sophie's parents joined him. "What's the matter? Has she had another setback?" Sophie's mother grabbed his hand as they waited patiently for Gail to give them an update.

"No, No Kyle she's actually awake. She's not fidgeting around, or even fighting her restraints anymore. She's much calmer now than she was yesterday. I think the extra day has given her some needed rest and strength."

Sighing a breath of relief, Kyle ran his hands through his hair. *Thank you, God; I knew you could pull her through this. I never doubted you in the least.* "When can I go back and see her?"

"I think we can arrange for a very brief visit. As long as you don't upset her."

"What about Sophie's parents; can they go back too?

"I think she needs to see you first then we can get her parents back. Hopefully, if she does well, we can think about moving her from the ICU to a more private room."

"She hasn't asked about her injuries yet. I'm going to have to tell her, but I think she needs to see you first."

"Agreed. I just need to let her know that I'm here for her." He was a little anxious to say the least, but he had to show Sophie that she meant the world to him.

Time would heal her wounds, but was she ready to take the next step in her life, with him.

She was everything he'd ever dreamed of in a woman. She had strength and courage that he hadn't seen in a woman before. She was not afraid of challenge or to surrender, a woman of kindness and passion. A woman so beautiful inside and out. She could fill every day with wonder and joy for the rest of his life. She was that and more in every way. He had to make her see that he was the man, Dom, and Master of her life.

Anticipation built inside of Sophie's chest, as she waited to see Kyle. Taking another set of vitals, nurse Orja asked Sophie if she would like a fresh warm blanket. Nodding her head just slightly, Sophie suddenly felt she needed to be warmed, it wasn't from a blanket, and she needed inner body warmth from human touch.

Just as she started to get comfortable, she closed her eyes and drifted back off to sleep.

Hearing the sound of metal sliding, she suddenly woke up from her brief nap. Slowly opening her eyes, she saw the only person who could comfort her…Kyle.

Feeling his presence in the room sent tiny goose bumps up and down Sophie's restrained arm. Tears started to trickle down her cheeks, feeling the sudden emotions all bundled up inside of her heart; she had nowhere to run to, or hide, except to Kyle.

She looked at him as if she were a lost child. Her long lashes fluttered open as she was about to speak, when Kyle placed his index finger over her mouth.

"Shhh baby, I don't want you upsetting yourself and getting me kicked out so fast."

Sophie lightly nodded her head in acceptance of Kyle's words. By the look on her face, the mental wall she had when she walked out on Kyle, a few days ago was now lifted.

"I just want you to lay there and heal. We have forever to talk about what happened but for now, I just needed to make sure you're okay."

Thinking back to when she walked out on Kyle, she knew she had made one of the biggest mistakes of her life. She would have to deal with that for the rest of her life.

"What day is it? Did I miss the awards banquet?" Remembering she had left Kyle's place late on Wednesday night, she didn't know what day it was now. "It's Monday afternoon, you've been sedated since last Thursday."

Fear gripped her. "Why was I sedated for so long?"

"Your injuries were life threatening. You became combative when you first woke up, so Gail decided to sedate you to allow for more healing time. So that brings us to today... Monday."

Shaking her head made Sophie just a little bit dizzy, trying to focus in on Kyle's words also made her realize that the surgery was not a success.

Thinking that her surgical career was most likely over, tears streamed down her face. In his most stern Dom voice, "I will have none of that, Sophie, your job is to submit and heal."

Chapter Five

Feeling like she might not be able to shake her emotions, Sophie did what most people would do, she asked Kyle to hold her as she cried, and she knew that her past indiscretion of running from Kyle had to come up at some point, but she didn't want the warmth of his body to go away. Sophie sighed, as she felt the guilt roll off her shoulders. Kyle held her tight in his massive arms. He held her as she cried; stroking the top of her head calmed all of Sophie's fears. Several minutes passed before either of them said a single word. All that could be heard in the room was the sounds of the beeps coming from the lifesaving machines and Sophie's sobbing.

Pulling slightly out of Kyle's warm clutches, Sophie had tears and snot streaming down her face. Imagining what she must look like, she didn't want Kyle seeing her like this. What was most startling to Sophie was that she couldn't even use her good arm to wipe her face or nose because it was still being held in restraints.

She was going to need to depend on someone else for the time being to help her through the roughest time of her life. *Hopefully, Kyle would be her right and left hand during her time of need.*

Always being very independent for the past two years since the death of her husband, Sophie had no other choice.

She had to ask for help. Looking into Kyle's big bright blue eyes, Sophie let the words flow freely from her mouth. Something about Kyle's demeanor had changed in the past few days. Sophie wasn't sure what it was but she did feel more comfortable with him than she did before she departed his company last Wednesday night.

Without hesitation, Sophie did the unthinkable. "Kyle I need you, to wipe my face please?"

Asking for help took everything inside of her. She wasn't used to asking for help. Instead, she always did things on her own. Giving up the reigns to the man she was falling in love with was a huge step in her submission to him. Yep, she finally had admitted it to herself. *She was falling in love with Kyle.*

Nothing felt better than having him take care of her needs. The truth be told, it felt fucking amazing having Kyle take care of her. A weight had been lifted off Sophie's shoulders. She closed her eyes as he wiped her face with a warm, damp cloth.

He wiped her face, then she suddenly felt him, lean forward, kissing her tenderly with his mouth. His kiss seemed to go deep into Sophie's soul, claiming her as he had done before. Melting into his kiss brought back feelings of when he first kissed her at The Cellar.

Unfortunately, Kyle's kiss was interrupted by Gail. She had come back to check in on Sophie and when she saw the two kissing, made a loud noise, as if clearing her throat. Gail politely came in on the opposite side of the bed with her stethoscope in hand.

Breaking off the passionate kiss and taking away the warmth he had just given her. Sophie felt loved and protected. Was this the Dom side of Kyle? If it was, she surely loved the way he was making her feel.

What flashed into her mind was the way Kyle made love to her. He had taken charge of the entire night as she surrendered to him.

"Your parents are outside in the waiting area." Kyle told Sophie. "Would you like for them to come back now?"

"I think I need to talk to Gail first. I was too afraid to ask her what the extent of my injuries were. Now that I have you back here with me, I need for you to hear what she has to say to us together."

"Baby, I'm not leaving you alone ever again. These past few days I've done nothing but prayed to get you back. Now that you're awake, I'm not ever leaving your side. Seeing you restrained just about killed me. I'm the only one who will ever have that hold over you." The Dom in Kyle was definitely showing.

Scared to hear what Gail had to say, Sophie turned to Kyle and mouthed the words thank you. Before Gail began to tell Sophie about her injuries, and what it was going to take for her to recover, Sophie politely asked Gail to remove the restraints from her left arm. Being in someone else's restraints was not helping the current situation.

"Before I remove the restraint from your left arm, I need for you not to move at all with your right arm. Do I make myself clear, Sophie; we have stabilized you this way for a reason.

Gail wasn't going to take any chances of Sophie screwing up the surgery she and Dr. Clancy had done to repair the gunshot wound.

"Gail you have my word. Sophie is not going to lift a finger until she is told to do so. That's an order I will personally make her follow." Kyle gave Sophie a grimacing look as she nodded her head in acceptance.

Feeling the restraints being removed, Sophie felt a huge weight being removed from her. "I was starting to feel a little claustrophobic with just that little bit of restraint." Sophie said to Gail hoping Kyle didn't get the wrong idea about future bondage on her when she was all healed.

"Now that we have that removed, are you sure you don't want to see your parents first? Then I can give you a full medical update. I need your visit with your parents to be brief."

Starting to think about why Gail was stalling, Sophie looked over at Kyle, he had moved off to the side while Gail removed her restraints. Giving him the saddest face she could, Sophie asked Kyle to come back closer to the bed.

I need you more than ever. Please don't leave me alone. "As long as Kyle stays with me you can send my mom in first."

Both Kyle and Sophie watched Gail walked out of the ICU to retrieve Sophie's mother.

Minutes later, seeing her mom for the first time in over a week brought back memories of the last time she had spoken to her mother. Not a really good memory for Sophie to remember. Kyle had arranged for her parents to hide out at his mountain house while he tried to find out who was threatening Sophie. Not a good memory at all.

Josie looked tired. The circles under her eyes told Sophie her mother had been worried. Sophie never liked for anyone to be worried about her; she liked to be the one who worried about them.

Guilt, remorse and a feeling of total let-down was written all over Sophie's face and her mother could see that in Sophie's eyes. Feeling her mother stroke the side of her head, instantly squelched those horrible feelings Sophie was harboring deep down.

Niceties were exchanged between the two women before Josie lashed out at her. "Honey, I'm your mother. I wish you would have come to me months ago when you first were being stalked, your father could have assigned some of the security people from Volkov Security to protect you, darling."

"I know mom, I just didn't think it through, that's all."

Josie didn't hold back, and laid into Sophie with her vile tongue. Her words pierced Sophie's heart, just like she had always done in the past.

The bile in her stomach started to churn. She felt like she might get sick.

"I assure you, Sophie is good hands now. Mrs. Spencer, would you mind sending in Coston for a brief visit?"

Her mom might go on for hours about how upset she was for not contacting her family for help or support and she didn't need that lecture at this very moment. "Mom, I know you and dad love me very much. I should have said something but I didn't. We need to move on from this. Agreed?"

"Agreed, for now." Josie kissed Sophie on her head, turned and walked out of the room.

Kyle rushed to the head of the bed. She wondered if she was starting to look a little green.

"Baby, what can I do for you?" Hearing the words escape from his lips calmed Sophie down enough that her stomach seemed to settle down. "Just having you by my side is enough for now. I knew seeing my mom was going to be tough. She's pissed and worried, but I never realized how old she looked until she walked in."

"Sophie, do you realize your family has been worried sick to death over what has happened to you? You can't begin to believe how many other people in the past week have come to sit with your parents.

You're loved by so many. Sometimes it takes almost losing someone, before that person realizes how important they really are. I hope that you'll see what everyone has gone through and I hope you understand how important you are to everyone. Especially to your parents."

In his most stern DOM voice Kyle said, "You owe me two sets of punishments. We're going to talk about the repercussions, Sophie... but not tonight. I aim to collect my debt when you are able to understand the reasons behind punishments."

A tingling of excitement bloomed deep down in her heart. Grasping at what Kyle just proclaimed. He still wanted her. "I never meant for any of this to happen. You must believe me when I say that, Kyle. I was mad at you, when I ran from your house; never did I think I would put Lexi or myself in harm's way."

"Let it go for tonight, Pet. I promise you. We'll revisit your indiscretion as soon as you're fit."

Tears streamed down Sophie's face, as she heard her father enter. Just feeling his presence in the room, Sophie finally let her pent up emotions go. She wept for what seemed liked forever. Kyle wiped away her wet face and cheeks, he then held a tissue to her nose and said, "Blow." Coston Spencer never looked a day over fifty, but in reality, he was going to turn sixty-five in a month.

Coming to Sophie's bedside, Coston stroked his daughter's leg in a soothing fatherly manner. Sophie slowed her breathing down as soon as she felt the warmth of his hand.

Having two men again in her life to take care of had definitely had a different effect. She felt wanted and loved. Her father stood by her side after the fatal car accident that took her husband's life a little over two years ago.

Coston had been Sophie's support and life line at that time. Even though she had always been close to her parents, it was her father's kind words and soothing touch that always seemed to center Sophie when she was at her worst.

Feeling or being in pain had never affected Sophie until after the horrible car accident; her left kneecap had been crushed which required multiple surgeries, several months of rehab, and heavy dosages of painkillers.

Her father was her chauffeur to and from her doctor's appointments during that time. But as soon as Sophie was able, she isolated herself from him too. All because of her depression and hidden anxiety attacks. She was great at hiding her panic attacks and emotional issues from not only her parents, but especially her friends.

It was only until her friends forced her out on a spa day that Sophie snapped out of her funk and was back to her natural self. Meeting the guy of her dreams had not been in the big picture, but behold Kyle walked into her life and she was hooked.

Looking into her father's big blue eyes Sophie saw the kind man her father had always been to her and her siblings. "Dad, I guess you've already met Kyle." She paused just a few seconds when she said, "This is not how I wanted the two of you to actually meet each other." She smiled.

"Yes, baby girl, I've met Kyle, but we actually have known each other for years."

"Oh, that's right. Volkov Security. How could I have forgotten that?"

"Honey your dad and I really haven't known each other that well. It's been at best a business relationship, but that's already changed."

"What do you mean?"

"That's for us to know!" She could tell by the tone in Kyle's voice he was operating now in a more relaxed mode. He was being a little mysterious, and boy did she like it.

"Sweet Pea, I'm going to go round up your mother, brother and sister and take them out for some lunch. You need your rest. As much as we all love you and want to hover over you, that is not going to make you heal any faster. I think you're in good hands with Kyle at your bedside."

Sophie loved it when her father called her Sweet Pea. It reminded her of when she was little. Her father would take her to see the circus when it came into town.

The circus animals would always arrive by train a few days before the circus actually opened. All the animals were taken from the boxcars of the train, walked down the streets of Baltimore until they reached their final destination: The big top circus tent.

She absolutely loved the alone time with her father. Her dad even took her out of school when the circus came to town just to see the animal's parade single file. It was a big deal to Sophie, a memory she would never forget.

"Dad, I love you. Thanks for being here. How long have Laura and Joseph been here?"

"Joseph got here on Friday and Laura came in Saturday afternoon. They're staying at the house. Don't worry about them. You'll see them when you are moved to a private room. Now promise me you'll get some rest while I'm gone."

Coston bent forward and kissed Sophie on the forehead.

"Sorry to interrupt you Mr. Spencer, but Sophie needs to get her rest if she's ever going to move out of the ICU." Gail graciously said. "How about you take your beautiful family out for a picnic lunch? I hear Candy just dropped off a lovely spread of food."

It was amazing to Sophie how everyone had come together to take care of her family during this difficult time.

"Dad, I think you're getting booted out for a little while. Go spend the afternoon with everyone. I'm fine. I don't think I'm going anywhere anytime soon."

Watching her dad walk out of the ICU put a different perspective on Sophie's recovery. She had to do everything in her power to recover. She didn't like the idea that her parents had been caught up in her problems.

Feeling increased pain where she had been shot, she knew she had to let Gail know. That way, they could manage her pain a little more aggressively. Asking for help wasn't heard of from Sophie, but she was going to lean on her friends more than ever.

Chapter Six

Sophie informed Gail of the increased amount of pain she had been experiencing. Being a physician, Sophie knew the key prescription to healing was taking the correct amount of pain medications for the first few days, relaxing and sleeping as much as possible. That's exactly what Sophie was going to do. She was going to submit to her recovery just as she had submitted to Kyle on their date.

Gail made all the necessary arrangements for Sophie to be transferred to the private suite that Kyle had demanded for her, but before that happened, Gail had promised to give Sophie a full update on her condition. That time was now, and Sophie knew it. Making sure her pain was more tolerable, she was as comfortable as she was going to get.

Gail walked over to Sophie's right side, while Kyle stayed on Sophie's left side. He had not let go of her hand and Sophie loved the way Kyle made her feel. He slowly caressed Sophie's left hand, moving his fingers all over hers, trying to help her relax as much as possible while she listened to Gail's description of her injury.

Gail pulled her IPad from her lab jacket pocket. On the screen were several X-rays of Sophie's arm, neck, back and chest. Gail took her stylus and drew the path of the bullet's destruction. It had entered Sophie's right arm, shattering into multiple fragments and tearing up everything in its pathway. Arteries, veins and muscle had all been damaged. Several fragments still remained in her right lung, along with a very small pulmonary embolism, which happened following the fragments entering her lung.

Sophie started to water up again as Gail explained to her how lucky she was to survive. Gail pointed to one of the X-rays and told Sophie if the bullet had entered just a centimeter to the left Sophie would have lost her right arm completely, but with the help of the Vascular Surgeon, they were able to retrieve all the fragments from her arm, saving her function.

It is going to be a hell of a rehab to make everything work again, but as far as everyone else could see she was going to recover from this horrible injury. With time and patience. *Sophie had heard these words from Kyle just a week before, hearing these two words again were going to be her favorite words to live by, TIME and PATIENCE. Yes, she would do it.*

Kyle clutched her good hand, listening to Gail tell Sophie how close she came from not being with them anymore.

"Now that you told me the bad news, Sophie took a deep breath in, tell me the really bad news. I know you're holding back something. I can see it in your face, Gail.

Give it to me. I'm a big girl. I can handle anything you tell me at this point."

Sophie looked over to Kyle, "I have Kyle and my family to help me through whatever challenges or hurdles I must concur. I know that I'm not alone anymore."

"You've heard the worst, Sophie. Your recovery is going to be slow at first, until you get feeling, function, and strength back into your arm. Eventually we hope that will all get better in time. Once we get you settled in your room, we'll start with having some lite therapy. When you go home, therapy at the house, and down the road when you're stronger, you'll venture to a therapy center, but for today let's take it one step at a time.

You'll most likely experience some shortness of breath; you were on a vent for two days following the surgery, only because of the pulmonary embolism we found in your lung. You didn't need a Greens Filter implanted; you threw the clot just as we were trying to aspirate the bullet fragments from your lung. And no... before you even ask, you're not on any anticoagulation therapy. You don't need it. We didn't get the clot completely out of your lung, but it's so small it will just reabsorb in time. Your biggest problem at this point is letting others help you.

You're going to need more help than what you think. No, and I repeat, no being upset or frustrated when a challenge comes your way that you can't handle. You'll need to ask for help.

The rest of the team will stop by later today to do rounds. I want you just resting once you're moved to a private room. Not a lot of visitors for a couple of days, until you're more stable. You'll have plenty of time once you go home for your friends to visit."

Breathing a sigh of relief after hearing those words come from Gail's lips was sweet music to Sophie's ears. She wasn't totally out of the woods yet. The big question burning inside of Sophie's head now was staring back at her.

Kyle hadn't said a word to her the entire time Gail went over her injuries. He just stood caressing her hand. Feeling like the air was being sucked out of her lungs, Sophie began to feel a burning pain as she took a deep breath in. *Control your breathing* is all Sophie could think about until the pain subsided.

Kyle felt Sophie start to tense up. She had a look of sheer pain across her face. Trying not to startle her, he encouraged her to close her eyes. With his deepest Dom voice, he described the field they had walked through on their first date. He pointed out how she danced so lovely around with the butterfly. He could tell that his words were starting to settle her down. Watching her fall asleep also calmed his anxiety of seeing his girl fight through her pain.

Remembering how she submitted to him was just what he needed to filter through his mind. Looking forward to taking his girl home, having her for the rest of time was what he had to focus on now.

Making love to his dream girl for the rest of his life would be his ultimate pleasure. Before he could do that, he had to make sure the gang members who ambushed Sophie and Lexi stayed in the custody of the local police. Hopefully, they would be put away for a long time. If Kyle had anything to say about the criminals, both would spend the rest of their lives behind bars.

He watched as Sophie slept peacefully for several hours. Not once did he let go of her petite hand. Watching her finally release herself, all of his pent up stress slowly lifted. She was the calm he needed. It was only when hospital employees were about to move her to a private room that Sophie slowly woke up. Kyle watched her beautiful dark emerald eyes open and she let a slight yawn escape her mouth.

"How long have I been out?"

Bending down, Kyle kissed her forehead. "Long enough for me to enjoy watching you finally sleep peacefully."

"You're going to make me blush with your kind words. I probably snored up a storm."

"You were pretty loud at times, but it was music to my ears. I was relieved to hear such beautiful music coming from your mouth." Kyle felt more at ease the past few hours knowing that he could watch over his Pet. To his eyes, Sophie looked more peaceful, now that she had slept.

Sophie tried to reach for his chest and winced in pain. Kyle tried to reassure her that she would have plenty of time to touch him. Confusion was written all over Sophie's face. Before she could move, Kyle let her know that she was still in the hospital. Being reassured was all Kyle had to do to settle Sophie's precious mind.

After transferring Sophie to a private room, the team who had worked fiercely to save Sophie's life made their round. They updated Sophie and Kyle on her condition and what she needed to do to make a full recovery. Each specialist told them that her recovery depended totally on Sophie's will to recover. She was the only person who could make it happen.

So many unanswered questions swirled around in Sophie's head. She spent most of the remaining part of the day visiting with her brother and sister. She was so excited to see both of them. This was definitely not the reunion she'd hoped for, but boy, she did enjoy seeing them.

Her room was starting to look like a floral shop. All afternoon, delivery after delivery of flowers, stuffed animals, and get-well cards had arrived, some from people she hadn't even met. Kyle told her that some were friends of his. She felt loved because of all the kind gestures.

Just as things started to settle down, Kyle's cell phone rang. She watched as he answered, all she could hear him say was, "Yes she's still awake. Sure, I think she's up for that." Watching Kyle pocket his cell phone, Sophie asked him was everything okay. "Yeah, baby, why are you asking?" Sensing that something was wrong, she hoped it was nothing serious with his business or his family.

"You just looked so intent with whoever was on the line."

"I have a little surprise for you. That's all." Excitement filled her. *What kind of surprise is Kyle planning?*

"I figured you would want to spent a little alone time with your next visitor, before you hit dream land tonight." With just a slight smirk on his face, "If you think you're too tired I can always call her back and tell her to come tomorrow."

"No…No I'm not tired yet. I'm up for one more visitor tonight." Kyle bent down and kissed her on top of her head, sending goose bumps up and down her spine. Kyle sported a wicked smile. Sophie missed seeing him act this way.

All day the look on Kyle's face changed from serious, to a calmer laid back guy she remembered watching fireworks with. She hadn't brought up the fact that the last time she saw Kyle she yelled her safe-word.

Kissing her on the forehead was nice; she wanted more than just a peck on the head, though. Sophie let a moan escape her lips when Kyle ended the kiss. Feeling like she was going to burst, Sophie finally couldn't hold back her thoughts anymore. "Why have you only kissed me once on my lips today?"

"Pet, you've been through so much in the last few days. I didn't want to push myself on you. I've felt the burning desires to capture your lips with mine ever since I walked into the ICU. I know you need time to heal first.

Every time I touch your skin, it reminds me of warm velvet. You're correct. I have waited too long. Fuck it. I must reclaim what is mine." Never before had she felt so cherished, loved, and safe; that's the affect Kyle had on her. *He loves me. God…everything is going to be all right. It has to be.* Looking into his eyes, she saw her future. She repeated the same words over and over. His words eased the fear that was brewing in her mind.

Just as Kyle went to bend down and kiss her on her lips a knock came from outside of her room. "Hold that position, Pet, let me go see who's at the door."

Letting out a sigh, Sophie watched Kyle walk over to the door. Not wanting for him to leave her side, desire grew within her soul. She watched as Master's ass swayed in front of her. Yep that was the first time she had those thoughts…her future, and boy did he look fucking good.

She needed to get the nerve up to tell him about her past fears and insecurities. Only then, is when she would be able to move forward.

Looking pensive, she saw who was being wheeled in. Sophie no longer had to wonder how her best friend Lexi was doing. Tears streamed down both girls cheeks. She realized whom Kyle had spoken to earlier.

Sophie stared at Bryce as he wheeled Lexi into her room. She saw the sheer exhaustion plastered all over his face. Kyle walked over to Lexi and gave her a kiss on the top of her head. "You look lovely today." Kyle stated affectionately.

"Thank you, Sir. I feel much better today."

Sophie took in the exchange of pleasantries between the two. She had called Lexi begging her to come rescue her from Kyle's house. Even though Lexi's injuries were not as severe as Sophie's, she still required surgery to retrieve the lodged bullet. In no time, Lexi would make a full recovery.

Kyle made his way back over to where Sophie sat up in the hospital bed. The four began to talk about the past few days' events. As the conversation wore on, Sophie's mind began to wander just a bit. Now knowing what was going to be her future, she knew that her friendship with Lexi would never be broken.

Seeing Lexi come to her aide, putting her life in jeopardy was the true bond of sisterhood. Sophie felt tiny goose bumps run up and down her spine when thinking about such heroic measure.

Feeling Kyle place his hand on top of her good hand instantly sent a calming feeling throughout her body. *God how did he know just when she needed to feel his touch.* It not only soothed her, but it also pulled her out of her thoughts and brought her back to the conversation in the room.

After about an hour of talking and joking with the three most important people in her life, Sophie felt an uncomfortable feeling starting at the center of her collarbone traveling down her right shoulder.

Shifting from side to side in the bed, she tried to find maybe a more comfortable position. Still not getting any resolution, not wanting to say anything to anyone that she was in pain. Sophie continued to squirm around impatiently, trying to remember when the last time she asked for pain medications.

Kyle shot Sophie a perplexed look. She knew she should tell him that she was in pain, but before she could say anything, Kyle hit the nurses call button.

Before she could choke out a signal word, she listened as Kyle asked for her pain medication. Sighing with relief, Sophie mouthed to him, "Thank you."

"Pet, Bryce is going to take Lexi home now. She needs to rest just as much as you do. Once the two of you are strong enough, we'll all get together for lunch. How's that sound with everyone?" Both girls said at the same time, "GREAT!" The two Dom's just shook their heads.

"I see trouble in our near future with these two." Kyle said directly to Bryce.

After receiving pain medication and eating a small amount of chicken broth, Sophie wondered if Kyle would pick back up where he had left off, when Lexi came to visit her. She surely hoped so, but before that happened, she drifted off to sleep.

Chapter Seven

Sophie survived the next several days without losing her cool. She felt safe when it was just her and Kyle together. The only time Kyle wasn't by her side was when he had to go take a call or deal with getting things ready for her discharge.

Sophie started becoming panicky. She didn't like the idea of being left alone. Nurse Orja stayed with her when Kyle had to leave, which wasn't for more than an hour, but that seemed like a lifetime when it came to Sophie's wild imagination. She started looking over her shoulder constantly. What would she feel like when she was on her own again?

Everything seemed to hurt. Not really liking how the pain medication made her sleepy all the time, Sophie tried to cut back on the amount of pain medication she received. Backfiring in the worst way, it took twice as long for the medication to ease her back to a happy place.

Kyle picked up quickly on her little scheme. He set a timer on his phone that buzzed when it was time for her medication. She'd watched him pick up the call button, and kindly ask the aide to bring her pain meds.

He was on top of everything. He knew when it was time for therapy, time for her breathing treatments, even down to when her meals would come.

Sophie grew very tired of having people taking care of her. It was always the opposite, and she took care of others. Her patience was slowing big time by her fifth day in the hospital, not able to stay still any longer. Doing another crossword puzzle made Sophie see stars. Her temper was getting shorter and shorter as each therapist or tech entered her room.

Sophie asked Kyle if he could go and get her IPad from the apartment. What she really meant was she needed him to take a break from being by her side 24/7. Her plan backfired, though. Kyle saw through her scheming so he pulled his IPad out of his briefcase and told her to use his. "I don't want yours I want mine Damn it, she screeched at the top of her lungs."

"Pet, what's the matter? You've been extremely agitated all day. I've watched you not eat your breakfast. You pick at your lunch, barely drink anything. I see you're on the brink of exploding. Tell me what's wrong NOW."

Sophie twisted and turned feeling the pressure of telling Kyle what was the matter was harder than she imagined. She knew she just had to come clean and tell him.

"I'm so bored I can't even see straight. Every time I go to sit up, turn over, or even try to take a deep breath in, I either get exhausted or I'm hurting so bad I just wanted to scream at the top of my lungs."

She watched as Kyle shifted slowly from the chair he was sitting in to coming closer to the bed. "I'm so fucking sore. It's not funny. I just wish it would go away." She was laying it on thick now for Kyle.

Tear, snot, and saliva all seemed to be spewing from her face as she said the next statement. "I wish I hadn't woken up. I've put my family and loved ones in harm's way.

Not only are they worried about me, I might not be able to live up to their high expectations anymore."

Really sobbing now, Sophie's filter hadn't stopped either; she spouted vile things from her mouth. "What if I can't practice medicine anymore? What am I going to do? If I can't handle being stuck in a goddamn hospital for five days what will I be like in a year from now? When I don't have anything? What type of person will I be?"

"Are you done yet, Sophie?"

Looking into Kyle's deep Caribbean blue eyes instantly calmed her fears. She loved how he could one minute have a stern look in his eyes, and in the next minute, his eyes were creamy just like a wave hitting the surf.

"God, Kyle, what is wrong with me? I should be grateful, but all I can think about is not being able to stand myself if I don't get the function back in my hand. It horrifies me to think I will not be able to put my hands inside someone's chest.

Fixing a human being's beating heart has been the most important concept in my life since…" she realized at that moment, all of her life. "I've always been fascinated how powerful a single person can be, and I've been that person for years now. I've been the person in charge of everything."

"Pet, you just answered your own question." Confused, Sophie thought about what he just said.

"Think about what you just said, Sophie darling. You're scared. You have to rely on everyone else to care for you. You think that's a bad thing, but ultimately it's giving your body a chance to heal. You don't see the love that each person is giving you. You see it as a burden."

All she could see was Kyle getting more infuriated.

"You're fucking scared out of your mind thinking about what the future will hold for you. Instead, you should be thanking God for saving your ass. You put not only yourself in danger, but you were willing to sacrifice your best friend at the same time.

Baby girl, instead of having a one-person pity party, do something worthwhile. Help yourself get better. Stop fighting yourself. The whole starvation thing isn't working for you either. Remember the clinical psychologist in me sees straight through your temper tantrum." Sarcastically Kyle said in a huffed voice, "Guess what darling? I'm not buying into your tactics. Let me tell you what's going to happen for the rest of tonight."

Feeling all sorts of emotions bubbling up inside of Sophie, she realized Kyle was onto her. Big time. She had never been around someone as persistent as he was. He was like a raging bull. All she could see was steam coming out of the top of his head when he told her how she was acting.

She really had fucked up. Amazingly, he hadn't walked out on her.

No, instead he stood by her-side, stroking her head, wiping the tears and snot from her face. Never had she allowed anyone in her life to do these simple acts of kindness, not even her dead husband. Whenever she needed a good cry, she would escape into a hiding place. She'd isolated herself from everyone.

It only took Sophie a few minutes to figure out he wasn't going anywhere. She pulled herself back together as best as she could in this situation, thinking more clearly now that she had spoken her mind. She knew what she had to do.

What started out as a little peep coming from her mouth, the words that she hadn't spoken since yelling her safe-word? She closed her swollen blood shot eyes, tilted her head downward showing Kyle she was ready to surrender to him.

"Master, can you ever forgive me for what I've done?" Not moving a muscle in her body, she stilled herself just as she had done during her ordeal at his condo. She remembered kneeling down in the center of his living room with no clothes on in a full surrender position. Kyle had instructed her to do so. She'd had to put all of her cares, worries and feelings aside until she could face her inner demons. It worked that night. There was no reason why it wouldn't work today.

All she heard was the IV pump clicking as it continued to administer medication and fluids into her veins, hearing her own heartbeat via the heart monitor gave her an eerie feeling. Her heart was beating rapidly waiting for a sign from Kyle that she was forgiven.

She knew Kyle had been worried sick about her. Never had someone expressed that kind of devotion to her. She was acting like a brat. Reading online so many times when doing her research about the lifestyle, she'd discovered most Dom's wouldn't tolerate that kind of behavior coming from their partner. Kyle was no different. He put his foot down as soon as he witnessed her being a brat, and he would most likely do it again. Until she got the picture.

Several minutes went by without a single word spoken between the two of them. Sophie knew she had to wait until Kyle was ready. It wasn't her decision at all. It was fully up to her Master to accept her plea. So with her head lowered, eyes closed, her left hand laying palm up, she did what she had been taught. That was WAIT. She had to be patient.

Hearing Kyle move toward her, smelling his musky cologne getting closer and closer to her. She let out a huge sigh of relief when he finally spoke.

"Open your eyes, Sophie. I want you looking at me when I talk to you. You will respect my decisions on how I take care of what is mine. You did not take care of my property."

Each word that he spoke sent shivers down her spine. Her stomach tightening in a wound up ball, instantly Sophie felt like she was going to vomit. Feeling herself start to shake from head to toe, she knew she had nowhere to run.

She had to accept what Kyle had in-store for her. She had to face the consequences.

Not wanting to lose the man standing in front of her she slowly opened her eyes and listened to every word. Her heart was being broken in two by the man she now knew loved her. This just wasn't just some fly by night guy who had stepped into her life; no he was The Master who planned on keeping her forever.

"You will never put yourself in danger ever again, Pet. We will need to work on your communication skills, and when you think we're done, you'll realize I'm only just getting started. You should have no reason why you can't tell me what's wrong when I ask a simple question. You were rude today, not only to the staff but also to me. One thing you will learn very quickly about me is I can't stand for someone not to show respect to someone who is trying to help them."

Feeling his words hit her even harder. She forced herself not to cry. His words were true or he wouldn't be having this discussion. God how stupid could she have been? Leaving her would almost be the responsible thing for Kyle to do. She didn't like that thought at all.

"You owe me three separate punishments when you recover. I vow as your Master I will collect each one on my terms only, Sophie."

Now fully shaking from head to toe. Nowhere to go, nowhere to run. She accepted his words as truth. Feeling his large hands take hold of her neck, he claimed her as his, placing his mouth over her soft lips. She slowly opened herself up to his passionate kiss. Moaning a happy noise into his mouth as he devoured her. As he started to pull away, she felt the heat coming off his hands spreading down to her clit as it had its first twinge of sensation.

Kyle surely knew how to possess a woman with his magical hands. Having the courage, Sophie used her left hand to clench his shirt, not wanting to let go. She felt him dive back into her mouth. Holding on for dear life, he was her lifesaver, her float to keep her head above water. He would always be there to pick her up when she fell. She knew that for sure now.

"I've missed the warmth you give me, Kyle. I feel like a total ass."

"As you should, but for now your job is not to worry about anything. I will be doing all that for the two of us. Understand, Pet?" She didn't know what it was, but boy, oh boy she loved it when he called her Pet and Darling. Her insides seemed to heat up life a fiery inferno, ready to erupt. "Yes, Master." Just those two words brought back the submissive side of Sophie. She hadn't said them often but when she did, she meant it.

Sophie had several visitors later that evening, making her even more tired than what she was earlier. She really was tired of having hospital food. She'd never been a processed food person. She loved being a meat and vegetable girl. Eating the food and being on painkillers, brought up a serious question in her mind. *She hadn't had a bowel movement in six days.* Knowing that she wouldn't be able to go home until she had a poop, she did the unthinkable. Pulling the nurse call bottom from the side of the bed, Sophie asked to have nurse Orja come to her room.

As Nurse Orja came in Sophie had to think fast, how she was going to be able to ask for a stool softener in front of Kyle. So she did the unthinkable. "I know this is probably a bad idea but I was thinking if Orja could help me get into a shower, she could help me clean up just a bit. I just might feel somewhat like a human."

Not knowing, if he would leave her alone that long or not, she just started in on the next part. "I'm really hungry too, but not for hospital food. I need real food. Something… maybe from Jimmy's Seafood."

Getting more and more excited as she expressed her point. Sophie began to breathe a little harder as she worked up to the next part. You could call the order in and then run over to the condo. Maybe get a shower yourself, grab me a night gown or two, a pair of yoga pants, and perhaps by chance some warm socks."

She started to bat her puppy dog eyes at Kyle. "My toes are so cold." Getting the hint, she could tell Kyle was thinking over her requests.

"Baby, when you put it like that, if you're hungry all you needed to do was ask. I'm at your disposal to get you whatever you want."

Really pulling out the charm now, Sophie was sitting on her good hand with her fingers crossed that Kyle would get the hint she needed some alone time.

"I like the way you're groveling and begging, Baby. Can you think of anything else I could have Jake pick up for you? I'm most sure he wouldn't mind at all." Looking like she had just had her favorite balloon popped in front of her, she shook her head from side to side in disapproval.

"But on the other hand, you know I think some real food sounds terrific. Let's do this. Tell me what you think you can handle. I'll have Jake swing by the hospital and pick me up. He can drop me off at the house so I can drive back on my own, stop off at Jimmy's, pick up the food all while you're getting cleaned up.

How's that sound darling?"

"Sounds like a wonderful plan to me. What about you, Orja? How's that sound to you?"

"I think I need to go round up some supplies, so we can make you feel more comfortable tonight." Sending a quick glance over to Orja, Sophie mouthed thank you as she turned and walked out the door.

Before, Kyle left Sophie's side he made sure under no circumstances was she to run from the hospital. All she could do was laugh. "Yeah me running outside with my ass hanging out… No that's not my thing."

Going over the list one more time, making sure Kyle had everything she needed. She sat up in the hospital bed, looking at how close she had come to fucking up everything. She took a deep breath, making sure she had direct eye contact with him.

"I love you, Kyle. Thank you for being by my side." As she finished her words Orja came bobbing into the room holding everything they would need to make Sophie feel better.

"I love you too, Sophie Spencer."

Getting her life back together was Sophie's number one priority. She had to get stronger, and in turn, her injuries would heal. She saw her future and that was with Master Kyle.

Orja had been taking care of Sophie since she got out of surgery. Kyle had made sure Orja was in charge of Sophie's care at all times. Getting to know her at first was a little rough for Sophie.

Sophie's first encounter with Orja wasn't the best; it was plain out scary. Orja was a small woman in body structure, and had a loud voice just like a big burly drill sergeant, but after a few days Sophie realized Orja was as kind as a kitten. She did have claws like a lion when she needed to get her point across to Sophie, though.

The first thing that needed to be accomplished was getting a laxative to help her stopped up bowels. Maybe that's why Sophie had become so cranky this afternoon. No time like the present. Feeling a little embarrassed, asking another woman to stick something up her ass had to be a sign of desperation in Sophie's eyes but she knew it had to be done.

After a nice hot long shower, getting her hair washed, feeling her stomach grumble like Mount Saint Helen's,

Sophie felt it was better to stay in the bathroom until the impossible happened.

Orja and Sophie seemed to be forming a closer bond. They both had a lot of things in common.

Orja had lost her first husband to a drunk driver fifteen years ago. Already being in the lifestyle, Orja explained how she lost all interests in every aspect of living. She went through a long bout of depression.

Orja was no different from anyone else who had ever lost a loved one. After several counseling sessions with Kyle, she explained to Sophie, he challenged her to go to a support group called Al-Anon. Sophie new exactly how Orja felt at that time. She had just had the same epiphany.

It took Orja several months before she was convinced that Kyle was right. What a blessing for Orja. It was as if a light bulb turned on in her head. She woke up one spring gorgeous morning, reality hit her that she had no one to spend the day with, and she told herself she was done with grieving. Braving all of her inner demons, Orja picked up the phone and called Kyle. He met her for coffee, convinced her to go to an Al-Anon meeting together.

She told Sophie how nervous she had been stepping into her first meeting. Now she often reminisces back on her first couple of meetings as a blessing.

If it hadn't been for Kyle seeing to her needs, like a good Dom, she probably wouldn't be worth anything, especially not a slave, wife, mother to three wonderful boys, and a caring nurse that she is today. She says it was like fate when she ran into Master Don at an Al-Anon meeting. He had just lost his wife to a drunk driver.

He too had been in the grieving process when Orja asked if he needed a shoulder to cry on. It was love at first sight for Master Don. He courted her for a year until Orja saw the bigger picture, her future with Master Don.

After hearing Orja's story, Sophie deeply felt the words hit her soul. She was no different from Orja, a lost person who now had found true happiness. It was only after their talk that it hit Sophie. *Oh my God. Orja wrote the Surrender Poem.*

Surrender
As the words leave his lips,
Her heart knows what she must do.
Surrender
Her mind releases all notions of defiance. For who else captures her thoughts so completely
And peers through the glass that is her soul.
Surrender
On her knees, bent in deference to his power,
The mind, the body and the soul know absolute peace.
Only
In
Surrender.
No, it can't be the same person! Could it be?

The waiting game for the big explosion didn't take as long as Sophie had expected. Orja even gave Sophie some lovely air freshener to mask the odor from the bathroom. Not wanting to take any chances Sophie stayed in the bathroom for what seemed like forever but it was enough time for Orja to change the sheets on Sophie's bed, grabs some fresh pillows, and refresh her water pitcher.

Sophie now felt more like a human than she had two hours ago. All she needed now was some non-hospital food, her own clothes, and her man to return. She was amazed how well Orja and she were getting along.

It meant something to Sophie at how easily Orja opened up like she did. Sophie was starting to see how closed off she had been. That was not who she was at all. She would repay the kindness that everyone was showing to her somehow in the future.

Getting settled back in bed was the last thing Sophie wanted to do. Instead Orja rearranged a chair with several pillows, making sure Sophie's arm was fully protected. Her back and her legs were getting crampy just lying around in a hospital bed. Giving her body a different position felt wonderful. Subtle changes did make a difference to Sophie.

Looking fresher, feeling stronger, Sophie drifted off while waiting patiently for her Master to return. It wasn't more than fifteen minutes when she was woken up by a kiss on her forehead. Looking super-hot as always, Kyle had shaved, changed clothes, and was carrying a lot of goodies for Sophie.

"Something smells delicious."

"I hope my girl is hungry, because I had Jimmy make you several dishes."

"I'm starving. I could eat a horse." Giggling like a schoolgirl Sophie shook her head, "No not a horse at all, but whatever you got! God smells so good."

"Do you think you can handle sitting in the chair while you eat or do you want to get back in the bed?"

"I want to stay in the chair for now. I only want to get back in the bed when it's time to sleep."

"Baby, I don't want you over doing it." Sophie watched Kyle's expression change from loving to concern.

"I promise when I start feeling tired, I'll have you tuck me in. It feels great just to be able to sit upright. My lung is expanding better this way."

After eating her meal, Sophie did as she promised; she had Kyle help her into her nightgown. Surprisingly to Sophie, having her own clothes on did add a layer of comfort. She'd need to remember that for the future, when she reminded a patient to bring some comforts from home. Most likely, it would help with their recovery.

Kyle did as Sophie asked him to do earlier. He pulled out a pair of warm comfy socks from the suitcase and placed them on her feet, then covered her up with a Sherpa blanket that he brought from home. After all the fuss she had raised earlier in the afternoon, Kyle pulled out one more thing from the suitcase… Sophie's iPad… With tears running down her face and barely able to speak, she did what any slave would do, she bowed her head in pure resolve to her Master's attentiveness.

Catching up on the past week's emails, then looking at current news in the world, Sophie tired out. Hitting the nurse call button to ask for pain medication hadn't slipped her mind.

She made a promise to Kyle earlier she would be more attentive to her pain, instead of letting it get so fucking bad. Before signing off for the night, Orja checked back in on Sophie and Kyle before going home, telling both of them she would be back bright and early tomorrow. Sophie appreciated everything Orja had done for her in the past few days.

Most nurses come to work because of a paycheck, not Orja. She came because she had a need to help others. This was a true gift Orja possessed.

"I hope I get a chance to meet your Master, Orja, when I get out of the hospital. I would like to have the two you over for dinner." Looking over towards Kyle, Sophie shrugged her shoulders in his direction.

"I'm most sure Master Kyle and Master Don can arrange a time when you're feeling better Sophie. I will tell him when I go home tonight. I'm really glad you're feeling better tonight."

"Me too. Thank you for everything you've done for me today. Be safe going home." Sophie watched as Kyle stood and walked over toward Orja. Both hugged each other. Watching the two exchange such a friendly gesture warmed Sophie's insides.

It had been a craptastic day, but when it was all said and done, the man who was still sitting beside her was her Master. How much more could a girl ask for?

Sitting in the passenger seat of her sporty BMW, Sophie watched as the hustle and bustle of the city traffic passed them by. Carl had decided to drive her car this evening instead of his huge manly pickup truck. Meeting up with Lexi and Bryce for dinner was on the evening agenda, but before they could meet with them, the contractor of their new house asked if Carl could stop and look at the new addition. Kill two birds with one stone as Carl said to her, no need to make two trips. She would just have to wait in the car, plus it would add to the excitement of not being allowed to see the house.

Full of excitement, Sophie tried to imagine why the house was taking so long to complete. She'd ask Carl every so often, all he would ever say was it was a surprise. For the past month, she wasn't even allowed to go visit the construction site.

Before, leaving their apartment in the city, Carl made sure that Sophie had a scarf with her; he wanted her blindfolded while she waited in the car. He even joked, no peeking while he was inside the house, or she would get a spanking. Sophie giggled, trying to hold in the excitement of his words of getting a spanking. She had received a few of those in the past few weeks. She wasn't complaining one bit.

The weather has taken a turn for the worse as they headed out for the evening. The skies grew dark, the wind began to blow, and large drops of rain hit the windshield. Hating to drive in bad weather, Sophie wiggled back and forth in the passenger seat, looking out the window. The long winding roads gave her the willies; she wasn't sure how she was going to handle the roads when she had to commute back and forth to work. No taking these roads at high speeds when running late. That was for sure.

The storm didn't look like it would let up anytime soon. Crackling sounds of lightning bolts lit up the evening skies. The deep rumbling of thunder was heard in the distance with frequent crashes indicating the storm was getting closer and closer.

Sophie had stopped making small talk a few miles back when the road narrowed just a bit. Carl needed to concentrate on driving. Fidgeting in her seat, Sophie could no longer keep quiet, "Only few more minutes until we arrive. I hope we get there soon, before it gets any worse."

Carl just nodded back at Sophie. "Yup."

It was nights like this she'd rather be at home cuddled up on the sofa with popcorn watching a horror movie with Carl at her side.

As Carl made the last turn onto the country road, seeing out the front windshield had become almost impossible. The windows had fogged up, most likely from Sophie's heavy breathing. Carl tried to reassure her by singing along with the radio. All Sophie heard was the rain, lightning, and thunder.

The rain hit the window even harder. Sophie had a white-knuckle grip around the door handle. All she could think of now was hopefully they would get to the new house. Carl drove the small sport car on rare occasions, he handled it like a racecar driver, and she loved how he could look so damn sexy behind the wheel of any vehicle.

The car picked up speed as it went around a winding curve in the road. She looked over at Carl. He loved taking some of the turns just a little faster than what Sophie liked. He would hit a certain crest in the road making the car go a little airborne just to get a rise out of Sophie. Feeling her stomach jump up into her throat always gave Sophie a big thrill but tonight she just wasn't feeling it. Knowing that Carl would never put either one of them in danger. Sophie scooted as far back in the seat as possible, closed her eyes wishing they would get to the house soon.

Steering down the narrow country road, trying to slow the speed of the car down, she saw the panic all over Carl's face. Blinking back fear, Sophie asked Carl what was wrong. He tried to slow the car down to a more controlled speed, but finally yelled, "No brakes, baby, brace yourself!"

Sophie screamed and kicked the nice warm Sherpa blanket off her body, trying everything in her power to escape. Feeling like she was trapped. Sophie slowly opened her eyes to Kyle's soothing voice.

"Baby, you're okay. I need you to open your eyes. You were having a horrible nightmare." Slowly reality hit her, she wasn't just in a car accident, but rather she was recovering in the hospital from the gunshot wound. Kyle eased her back to sleep.

Seven days had passed since Sophie had been shot, on the day of her discharge her nerves were on high alert. She was being protected by the hospital staff and Kyle. But today she would be finally released.

She would be free from the restraints of the hospital. She'd had several visits from the Baltimore City Police Department, the gang member squad and even the chief commissioner. Kyle told her that the commissioner was a personal friend of his and would be handling Sophie's case himself.

Sophie's general demeanor on the day of her discharge was up one minute down the next. She had so many emotions running through her mind, fearing of being attacked again by the gangs.

She worked herself up to the point she got sick and had to have Orja help her clean herself playing it off that she might be coming down with an infection or had a stomach bug. She hoped Kyle didn't see right through her fears. Sophie said a silent prayer that Kyle would protect her forever.

Kyle did his best to assure Sophie that the CCTV he had installed at her apartment had caught the two teenage gang members doing their dirty deeds. The Baltimore City Police Department had the two minors under lock and key at the juvenile detention center ever since. Luckily for Sophie, she had Kyle by her side or she would have fallen apart. Knowing these two boys were so young disturbed Sophie. Why were they sent to do the job that should have been handled most likely by someone else higher in the gang's leadership.

Sophie balked at whose house she would go to once being discharged from the hospital. Her parents wanted her to come to their house; Sophie wanted to go back to her apartment.

The Dom in Kyle put his foot down in front of everyone. He told her under no circumstances would she be returning to her apartment to stay by herself. So, he did what any Dom would do, he chose his house in the country for her recovery. Sophie had only been there once, filled with its ups and downs, and she knew they still had to work out their relationship.

Having to put her career on hold was going to be a challenge for Sophie. She had to figure out how to heal as quickly as possible. She would work on her therapy when the therapists weren't standing over top of her being a drill Sargent.

Chapter Eight

Sophie arrived at Kyle's country home eight days after being shot. Her discharge instructions were very clear. Do everything the therapist tells you, no ifs, ands, or buts. No sexual penetration for at least two weeks or until she could walk up and down a flight of ten steps three times without becoming short of breath.

Sophie shook her head when she read the last instruction, which was penciled in by Gail. No use of any electronic sexual toys without your Master's permission or his help. Finding out that Gail was a Domme had been news to Sophie. Even though they had been working friends for years, Sophie had no knowledge so many people with power were actually living the lifestyle 24/7.

She had accomplished a lot in the past few weeks. She was able to walk farther and farther each day without being as short of breath. Kyle's home had the best security system money could buy. Especially since it came from Volkov Security. Kyle had several of his security team doing perimeter checks. Just to make sure his girl was safe he told her on several occasions.

She loved taking an afternoon stroll just around the large property. Or as she had come to call it, the compound. She knew she was being watched by whatever security guy was on duty at that time. It gave her time to think about life as it was for her now. The problem with that was Sophie still didn't know what life had in store for her.

Sophie had friends and family members come over to visit during the day. Kyle turned his home into their home in just a short time. He made sure she didn't lift a finger to do anything when her friends came over to visit.

Kyle hired a temporary housekeeper, Daisy, who arranged everything in his house, from cleaning, cooking, shopping, and laundry. He told Sophie that Daisy had been employed by him for several years at the club.

You name it, Daisy did it. Each time Sophie had someone new over, Daisy out did herself to make them feel welcome. Even down to arranging Sophie's physical therapy schedules. Sophie was told to let Daisy handle everything and she was to report directly to Sophie.

Daisy's main job was to make sure Sophie was comfortable. Sophie had never had anyone fuss over her as much as Kyle did.

Some days Sophie loved it, but here lately it was beginning to set off small little land mines inside of Sophie heart. Would she ever be enough for Kyle? Yes, she had been a terrific cardio-thoracic surgeon up until a few weeks ago, but that wasn't even a definite that she would ever practice medicine again due to the injury in her left arm.

Growing up, her mother ran the house while her father worked. They didn't have any type of help. Neither did the Volkovs. The wives took care of everything. This was new for Sophie to have people waiting on her.

It still remained a mystery to Sophie. What was her relationship between her and Kyle anyway? Was she his girlfriend? His submissive? She called him Master or Sir when he gave her a direct order, but when her family was over he was just Kyle.

What were they, or were they just friends? Stepping into uncharted waters of having a large house and a temporary housekeeper added more and more stress to Sophie.

After a full day of therapy and a nice long walk around the grounds, Sophie was ready for bed. Still having to sleep in a hospital bed was getting a little old. Even though Kyle held her several times during the day, she just wanted to be able to curl up under his arms and feel his body next to hers. Kyle had the hospital bed set up in the middle of the large family room; a pull out sofa was directly across from where the hospital bed was situated in the room. At least they slept in the same room.

Kyle slowly made modifications to small things in Sophie's everyday life. He set out her clothes in the morning. He only allowed her special sweet treats after she completed a task designed by her therapist. At night he allowed only a t-shirt of his. No nightgowns or underwear. He told her when she was totally healed she would no longer need the barrier of fabric between them. She wasn't too sure about sleeping nude, but she said she would try. Snuggling under the covers it didn't take Sophie long at all to drift off to sleep.

"No brakes, baby, brace yourself!"

Time seemed to stand still as those words sank in. Just as he stopped speaking, a large utility truck came barreling towards the car. Nothing could keep the two vehicles from colliding. Hearing screeching metal grinding together, tossing from side to side, being held in by her seatbelt, Sophie saw her world ripped apart.

Screaming at the top of her lungs, Sophie thrashed back and forth in the bed. She felt Kyle's hand on her left arm slowly waking her up from a nightmare. Sophie gripped the sheet with her good hand, frantically looking around the room trying to figure out where the hell she was. Why was she being haunted by this old nightmare? Something had been triggered in her subconscious mind after being shot.

Sophie had been having the same nightmare for the past two weeks since her discharge from the hospital. Kyle rushed to her side night after night. He'd console her until she fell back to sleep, and watching her obviously having nightmares about being shot didn't set very well with Kyle and Sophie knew it. Caressing the top of her head, easing her back to sleep had become Kyle's gift to her.

She was sure Kyle would use his trained skills in psychology to get her to talk about her nightmares, but she managed to tell him she couldn't remember what she was dreaming. She wasn't sure how long she would get away with that, but she wasn't about to tell him that she was dreaming about her dead husband.

Sophie felt safe when it was just the two of them together. She wasn't looking over her shoulder constantly. What would she feel like when she was on her own again?

For the next two weeks, Sophie and Kyle spent most of their time talking about everything under the sun, from work, to hobbies, likes, dislikes, sexual stuff, BDSM, how he got started being a Dom, opening The Cellar.

Most topics were easy for both of them to discuss openly. When it got to the more detailed sexual stuff, Sophie wasn't quite up to the challenge of knowing what she wanted, so Kyle, being the good Dom, gave her a list of over three hundred different kinky sex acts. Her homework was to research them to see if they could be on a list of possible dos or don'ts.

He even made arrangements for Lexi, Orja, Daisy and Candy to come over for lunch so Sophie had time to have girl time. She could ask them anything her heart desired. None of the ladies were ashamed to talk openly and freely about kinky ways.

She still had haunting nightmares that filled her sleepless nights. Life is fragile, she was most definitely fragile, and nothing was as it seemed on the inside of Sophie's soul.

Each night before tucking Sophie into the hospital bed, they would discuss at least five of the items on her list. Kyle called it her soft and hard limit list. It had been almost a month since either one of them had sex.

Sophie was sure it was the lack of sex or the nightly topic of sex was making her super horny. They made out several times, with a little lite touching of her breast, always over top of his t-shirt that she wore to bed.

She needed to have him touching her with no barrier. Skin to skin. Kyle knew just how to bring her sexual desires to a pinnacle, but each time he seemed close to doing something about it, he would leave Sophie extremely frustrated.

What good was it to talk about soft and hard limits if they hadn't progressed to first base? Was he ever going to hit a home run out of the ballpark? Damn she needed sex bad.

Her pussy was aching to be touched. She went to sleep most nights dripping wet. Kyle had to know how she felt, or had he given up on the two of them?

Some nights she had the urge to tackle him, but he constantly reminded her that she had to be patient with his Dom decisions; sex was when he felt she could handle it. In some ways she resented him, in other ways it just made her want him even more.

Therapy seemed to be improving Sophie's range of motion and flexibility. Having therapy three times a day at home was more than most patients received, but Sophie was no ordinary patient. She tackled going up and down ten steps at least twenty times a day. Still no sexual action. She was most sure her battery operated boyfriend, or BOB for short, was missing her too. Unfortunately, BOB was still at her apartment.

Kyle often told her she looked beautiful, which reminded her he still was interested in her. But still no fucking sex. He made sure Sophie had the best care that money could buy. Everything was provided for her; all she had to do was ask, and he'd have it at her fingertips.

Remembering her conversation with Gail before she was released from the hospital about how her lung needed about four weeks to heal, and if she experienced any shortness of breath, not to be alarmed. She hadn't lifted a finger to even get a little winded.

Day in and day out, Sophie dealt with her recovery; things seemed to be moving along very nicely. Feeling a little apprehensive today, she was going to be leaving the compound, as she called it, and venturing back to the hospital for a few checkups. Hopefully she would get the all clear checkup today.

God she hoped that's why Kyle hadn't made any sexual advances. She'd done everything the therapist had taught her. Now the proof would be convincing everyone she was ready to be on her own again.

Hopefully, that would free up Kyle to go back to work in his office versus seeing his patients at the house. Fortunately for Kyle's patients, none of them minded coming out to the compound for their counseling sessions.

She hoped she could even convince him to spend some time at The Cellar. Kyle hadn't complained at all during the past four weeks. She hoped he'd didn't resent her in the long run. Only time would tell.

Remembering one of the conversations she had with Kyle during one of their late night chats, Kyle had mentioned the possibility of finding his father the night she'd been shot, and how he aborted the mission to get back to Sophie ASAP.

She knew he wanted to put closure to that piece of his life. Sophie felt she was holding him back from doing just that. He'd been babysitting her for the past month. It was time he got back to his normal daily life.

Sophie asked him several times if he needed to finish what he started that night, and his response had been, "There is time for that later, my priority is you." God she loved hearing his manly voice when he went all Dom on her. It turned her insides into Jell-o every time. Yes, she was becoming aware of her inner submissive needs, her need to serve him and to be transparent.

Sophie checked her new IPhone. It had more features than she knew what to do with. Some of the apps Kyle had insisted she have on the phone were for her safety. He made sure she had the latest and greatest GPS tracking system. It gave her hope that one day she wouldn't feel like she was being held hostage just because of the gang threats.

Checking the phone to make sure it was fully charged, she didn't want to be without modern day luxuries. It held stored information that she wasn't ready to depart with yet. Daisy made sure Sophie knew just how to navigate from screen to screen, and having Daisy around was a Godsend. She really was a wiz at everything. Even though everything was now securely back up on the iCloud Sophie felt she needed to have them in two different locations.

All of her old text messages, photos remained on her phone, including the ones from the gang members telling her that they were watching her. She had met with the state's attorney just yesterday. He gave her all the information on her shooters.

Even officer Ferguson had stopped by Kyle's to check up on her.

Daisy was such a talented and creative woman. She made sure Sophie's daily schedule was updated to her Google calendar, something Sophie never did before, not even her secretary at the hospital could keep her calendar up to date.

These tiny tasks that Daisy did for Sophie were great. Not like Sophie had any important engagements anytime soon, but she did have a boatload of birthdays and anniversary parties that she potentially might not be able to make in the near future.

Getting to know Daisy was a win-win for Sophie. It gave her the opportunity to learn some needed skills.

Besides keeping a calendar Daisy was super genius in the kitchen. Sophie still couldn't hold anything with her right hand, but what she could do was learn Kyle's favorite dishes.

Sophie learned that Daisy had been in the lifestyle for about six years. She was a submissive through and through. Not in a full time contract at the current time, so instead she was collared to the club. Daisy was hopeful of finding her Master someday soon.

Glancing back at her phone, Sophie noticed she only had two doctors' appointments today at the hospital. It had been four weeks since the shooting. Looking back again at her calendar, Sophie realized Daisy had entered a few new birthdays of importance.

AUGUST 26: Kyle's 35th b-day…that was exactly three weeks from today.

Chapter Nine

Excitement rose up in her chest. She hadn't felt this giddy since the night she'd submitted to Kyle. She'd had to get the all clear from the doctor. *How else could she throw Kyle the best party ever?* It came to her like a bolt of lightning. She would use the resources around her, but first she needed to get cleared, then she would enlist the help of four of her newest friends.

Kyle drove like he was going to a funeral. She had never been driven this slow before. He made sure he didn't hit a single pothole. He reminded her of Carl in so many ways.

Carl had been an excellent provider, wonderful lover, and supported her in every decision she ever made even if it didn't work out to her favor. Kyle had the same traits. Finally, she said to him, "You know I'm not made out of egg shells. I can take the bumps in the road." He just smiled and continued to drive.

She felt like he was *Driving Miss Daisy*. God, if he continued to drive this way, it would take them forever to get to her appointments. Worse than that, she was getting carsick too. She reached in her purse and pulled out a pack of orange certs. They were her go to candy when she needed a little pick me up, plus orange was her favorite flavor in the certs candy line.

All seemed to work out at her doctor's visit, up until Sophie asked to speak with Gail alone. Sophie watched as the look on Kyle's face turned to a stern cross look. Sophie immediately told him she had work-related issues that needed to be cleared up. Knowing that wasn't the case at all, Sophie waited until Kyle exited Gail's office before she spoke her mind.

Bracing herself for some of the hardest questions, Sophie knew she had to get then off her chest. Looking like a deer in the headlights of a car, Sophie proceeded with the least amount of encouragement from Gail.

With a nice pink blush spreading across her cheeks, Sophie took the leap of faith by letting all of her pent up anxieties explode from her inner soul. "Gail this is so hard to ask you, but since you've known Kyle on a more personal level for many years, can you tell me… what kind of Dom/Master Kyle is? I'm so confused about the whole lifestyle thing. He keeps telling me that I'm definitely a submissive."

"So what's the problem, Sophie?"

"It's not really a problem, I just…with clear hesitation in her voice…I don't know that I'm the kind of girl that can give up total control 100%, to him, just yet."

"Look at it in another way. He wants to take all of the burden away from you. Sometimes when submissives have too many choices it becomes overwhelming to them, Kyle's not the type of Master who takes all your choices away. He's the more protecting loving type of Master. He doesn't want a doormat for a partner, he wants someone in his life that's able to protect, think on her own, and most of all be someone he can trust with his heart. Power exchange is a funny thing Sophie; it's not something that happens overnight. The two of you'll need to come up with rules and boundaries that will work out for the two of you.

Just think back to when you were married to Carl. He knew where you were at all times. Correct? You never went out after work with just the girls for a drink." Shaking her from side to side, just that gesture answered Gail's question.

"That's right, Soph, you didn't. Why's that?"

"Because I didn't want Carl worrying where I was, and it was polite."

"That's correct. It's the same thing in a power exchange. The only difference is when you break a rule you'll need to pay the consequence, usually with some kind of punishment that has been established by the two of you.

Sophie you hold the key to your own happiness. You have the final say in this type of relationship. You're not a yes girl all the time; you can say no. Just like in your marriage, you could have walked away at any time. The same holds true in a power exchange. It's a lot of give and take between the two of you. Once you see your inner submissive side, you will find Kyle needs his Mastery over you. It's a two way street. You're his Yin, and he's your Yang.

The best thing for you to do now is get to know some of the submissives that come to The Cellar. You already know a few of them. You'll be surprised submissives come in all different genders, shapes, sizes, abilities, traits, backgrounds, and careers. But what you'll find with all of them is an inner calling, a desire deep down in their soul to serve. Once those fears are relieved, you'll find its easier than what your first thoughts were.

I'll let you in on a big secret. Your journey will have its ups and downs just like anything else in life. Surprise, surprise. We all have room for growth in our personal journeys. You're no different. This is a new path you must decide to take. I bet once you get to know others, you'll find you're no different than anyone else.

Kyle's a wonderful, kind, loving man. He does live the lifestyle 24/7 which scares the hell out of a lot of women.

once you get past the doubt within yourself, you'll see it's a special bond between the two of you."

Letting the words of encouragement sink into Sophie's soul, sparked another question in her burning head. *How does Gail know so much about Kyle? Wow, I'm really afraid of this answer. Yes.* She just her no filter was beginning to turn back on again. "Gail, did the two of you…ever, you know, do it?" As Sophie asked the question, she saw the mirrored hesitation written all over Gail's face.

"When I first entered the lifestyle, I didn't know what was up or down. I did all the possible research, just like you're doing now. Trying to make heads or tails out of everything, I braved the inner side of my demons, thinking about typical stereotypes of modern society where whites were with white and blacks with black, guys with girls kind of stuff. Nothing out the norm.

At first, I only dated white dominant guys. Kyle happened to come across my path, just like anything else, he was white, he fit the bill so to speak, but something just didn't spark between the two of us. Well that's not true. Sex was out of this world."

Sophie became really uncomfortable with her confession.

"Sophie, I would crumble at his feet for days. Then I realized I was fighting the demons insides myself. I wasn't being true to myself. I had always fantasied about being in charge. I wanted to hold all the power, but never put that out there when I was first exploring. Kyle immediately saw that side of me. So he did the most amazing thing, he took me to the club, made me kneel at his side, instead of the two of us doing a scene, he arranged for us to watch a beautiful scene between a powerful Dominatrix and her male submissive.

I watched her scene so intently; it still brings tingling sensations up and down my spine, just thinking about it. I still remember it to this day. It was the most beautiful thing

I had ever witnessed. She held all the power in her hands as she flogged her submissive's back.

The energy that was released between the two had a lasting effect on me. I turned to Kyle. He kissed me on the top of my head and asked, "Do you see it now?" I knew exactly what he was saying; after the dominatrix was done with her scene, Kyle introduced me to her and her husband. We made arrangements for Mistress O to train and teach me everything about being a female Dominant.

So to answer your question, yes Kyle and I had a thing for each other. It only lasted for a short time. He saw right through me. Generally, his instincts are dead on. When he sees something worthwhile, he uses his Mastery to make it work. He saw that in me, that's why he forced me to see a different path without him. We are closer than ever, but that's not saying we don't have our differences. We don't always see eye to eye on everything." Gail snickered.

"Is it hard for you to see people at the club that you've had a connection to, but know they're with someone else?"

"If you're asking if I'm jealous? No not at all. I look at it as a learning process. Some people are meant for each other and some are not. I do see you and Kyle being meant for each other, if that's what you're asking.

Kyle has come in contact with a lot of submissives at the club. Some hold special bonds with him, but what I can tell you, he's been looking for that special someone to complete him.

I most sure that's you Sophie. I saw it in his face when we almost lost you. I had never seen him look so devastated. You've won his heart. You need to trust your heart. That's where trust comes into the picture."

"Wow, I've been so blind at times. I think I'm beginning to see a clearer picture now. I hope you didn't mind me coming to you with these questions."

"Not at all. Hopefully you'll find that asking questions first instead of jumping to conclusions will only benefit you.

Most, not all, people in the lifestyle are here for each other. Use them as resources, just like in medicine when we come across something questionable about a specific treatment for a patient, we seek out advice from our colleges. Do the same with kink."

"I know it's probably way too soon to tell, but what do you think my chances are of still practicing medicine."

"That's going to totally depend on therapy. No one will be able to tell until you get full use of your hand back. It's going to take more time. So in the meantime, work on your therapy, like you've been. We'll recheck you in a month."

"Are you willing to speculate at all?"

"I'm thinking by Christmas I'll see my favorite Cardiac Thoracic Surgeon in her blue scrubs, sporting a collar around her neck and a ring on her finger."

Blushing with excitement, Sophie watched as Gail came from around her desk. The two women had been friends for many years, but Sophie learned more about Gail in the past fifteen minutes than she had in the last six years.

"I think your man is going to wear a hole in the floor outside if we don't tell him its ok for him to take you home."

"Gail, one last thing. I'm cleared for sexual intercourse, right?"

"Why I would have thought the two of you would have been doing it like monkeys by now."

"Not in the least bit. I think he thinks he's going to break me or something. If a little gunshot didn't do me in, I really don't think sex is going to kill me."

"God I can see the eleven o'clock news now, *cardiac thoracic surgeon died while having sex with prominent doctor/ businessman/24/7 Master.*"

Both girls broke out in loud laughing.

Kyle could no doubt hear them joking and laughing at this point. Sophie opened the door and gestured for him to come back in the office. Just seeing his sparkling Caribbean blue eyes melted Sophie's insides.

"I think our patient is healing just fine. She still has a long road ahead of her. I already told Sophie I'd see the two of you back in a month to reassess her progress. She still needs to ask for help, no lifting over ten pounds.

Got it? Hopefully by then I won't have to hear how her delicate little flower between her legs hasn't been deflowered yet."

Shocked to hear what Gail had just called her pussy, Sophie diverted her eyes directly down to the floor. She couldn't bear to look at either one of them. Gail reached in her desk drawer and pulled out a business card. She handed it over to her. Sophie read the card with hesitation written all over her face.

"Since you've had two major life altering events that have had strong impacts on your life, I feel as your doctor you need to talk to a professional."

"I saw Dr. Pollock after the car accident. Couldn't I just call him and make an appointment?"

"Lisa happens not only to be a psychologist but she is also in the lifestyle. You'll find that most trained counselors that aren't in the lifestyle have no clue what the lifestyle really is about. Take Kyle for instance. He practices both, but he happens to be your partner so it's going to be harder for you to break down some of the barriers that you've built up.

Lisa is an amazing woman. I think the two of you will be able to work out a lot of issues that are still stored deep down in your soul."

"If you think it will help, then I'll make the call." Sophie looked over at Kyle his eyes sparkled with delight.

"Sophie, if it helps, I see her partner occasionally. After I was discharged from the military, I kept having flash backs of the horrible things that happened in the hot zones, plus the combination of looking for my father had been bottled up for so long I thought I was going crazy. So with the help of Lisa's partner, I was able to talk through my issues. Now look at me."

"All I can do is give it a try."

"That's my girl."

"Oh by the way, Kyle, do your club rules still…"

Before she could finish her statement he said, "What have the two of you've been up to while I was outside?"

"I just needed to mark my calendar with today's date that's all."

"What are the two of you talking about?" Sophie squeaked.

"Ask your Master on the drive home, Sophie. He'll fill you in."

Sophie would never have been able to survive her injuries if it weren't for the expert skills of her friend, and colleague Gail. Knowing that she owed her big time, flowers would not do in this case. Every doctor got flowers two to three times a week from their patients. A flash went off in Sophie's head. She'd remembered seeing a kinky clothing website online. She could pick something out for her online as a thank you. Now she was using her head for something good.

On the drive home from the hospital, Kyle took Sophie out to lunch. Phuong Duck's was one of the oldest Chinese restaurants in Baltimore City. She often talked about her love for different ethnic foods. It seemed that Kyle had that same love as she did.

Mr. Chang had been a patient of Sophie's a few years back. After his open heart surgery, Sophie made it a point to stop into the restaurant at least once a week to check up on Mr. Chang. Plus she enjoyed sipping her favorite jasmine tea while the two discussed everyday life. It happened that the restaurant was only a few blocks away from her apartment. When planning out their day, Kyle told her he had already called a head of time to let Mr. Chang know that they would be coming in after her appointments.

Sophie had asked if they could stop by her apartment. She had some important stuff she needed to pick up. The only thing that came to mind was BOB, and maybe she could dig around in her closet for a few sexy teddies she had shoved way back in the back. It had been a month since she had stepped foot in her apartment. Being a stickler for cleaning, she could just imagine the dust build up. She'd call a cleaning company when she got back to Kyle's place.

With her belly all filled from the delicious chicken fried rice, and three cups of Jasmine tea, Kyle turned the car into the parking lot of Sophie's apartment. Instantly Sophie began to sweat, and tiny beads of perspiration formed on her forehead. Not able to quite control herself, Sophie's knees started to pop up and down. She needed to run, but was afraid to even breathe.

Working herself up was the last thing she needed to do. "Baby, are you okay? Do you need to go home? I can get someone to come by your apartment and get whatever you need."

"I'm scared." That's all she could get to come out of her mouth."

That's all it took for Kyle to hear because the next thing she felt was his hand picking up her hand bringing it to his lips.

"Sophie, look at me, I'm by your side nothing is going to happen to you. The gang members who shot you are in jail. They're not getting out anytime soon. They can't hurt you any more, baby girl. I need you to do something for me Sophie. This is something as your Master I'm requiring you to do."

Listening to his words was like a switch had just been turned on in Sophie's brain. "What's that Master?"

"Very good, Pet, I see that I have your full attention. I'm pleased with your response. I want you to trust me." He didn't allude or beat around the bush when he said the word TRUST.

Sophie had a choice to make and it was probably the biggest step to conquer. Everyone around her recently used the word trust. It was more important that Sophie put her full trust heartily into Kyle's hands. She would need to surrender to his will.

"Yes, Master. I trust you." She watched as Kyle pulled out his cell phone. He hit an app on his phone, which brought up the CCTV. He started playing back the video that had been captured in the past hour.

Sophie had not seen how sophisticated the security system Volkov Security had set up. Feeling a little more relieved, Sophie reached into her purse and pulled out a tissue. She dried up her wet face. She indicated to Kyle she was ok and ready to go inside the building.

It only took the two of them about a half hour to get everything Sophie needed. Kyle told her they could come back in a few days to get more of her stuff. She had a feeling it would be only a matter of time before she had only her furniture left in the space. *That wasn't such a bad thing.*

After an emotional day, Sophie was tired more now than what she ever had been. When they got back to Kyle's place, he told Sophie he had some calls to make.

All she wanted to do was take a catnap. Kyle had helped her remove clothes before getting into the hospital bed. He kissed her, telling her that he was going to go to the den to make all of his calls. If she needed anything, she was to ring the bell that was on the nightstand. Sophie felt the exhaustion hit her like a brick falling from a collapsing building.

Her body sank down in the hospital bed. She snuggled under the covers until the only thing Kyle could see was the tip of her nose. She drifted off.

"No brakes, baby, brace yourself!"

Time stood still as Sophie replayed in her mind the two vehicles colliding. Screaming at the top of her lungs, NO, NO, NO! Twisting and turning from side to side in the hospital bed, Sophie felt large hands grabbing hold of her shoulders. Seeing herself pulled from the crumpled up wreckage. Looking over at her lifeless husband covered in blood. She felt again two large hands shaking her, "Sophie, darling, wake up for me baby. You're having a nightmare again. Blinking struggling to open up her eyes, she heard Kyle again say, "Baby, open up your eyes and look at me."

Sophie sat up, peered around vaguely confused. Finally focusing on Kyle's voice, Sophie knew she had just had another nightmare about her dead husband. *Why after two years was she being haunted by that horrible night? Would she be haunted for the rest of her life?*

Sophie watched as Kyle walked over to the bathroom. He came back with a glass of water and a washcloth. Slowly he held the glass to Sophie's lips as he told her to take a drink. Giving her just a sip of water, Kyle pulled the glass away from her lips. Taking the wet washcloth, Kyle placed it on her exposed bare neck.

The warmth of the terry cloth had Sophie purring like a kitten. "That's it, baby girl, feel the warmth seeping into your pores." Sophie closed her eyes, doing exactly what Kyle had just commanded her to do. *How did he know what to do to make her go from being scared shitless, to feeling completely taking care of?* "Are you okay now, baby?"

"I think so." Still feeling herself shaking inside, Sophie reached for his Kyle's hand. It was a huge step in telling him she needed him.

Chapter Ten

All through dinner Kyle watched Sophie intently, making sure she didn't melt down again. Every day since the shooting, he had made sure Sophie talked about her feelings and emotions. Today was like no other day. Kyle made small talk about her juvenile accusers.

Sophie expressed to Kyle she had mixed feelings about bringing charges up against the two young boys. He reinforced to her that he would be by her side through the entire process. Trying to get her to open up about the shooting had been a bust for him. Kyle suspected that was the cause of her recent nightmares. Tonight he wouldn't question her anymore. It could wait until to tomorrow.

Tonight, he had other plans for the two of them. He was sure glad that Gail had given the card for Lisa. He wasn't going to push her to set up an appointment, but he would drop subtle hints to her. *Positive reinforcement.*

Kyle walked with Sophie daily looking for signs of any type of breathing issues. She was definitely stronger than she had been two weeks ago. No, she wasn't at a hundred percent, but in time, he knew she would be. Not once did she show any signs of shortness of breath. Still being the good Dom, he needed to hear from Gail's mouth today that all Sophie's restrictions had been lifted, except for extreme bondage and suspension.

Tonight was all about rekindling his relationship with Sophie.

After dinner, the two enjoyed a long walk down to the stables that housed Kyle's pride and joy, Jake. Each day Kyle and Sophie spent time just walking the horses around in a big open field behind the stables. Tonight was going to be a little different. Kyle felt it was time to introduce her one of his favorite past times. Horseback riding.

Never had Kyle opened himself up to any woman as he had with Sophie in the past few weeks. He loved learning all about her likes, dislikes, hobbies, special vacations with her family, and even things her and Carl liked to do together. He felt it was only fair she learned about his likes, dislikes, and things special to Kyle's heart. Tonight she would be introduced to a few more things.

Kyle made sure the horses were saddled and ready to be ridden by the time they reached the stables. Clifton, the stable boy, had just finished prepping the horses when Kyle and Sophie entered the stables. Kyle watched Sophie's face light up with excitement. She looked as if she were going to jump up and down with glee. Instead, she walked over to the large American Quarter horse, bent to his ear and whispered something that only Jake could hear. Watching the two interact filled Kyle's heart with love.

Jake made all kinds of sounds that a horse could make as Sophie stroked his mane. "Baby, Clifton is going to steady Jake while I help you mount him."

"Kyle I'm not sure if I'm up to riding a horse yet. Plus, I haven't been on a horse in fifteen years."

Standing next to Sophie, Kyle stroked down Jake's back. "Sophie, do you trust me? Yes or no."

"Yes." Kyle reached over placing his hand on Sophie's shoulder, "Now that we settled that problem, Clifton will you show my beautiful sub how easy it is to mount Jake?"

Kyle watched as Sophie turned her face towards him with a puzzled look. Do you remember your safe-word, Pet?"

"Yes Master."

"Tell me what it is."

"Crash"

"My sweet little sub, do you remember what the definition of safe-word?"

"Yes, Master, the definition is: a previously agreed upon word, which when spoken during a BDSM role-play, tells the dominant partner to stop the activity immediately."

"Correct, baby girl, your Master is proud of you for memorizing the definition. Remember, when we talked about this at the pond, I told you that if you spoke your safe-word the scene would be immediately over. That still holds true. I need for you to understand that I will never put you in any type of danger. Some things I do to you will hurt, but I will never intentionally harm you. I need you to tell me that you understand what you're about to enter into. By agreeing, you fully understand anything that happens from this moment on. We're two consenting adults. You are submitting to my will."

Strangely enough, Sophie had a glow to her. Kyle watched as her nipples began to poke through her light cotton shirt. Seeing the change in her skin color gave Kyle a positive charge throughout his entire body.

Letting Sophie take as much time as she needed, Kyle just stood, like a soldier readying for battle. Giving her just another second to make her mind up, Kyle continued to stroke Jake up and down his back.

"We've gone over your soft and hard limits list for the past few weeks. Nowhere on that list did you ever have horseback riding as a hard limit." Kyle watched as Sophie nodded her head in agreement.

"Remember…when in a power exchange relationship, you need to be willing to hand over all power to your

Master. I know this is a tough decision for you. Control is one of your biggest downfalls when it comes to handing over your complete surrender. It's scary as hell for you. Remember, I cherish your gift of surrendering to me. Nothing is more satisfying to me than having your trust.

To clarify something for you, when we enter into a scene, the scene is not over until your Master deems it over. Since we've only scened once before, I would like to put a start and stop time limit on this scene. You are to address me as either Master or Sir. You will respect my decisions at all times. No curses or derogatory statements are to exit your mouth. Your right shoulder, arm and hand will not be used in any way that will cause more injury. Sophie, I need you to look directly into my eyes." He cupped her chin with his hands. "I want you to hand over total control of your body, mind and soul to me until tomorrow morning. Do you have any questions for me?" Kyle watched as Sophie shook her head. Sounding a little more stern than before, "Pet….what have I told you about shaking your head when I ask you a direct question?"

"Sir…I'm… sorry. You need to hear me answer your question with my voice not my head."

"Correct. For disobeying a direct command, you've earned two smacks on your ass.

Clifton I need you to retrieve the crop that is hanging over Buttercup's stall please."

"Yes, Sir." Kyle watched Sophie's cheeks turn beet red as Clifton went to get the crop. Sophie had never felt the bite of the crop. She was in for a big surprise on how much the crop stung after the impact was over.

Kyle motioned for Sophie to pull her yoga pants down to her knees. Without even having to command her twice, Sophie pulled her yoga pants down, leaving her black G-string in place.

"Pet, I want you to hold onto the metal stall, and you're to relax as much as possible. The more you tense up the worse the feeling will be after your punishment is over. You've earned two smacks with the crop. Do you understand, Pet?"

"Yes, Master."

"Let's get this over as quick as possible."

Watching her take a deep breath in, Kyle gave her barely enough time to get settled before flicking the crop over her ass cheek. An instant bite of red blossomed across Sophie's right ass cheek. She yelled out in pain.

"Oh God." Not giving her anytime to recover, Kyle smacked her left ass cheek in the same manner as he had the right side. She yelled out again as the crop impacted her ass.

Kyle rubbed both her ass cheeks. Seeing a lovely deep red imprint of the crop appear on her ass instantly made Kyle's cock twitch in his jeans. He loved seeing his mark on his girl. "Your punishment is over, Pet. Pull you pants up, turn and face me." Tears marked Sophie face. Kyle walked over to a table where a roll of paper towels sat. Pulling one off, he made his way back to Sophie, dried her face and had her blow her nose into the towel. Just as any Dom would do, Kyle took care of his sub's needs.

"Thank you Sir, for my punishment. I'm not perfect in the obeying area, but I will put forth every effort in my soul to make corrections."

"Your most welcomed darling. You have until the count of three to either get up on that horse or you say your safe-word. If you choose to use your safe-word, we go back up to the house and call it a night. We're losing day light. My horse needs to get his exercise with or without you."

"One...Two..."

"Master your sub would like to hand over total control of her mind, body and soul to her Master." He watched as Sophie, slowly tilted her head towards the hay filled ground.

He gave her a second to adjust to what she had just agreed to. Tapping Sophie's good shoulder with his hand,

Sophie raised her head. Kyle motioned for Clifton to help guide Sophie onto the saddle that lay on Jake's back, but before he allowed Clifton to lift her up, Kyle pressed his lips to her forehead. "Such a good girl, you are my dear. You've pleased your Master."

Sophie winced as Clifton sat her throbbing ass down on the leather saddle that rested on Jake's back. She wasn't sure how she would be able to handle a long horseback ride with her ass aching as it did. Not sure how to move on from her punishment, Sophie quietly sat on the back of the amazing horse. Processing the pain, versus the embarrassment she felt was disheartening. How could she have disrespected someone she was falling in love with?

"Don't beat yourself up, baby girl. I can see the steam coming out of your head."

"How did you know what I was thinking, Sir?"

"You have the look in your eyes. I've seen it before with other submissives who realize only after they have been punished what the true meaning of the infraction they committed."

"God. When you say it that way, I feel so horrible."

"Punishment is not to make you feel horrible, Pet. It's meant to correct your misgiving of yourself to your Master. I'll let you in on a little secret; punishment is meant to reconnect us back together as one. Not all punishment you receive will be inflicting pain; some forms of punishments will be purely mind games."

"I'm most sure my ass will be sore for at least a week."

"Yup, every time you go to sit down you'll feel sharp bites of pain flare throughout your ass cheeks. It will be a constant reminder to you of your disobedience."

With a sarcastic little smirk, Sophie replied to Kyle, "Great."

"I'm going to love watching each time you squirm back and forth from cheek to cheek. Your Master's firm hand will bring you back to reality every time you are disrespectful."

In time, Sophie knew the marks that Kyle had just given her would soon fade, only to have more of her Master's marking visible. Just that thought sent goose bumps up and down her spine.

The ride down to the pond wasn't as bad as Sophie had first imagined. Yeah, her ass smarted from time to time, but nothing she couldn't endure. Sophie realized she had to put some of her fears to rest. Just like getting on top of the horse, she let her fear become so over powering. She almost missed the opportunity of spending a beautiful night looking at the stars with her Master.

She was a strong-headed woman when it came to medicine, but when it came to her letting herself relax, she still resisted. This was something she needed to work on. Luckily, for Sophie when the two returned to the stables, Clifton had already done his chores and was gone for the night.

Sophie wasn't sure she could make eye contact with him for a while. Being watched during her punishment brought more shame and humiliation to her than what she had originally thought.

Sophie watched as Kyle slowly dismounted Sampson, the horse he rode. He told her that he was riding Sampson more and more since his most prized horse was getting slower. Sophie was truly honored that Kyle had let her experience the gentleness of Jake. Not once did he, buck her or even resist. Instead, he calmly carried Sophie on his back as if she were a princess.

Locking her eyes on his ass stirred up all kinds of hidden desires within Sophie's body. She was amazed how excited she was getting just by watching her guy. She hungered for sex in the worst possible way. It had been four weeks of no sex. So far, the only thing that the two of them had done was make out like two horny teenagers. Maybe tonight she'd get lucky.

Kyle told her to stay on her horse until he had Sampson secured back in his stall. Tracking each of his movements a stranger would have mistaken him for the stable guy instead of a successful billionaire. She was such a lucky girl to have an incredible man in her life. He had done everything for her in the past month. He could have sent her on her own after her discharge. Hell, he didn't even have to show up at the hospital at all. But, no, he stood by her side.

Chapter Eleven

Hearing Kyle walk back toward her and Jake, a beautiful picture flashed in her mind. She was kneeling at his feet, submitting to his desires, wearing a collar around her neck and a ring on her finger. As he stood in front of her, his blue eyes sparkled when the light hit them just right.

"I'm going to help you off the horse and when I put you on the ground I want you to go the bathroom. It's past the first stall on the right. Go pee and wash off with the supplies that I have left for you in the bathroom. When you're done, I want you to come back in here. You're to stand in front of the open stall next to Jake's. Do you understand the commands? Do you need for me to repeat any of the steps that I have given you, Pet?"

"No Sir, your submissive is to go pee, use the supplies to wash up, and then I'm to come back in here and stand over by the empty stall next to Jake."

"You've made your Master happy by remembering every step."

He slowly placed his hands around Sophie's curvy waist. Her nipple peaked to a tight point. Her clit became sensitive from just his hands on her hips. Feeling like a volcano, Sophie was sure to erupt. She remembered Kyle's command. No, it had nothing to do with having an orgasm, it was just getting off the horse. *Contain your excitement woman.*

Sliding her off Jake's back, the horse let a loud sigh come from his mouth. Puzzled by the way Jake was acting, Sophie spoke lightly to the old horse, "It's okay, boy, I'll be back. Go rest for now."

She managed to keep her composure as she slipped into the bathroom. Her heart began to hammer away in her chest as she looked at everything Kyle had sat out for her. On a small stool sat a neatly folded wash cloth, some of her favorite hand soap, a toothbrush, toothpaste, mouthwash, deodorant, a hair brush, a scrunchie, a tube of fire red lipstick, a red lacy bra, a matching G-string, and a silky robe.

God she had waited weeks to finally have her man back. Desire unfurled deep down in her belly as she started to undress.

After sprucing herself up, Sophie relieved her bladder as Kyle instructed her to do so. Before exiting the bathroom, Sophie painted her lips with the fire red lipstick. She pressed her lips together giving them added wetness from her tongue. Running her hands over the cold silk fabric teased her insides even more. *God she really did need to get a hold of herself.*

Leaving the inner sanction of the bathroom sent a chill up and down Sophie's spine. It wasn't cold outside. It was the beginning of August for God's sake. Why all of a sudden was she shivering like it was the middle of December and twenty degrees outside? Yep it was her nerves; they were coming to the surfaces ready to be set free.

Sophie walked methodically over to the stall next to Jake's as Kyle had instructed. She couldn't see Kyle clearly but she could make out his tall silhouette off in the dark side of the stable. She stood with her back to a steel metal gate just as Kyle had commanded. Her heartbeat ratcheted up in her chest.

Standing in only the lacy bra and panties, having the warmth of the robe cover her tingly body only comforted Sophie to a certain degree. She listen to the sounds of the room, hearing the horses breathe heavily, Sophie tried to match her breathing to theirs. She swore she could hear her heart beating in her ears. Never a big fan of bugs, Sophie heard the chirping of crickets in the distance.

All of the horses were now all settled in their stalls. What seemed like a lifetime was only sheer seconds that ticked by.

She watched as Kyle sauntered towards her. Each step he took brought her breathing up another notch, finally her Master stood in front of her like a warrior who had come to take what was rightfully his.

Sophie closed her eyes as she took in the musky smell of his cologne. She'd never tire of smelling him. She felt as she was under a hypnotic spell; it was as if she was already in bliss. She closed her eyes as Kyle drew even closer to her. He was definitely invading her space, God she felt her entire body light up like a firecracker as he placed his bear-like hands around her neck.

Sophie tried to slow down her breathing, fearing she might hyperventilate and pass out from all the extra oxygen that she breathed into her lungs. She felt a little dizzy, and it was all because of the touch of her man. It sent her head spinning.

Time stood still as the world around her only existed of her and Kyle, nothing else. Kyle slowly let go of her neck, then he pressed his body up against Sophie's stomach, pushing her back up against the metal gate. A low whimper escaped Sophie's mouth as he pressed his lips up against hers.

Instinctively Sophie opened her mouth to his, as both of their tongues did a slow dance, twisting and turning and sucking against each other. Sophie felt her juices slowly trickle down her inner thigh.

She had nowhere to run, being pinned up against the gate. Kyle used his entire body to secure her in a way she instantly felt safe. The air around her became charged from the energy that Kyle was expelling from his aura.

She felt his power and energy excreting from his body as he pressed even harder against her stomach. She felt his cock twitch as their bodies became one. He radiated warmth from his body and Sophie was no longer cold. What was she in for tonight?

Breaking off the kiss, Sophie stared at the man who stood in front of her. Her body had come to life just from his kiss, her nipples grew to large points, she felt them poking through the lacy bra. Her arousal had been definitely woken up.

Speaking to her in a baritone voice Kyle asked, "What is your safe-word?"

"Crash, Sir."

"Very good, Pet. I want you to put on a show for your Master, seduce your Master with your beautiful body. Sophie at first couldn't move a muscle. Everything in her body felt paralyzed. *What was her Master asking her to do?*" Kyle's tone deepened "Either obey my command or say your safe-word, Pet."

Deep down Sophie was extremely excited, though something about the situation rubbed her the wrong way. Trying to jog her brain with a snappy little burlesque number, Sophie began to hum out loud, swinging her hips from side to side, slowly she pushed down the robe off of her right shoulder, looking at the scar she now sported was a real eye catcher.

Not wanting to dampen the mood, she switched to her left shoulder and did the exact same thing, clenching the robe at the tops of her breast. Teasing her Master as he wished.

She slowly turned her back to her Master; taking her left hand, she grabbed the metal gate. Gyrating her hips in a seduced move, she slowly shimmied down to the floor.

Her back barely exposed, she released the ponytail holder that held her hair up high on her head. She swept her hair to the side of her neck. Twisting and twirling her hair from side to side, she ran her fingers through the long strands. *Damn, she wished it were her Master's fingers instead of hers.*

Singing and giggling out loud was all new for Sophie, because she had been so dark and low for so long. Tonight she finally hit a level of confidence that was exceptionally rewarding to her heart. This was her total submission being presented to her Master.

Gracefully, Sophie let the robe drop to the ground; her back now facing her Master, rotating, gyrating, and swaying her hips to sound of her own voice, transformed Sophie into another world.

Her body was on fire, her nipples throbbed to be touched, the tiny g-string she wore was sopping wet. She was sure her Master could sense her excitement.

Pivoting around to face her Master, she saw his large hands stroking his cock, through his jeans. Her erotic dance was working. She saw how hard he was. She still had her under garments on. She needed his large hands on her breasts, instead of his cock. She shimmied up close to him. Taking his hands off of his cock, Sophie placed them on both of her breasts.

She let out a soft moan when his fingers started squeezing her already plump nipples. She rotated her hips, pressing them up against Kyle's thighs. Taking her hands, she gently started to unbutton his jeans. Kyle removed his hands from her nipples, placing them on top of Sophie's petite slender fingers. "Feel how hard you've made your Master. You have pleased me, my little Pet, but you still have not finished my command yet. I need to see all of my beautiful slave."

"Yes, Master."

Just hearing his voice had a hypnotic effect on Sophie. The dominance exerted from Kyle when he used his baritone voice… Every time he spoke to her in that manor, her insides felt like gelatin. Her heart was beating so fast in her chest, she was sure to pass out. She hadn't felt this way in a long time.

She felt alive. Kyle had never referred to her as his slave; this was a new term. It made her feel even more excited. Passion burned through her; she needed to please her Master.

Sophie removed her hands from his zipper; scooting back, she lost the warmth from her Master. Braving her inner demons, she reached back and unclasped her bra. sliding the lacy material down and dropping it to the ground, she let her perky breasts fly free, exposing them for her Master's delight. Standing in front of him in just her G-string, Sophie never had an issue with her figure. Never having a modesty issue, she took her slender fingers, hooking them to the inside of the flimsy fabric and slid them down to the ground.

Need burned up inside of her, with nothing between her legs she was sure she'd come if she closed her legs together, instead she did what any slave would do, she slid gracefully to her knees, head tilted to the ground, palms laying on top of her thighs, legs spread wide apart exposing her glistening, wet pussy to her Master. She wasn't sure how long she could stay in this position, but she would do her best to please her Master. She was pretty sure once Kyle saw her sign of submission he would be all over her. Just like a bear, he would find his pot of honey, and it seeped between Sophie's quivering thighs. It was her own personal honey pot.

Taking a long deep breath in, Sophie settled herself even more into her submission. Sophie heard her heart pounding in her ears. Trying to ease her mind, she thought back to being held in Kyle's warm arms. Sophie had hit subspace for the first and only time when they had scened four weeks ago. She was surely on her way tonight.

Kyle had longed for this night, for the past month. Getting the all clear from Gail was the icing on the cake so to speak. He knew he had his work cut out for him, but he was willing to take the necessary time to build a strong M/s relationship with Sophie.

She was his everything; he just needed to guide her down the correct path. She had submitted to his will before and loved it. Now he just had to work through her nasty temper, and a bit of the sassiness she had acquired in the past few weeks. He loved a slave with a bite of sass.

She became more playful as her desires were met. What better way to handle his slave, than to administer her punishment she had earned when she ran from her fears, four weeks ago.

Kyle had to show her a different side of his dominance, but unfortunately for him that would result in Sophie receiving a much more serve punishment than her cropping session earlier. His mastery skills of working out a submissive's fear and trust were tools he had learned early on in his training. If a sub/slave couldn't trust her Dom/Master how could they build a long-term commitment?

Kyle saw Sophie as a long-term commitment; he'd been searching for her his entire life. Out of every one of the sub/slaves that he had been intimate with in the past few years, none of then held the characteristics that Sophie held.

She was beautiful beyond belief, her smoking hot body made him ache for her when she was in his presence. Not only was she intelligent, but she also had that sassiness to her that brought out the laughter in him. She was refined in a way that her easy laid-back life appealed to her sophistication. Her passion to serve others just put her on a pedestal.

Kyle often wondered if he could give the same of himself back to someone, since he still harbored abandonment issues from his father. It was still embedded in Kyle's soul, how his father just up and walked away from his family. Always having that thought , Kyle reminded himself often that he was nothing like his father. He could never walk away from Sophie or his future family with her.

Nothing was more important to him than Sophie. He would make the necessary arrangements to confront his father now that he knew Sophie could travel. He would get back in touch with Master Sergeant to set up another mission to Puerto Rico.

He could kill two birds with one trip. Confront his father first, then spend the rest of his time buried deep in Sophie's sweet pussy, nestled along a private beach in Puerto Rico. A little business with a lot of pleasure could be accomplished on this trip. Yep, that's exactly what he planned to do.

Focusing back on the beautiful woman who knelt at his feet, her exotic dance almost had him blowing his load in his jeans. She had that effect on him. He swore he could hear Sophie's heart pounding loudly. Knowing that she was the one for him, he had to reset his mind to what he planned for tonight.

Seeing that his girl was halfway to subspace, he tapped her on shoulder, forcing her to straighten her neck. Sliding his hand under her chin, he forced Sophie to gaze into his eyes. "Pet, I want you to stand, as much as I love you on your knees, I have other uses for you tonight."

He saw the goose pumps on her arms as he spoke to her. Her nipples grew to the size of erasers. Sucking on those beautiful buds were sure to bring pleasure to both of them.

Envisioning clover clamps on her nipples with a gold chain running down to her clit sent a twitch to Kyle's cock. Thinking back to when Sophie asked Kyle to use the clover clamps on her at the club brought back a delightful memory. Just attaching them to her little diamonds almost brought him to his knees. What if she let him pierce her buds? She didn't know yet but Master Kyle was very skilled with needle play.

He couldn't wait to train her to like all of his kinks. In the past few weeks he had ordered all different kinds of kink toys for his girl and his pleasure; he just had to hold out a bit longer to use all of them on her. After tonight, he would do just that.

Her scent from her sex filled the room; he could already taste her on his tongue. No, that too would have to wait. Tonight was all about punishment. Hopefully, she would open up to him by surrendering all of her fears. He knew this was a make or break moment in his life, the true Dom in him needed a slave that trusted him fully.

Night had completely captured the sky outside. Each stall had a small window that could be opened or closed depending on the weather conditions outside. Kyle had turned off all of the overhead fans, except for the one closest to Jake's stall. Just the correct amount of air circulated around the room with just one fan. He didn't want Sophie getting a chill.

His beautiful woman stood in front of him naked; she was the gift that you got at Christmas time that you cherished. Not the one you returned for a refund. She was a keeper for sure.

Kyle had already given all of the house staff off until tomorrow after noon, including the stable help. He had his work cut out for him. No time like the present to start.

Walking over to where a coil of rope hung from a hook, he took it into his hand, picked up a small stool, and a silver bowl that resembled a dogs drinking bowl. Sometimes a Dom had to do things to their pretty little subs that not only broke the sub but also broke the Dom.

Kyle was sure Sophie's punishment was going to strengthen their bond. He placed the stool next to Sophie's quivering legs. He motioned for her to sit on the stool.

She made a little squeal when her bare bottom hit the wood. "Did you like how that felt, baby girl?"

"Yes, Master but I'd rather have your warm hands any day."

"There's my bratty little girl. Tonight is going to be all about you.

You won't be feeling my warm hands until after breakfast. Kyle watched her eyes start to blink rapidly. Do you trust me Sophie? "Yes, Master why do ask me that question?" Kyle noticed as Sophie started to shift around on the small stool.

"Remember, I told you that I would take care of you no matter what?"

"Yes, Master. I still don't know what you're referring to, though."

"Let me jog your memory."

Kyle watched as Sophie looked around the room. He could tell that she was ready to run as she did before. "No matter what I say to you Sophie, your ass is not to leave that stool. Understand Pet?"

"Yes, Master."

"Four weeks ago, after a pretty intense scene, we both fell asleep; only to be woken up by a phone call. Is this jogging your memory, Pet?"

"Yes, Master." Sophie's face turned pale. Kyle watched her with intent eyes, making sure she didn't bolt.

I finished my call, to find you crumpled up on the floor in a ball crying, when I approached you to find out what was the matter you shut down, not letting me in, Sophie.

Do you know how bad that hurt me?" He was making some kind of headway, tears streamed down Sophie's face. When I tried to console you, you pushed me away just like a used newspaper."

Kyle watched as Sophie began to tremble, knowing the harsh words must be making a dent into Sophie's soul.

"I'm so sorry Master for shutting you out. I was…scared. Memories started rushing in my head and I needed to leave to sort them out."

In a protective move, Sophie covered up her chest with her arms. "Put your arm to your side. Don't cover up your body by hiding behind your arms, Pet. I want you open fully to me. Bringing himself closer to Sophie's quivering body, Kyle watched as she slowly removed her arms from her chest.

"Pet what you did was, you put yourself in harm's way by running. You didn't trust me enough to tell me what the matter was. Remember, I told you that trust is extremely important in a power exchange relationship. When you stood in front of me, I made you repeat that very phrase. You agreed, didn't you?

Sophie had a scared as shit look on her face.

"Answer my question Pet."

"Yes, Master."

"Instead you ran like a child from the situation. You closed yourself off just like you had been doing for two years. You didn't protect what was mine, and you put your best friend in danger.

All I asked of you that night was that you talk to me. Tell me what I did wrong.

Sophie could no longer look Kyle in the eyes. "Instead you shut me out."

"God I'm so sorry, I didn't trust you, let alone myself. You need to believe me. I never thought I was in true danger. I thought you were just overreacting, trying to be all macho, or even trying to impress me. I needed to surround myself with my stuff. I know that sounds childish, but I couldn't do that with you. It was too soon."

Kyle stood. He looked bemused at the way Sophie opened up to him. If she had said those words to him four weeks ago, he wouldn't be having this conversation with her now. She wouldn't have been shot. Kyle caressed the rope that he held tight in his hand because his plan for her punishment still needed to be enforced.

"Sophie, I need for you to understand something. When you give up your power to someone, you trust that person not only with your body, but also with your happiness. Without trust a relationship will never work. If you had realized that before, you would have trusted me with what was bothering you."

As he spoke those words, it pained him to punish her but he had to keep with his word or she would likely just form a bad habit. And that wasn't the type of relationship he wanted to build with Sophie.

Kyle smoothed the rope again, "Do you trust me Sophie?"

"Yes, Master I trust you with all of my heart."

"You're aware that your punishment will not necessarily be a physical strike against your body. You need to retrain your brain."

"Yes, Master. I understand fully."

"Good girl. I'm so proud of you. Once I bind your legs to the stool, you'll be required to stay put. Do you understand, Sophie?"

Watching her work through her faults was every Master's nightmare. This would be a make or break situation. Humiliation was a different kind of punishment that many Doms used on their disobedient subs; it would either open their mind up to what had clouded it, or their heart would be shattered to pieces.

Sophie had to trust herself above everything else, and only then could she trust Kyle.

Kyle knew this first hand. He had worked with many subs in the past, and this was the hardest thing for any of them to overcome.

He saw Sophie's true side of surrendering in the past few weeks. She had an incredible need to comfort others instead of herself. Her needs were second to everyone else's. Rarely did she allow anyone to take care of her needs. Kyle would make sure she knew the difference.

She had a nurturing side that always put a smile on his face. He saw them raising many children together. Living a long happy prosperous life together. Something he never envisioned with anyone else. He just had to get finished with this mind fuck of a punishment.

Kyle removed his belt from around his waist. He could hear Sophie breathing a little louder. Slowly he took his belt, fed it through the metal gate, and wrapped the opened end around Sophie's right arm. Tightening the belt, it pulled her arm back resting on the metal gate.

"You're being held by my bondage, Sophie. Your job is to trust yourself. You have the power to trust; it is deep down in your soul. At any time you feel you can't trust me, you'll use the arm you were shot in to remove my belt."

Sophie had the most perplexed look on her face. Kyle reached over and kissed her on her forehead. "Sophie, what you did to me when you ran tore my heart open. Getting the phone call saying you had been shot, nearly killed me. You needed to trust me when I said I would take care of you.

Now, tell me the truth about why you panicked and bolted as if I were some kind of mass murder? I need to know what triggered such a horrible outburst."

Sophie took a deep breath and tried to settle herself. "Where do I start? When I came back from the bathroom, you were obviously having a heated conversation with someone on the phone." She paused. Her voice had become shaky at best, blinking back tears. "I heard you talk about Volkov Security as being your company." Her pitch in her voice went up slightly when she said Volkov Security.

"You never said that you owned my husband's family business."

"Sophie, I own several businesses. Volkov is just one of them. I still don't see where that is the cause of you bolting."

"It was just a piece of the puzzle that I started to put together."

"Go on. I'm listening."

"It hit me that you already knew Carl. You were the Dom training him. Shaking uncontrollably now, Sophie squirmed on the little stool and tried not to fall off.

You already knew everything about me. What turned me on, like I had never been turned on to anyone or anything before? Realizing Sophie was getting more worked up, Kyle took a step back. He loved it when she sprung her cat claws out, and it showed him she had her will to fight back in her.

When I started putting everything together in my head, it felt like you had played me, Kyle. I just couldn't figure out what *you* got out of tricking me like you did. I started to believe you really didn't want me for who I was, but for who I was married to.

I panicked. I didn't know what to do, so I ran back to the place that made me feel safe. I thought I could close myself off to everyone.

How fucking stupid of me to think that way, but I did. God I'm so sorry. Please forgive me."

Kyle waited until she seemed like she was done spewing words from her mouth. He just looked at how she presented herself to him sitting on the stool.

The night had flown by. Several hours had gone by without Sophie having finally broken her fears down. She no longer squirmed on the stool, but looked peaceful sitting on the stool with her head held high, shoulders back, chest pointed to the sky. Not once did she reach for the belt that bound her to the gate.

Kyle had accomplished what he set out to do. He realized Sophie had already punished herself more than any physical punishment could be. She bore the permanent mark of the bullet wound.

Kyle reinforced during her entire punishment that he expected her to trust him and she had. She was to be truthful to him; she had done just as he asked.

He needed to make sure Sophie was ready to forge on with their relationship. Was she going to submit over her power to Kyle? He knew this was a tough decision for anyone, but more so for Sophie. She was going to have her ups and downs.

He would stand by her every step of the way. She had become very independent in the last two years; the hardest thing for her was having someone love her again. He saw the same twinkle in her eyes as he did the first time he laid eyes on her. Neither of them was ready to throw in the towel. Knowing that the time had come to accept her apology and move on.

"Pet, your punishment is over as of this moment. All is forgiven." He slowly unbuckled the belt from around her arm. He massaged her aching muscles; she had been bound for over three hours in the same position. He bent down and untied her right leg from the leg of the stool, massaging her calf down to her bare toes. He did the same to her left leg.

Kyle's hand sent a shiver down her entire body. After he motioned for Sophie to rise, she slid down to her knees, bent forward and kissed both of his feet, showing her sign of complete submission. He knew Sophie had been working with the submissive group from the club and she had learned so much in such a short amount of time.

Kyle let a sound of delight escape his mouth. She had pleased her Master by showing her grace, poise, and surrendering her heart. "Master, will you grant me a second chance of being yours?"

"Stand my darling. Your Master needs to show you pleasure. Sophie jumped up from her kneeling position, she threw her arms around her Master's neck hugging him, burying her head in his neck.

"I'm so sorry. Please forgive me."

Standing before her Master totally nude, Kyle positioned her back up against the metal gate. "You've taken your punishment Sophie; it is over now. I forgive you. Don't ever put me in that position again. You scared the shit out of me."

Sophie let out a slight squeal from the cold metal pressing up against her back. She had the cutest dimples when she smiled. Kyle took his lizard-like tongue and ran it across Sophie's dimple, swirling it in the divot of her right cheek. Hearing her moan instantly had his cock filling with blood. The head of his dick pressed into the zipper of his pants, constricting all of his movement. That's how his women excited him.

Kyle broke away from licking Sophie's cheeks. "Look at me," Kyle said with a snarl. Sophie did just as he asked. "Darling, you will not come until I give you permission. Is that understood?"

Stroking Sophie's shoulder to loosen her up, so when he took her, she would only feel his pleasure. No pain would her body endure tonight. Only his pleasure that he'd provided to her.

"Yes, Master I'm yours; this is your body to with as you wish. I trust you with all of my heart. I will not come until you give me permission to do so."

Kyle took his massive hands and toyed with her breasts, squeezing and plucking her breast one after another. "I love the way your breasts fit perfectly in my hands. Sophie just moaned as she tightened his grip on her nipples. I'm going to pierce these beauties myself once your arm is healed. Just hearing those words upped her excitement.

Licking her lips as he spoke to her, Kyle saw, without a doubt, pleasure written all over her face. Kyle lowered his mouth over Sophie's right breast, taking her erect nipple into his mouth. Instantly, his mouth felt the warmth from Sophie's skin. Licking and sucking sent more pleasure to the tip of cock. He felt himself grow even harder against his jeans. After he laved over her right breast he felt Sophie's entire body start to twitch.

She called out his name, which made him want her even more. Knowing her breasts were sensitive, trying to draw her pleasure out for as long as possible, he continued to add pressure to her very sensitive bits. Pulling his mouth from her nipple, it made a popping sound as he released his mouth from around her breast.

Savoring her other breast his mouth watered for more. Taking in her left breast, twisting and biting her breast, the beast within him had to mark his woman with his mark. He released her nipple, taking in the fleshy part of her breast and bit her hard. Screaming at the top of her voice, she wrapped her leg around his, humping him just as dog in heat would.

He began to move his leg up and letting her push her pussy up his thigh. Letting her ride out the sensation for several more strokes, Kyle felt the heat coming from between her legs.

Looking at her breast where he had just marked her, he knew she would wear his mark for several days. It pleased him to see she didn't pull away from him. Instead, she snuggled into him more.

Kyle took his index finger and traced the spot he had just marked her. Hearing her say "yours" just about made him explode in his pants. He had to be inside of her. He needed to feel her pussy pulsating around his cock, squeezing his come deep from his balls.

Kyle kicked her legs wider, giving him direct access to her hot, pretty, pink pussy. He separated her labia, stroking her clit with his forefinger. She quivered under his touch, almost losing her footing. Kyle pushed her harder against the gate, sending another moan from her mouth.

Feeling her clit harden under his thumb, Kyle knew she wasn't going to last much longer. He leaned forward grasping Sophie's hips giving her a little more support.

Pushing a single finger into her sweet opening, having her suck his finger up to his knuckle told him his girl needed more than just his finger. Making sure she was opened fully for his ten inch cock, he filled her with another finger, scissoring, stretching her walls wide open.

Slowly Kyle unzipped his jeans, pulling down his boxers, and releasing his rock hard cock. He reached back between Sophie legs, going for her wet pussy, removing some of her wetness on his fingers; he stroked his cock with her juices.

Not wanting to hurt Sophie by just ramming his cock into her cunt. He needed to feed his monster into her slowly. Stretching her open, feeding her inch by inch. He needed to be balls deep inside his slave. The sooner the better, because he wasn't sure how long he was going to last.

Gasping as he fed her his cock, she finally gripped his entire shaft all the way to his root. Struggling to hold back, Kyle gripped the back of her hair, pulling her neck into full view, pumping in and out of her, pulling out just far enough that the tip of his cock stayed buried inside of Sophie's pussy.

Kyle placed his lips on Sophie's lower lobe of her ear. Sucking on it as if he sucked a straw. Growling in her ear. "Come for me, baby. I want to feel your juices slick up my cock."

As he said the last word to her, he felt the inner walls of her pussy tighten up around his cock. Sophie cried out, "Oh, God... I'm coming, Master." As she started to shake from her massive orgasm, Kyle released his seed, bathing her insides, filling her up with his pleasure.

When Kyle had finished emptying his seed in her, the two collapsed onto the floor. He held her until they feel asleep in each other's arms. Post colloidal bliss was written all over each of their faces.

Chapter Twelve

Stirring from a peaceful few hours' sleep, Sophie felt warmth, not coming from the blanket that was laid onto her naked body, but rather from the large arms that wrapped around her torso.

Still inside the stable, she looked over at the horses in their stalls. She had never been one with nature but being around Kyle had brought that buried passion from her soul.

She let out a low yawn, not wanting to disturb her man. Just trying to listen to his breathing, she heard the rain hitting the outside of the barn. She felt the best she had in months.

She remembered back when she was little; her mother had a special quote she would say to Sophie when dealing with issues that were unpleasant. Thinking about a quote: Life isn't about how you survive the storm, but rather how you dance in the rain. It finally made sense, her time to dance in the rain was now, and the person that she would dance with was her Master.

Before she could dance, it hit her that she had to pee something bad. No longer able to hold her urges off, she slipped from under the warmth from the blanket, and made her way to the bathroom.

After relieving herself, Sophie stood at the barn door. Trying not to wake Kyle up, she slowly opened the door. The crisp freshness of a new day hit her nose. The early morning summer rain bounced off the grass, causing it to look as if the grass was smoking. Sophie loved to play in the rain as a child. She would jump from puddle to puddle splashing herself until she was soaking wet.

Josie, Sophie's mother made sure Sophie was always taken care of when coming in from the rain. She'd stand at the door with a warm towel and a hot cup of tea, to warm Sophie's insides.

She realized she hadn't spent that much time with either of her parents. It saddened Sophie to think how she had pushed them to the side. That was surely about to change; needing her parent's even more now in her life, Sophie had the perfect idea. She's have them over for an old fashion bar-b-cue.

The child in Sophie who had been buried for so long, needed to be released, so Sophie did the unthinkable. She opened the door and ran to the middle of field stark naked.

Giggling as loud as she could, dancing, twirling flapping her arms, she enjoyed the freedom of having her inner self freed from the hell that it once was trapped in. Feeling the rain hit her naked body, cleansed Sophie's soul. She'd never had a feeling like this. She was alive, and it felt damn good.

Stomping her feet in the wet grass splashed the water high in the air. Mud began to cover her toes. This was definitely what Sophie needed. The rain washed away all of Sophie's past fears, giving her a sense of rebirth. She had a purpose, something to live for. She would no longer live like a sheltered person, or the caged animal she felt like once. Instead, she would live life to the fullest.

Soaked to the bone didn't give Sophie a chill. Instead, her insides were on fire. She heard the barn door creak as it opened. Catching her eye was a beautiful, naked, tall man whose face had a look of happiness written all over it.

She saw the Master who had given her a second chance of happiness. She was truly thankful for him,. He'd opened up her eyes, and she finally saw the big picture. She'd missed out on so much in the past two years. No, not ever again would she go back down that road. She had a permanent scar that reminded her of what not trusting someone looked like. She made a promise to herself. *I will always trust Kyle. I know he has my best interests at heart.*

"Baby girl what are you doing out here in the rain?"

"I'm loving life to the fullest. Care to join me?"

"I would love that baby... but don't you think we could have done that under the covers." Blushing just slightly, Sophie twirled around in circles with her arm stretching up to the sky. It almost looked as she was giving herself up to the Gods. Kyle slowly made his way to her, she felt his large hands grab hold of her curvy waist. She loved the feel of his hands on her body. He could possess her entire body with just his touch.

"Good morning, beautiful, how did my girl sleep?"

"Wonderful. I don't think I've sleep that sound in years." Giving him her full attention, she knew she needed to be honest with him, and now was the time. "Having you hold me, made me feel safe. I haven't felt that way in years."

Kyle pressed his lips to Sophie's mouth, devouring her tongue. After their tongues twirled for a few seconds, Sophie melted into his touch. Pulling away to come up for air, Sophie felt safe.

"Hungry at all?"

"What man would want breakfast when I have a beautiful peach standing in front of me?"

"You're so romantic when you say things like that, but I need real food. I'm starving."

"Why don't we go up to the house, get a nice hot shower together. Sophie had the most pleasant look on her face. We'll grab a bagel, then my beautiful girl how about springing you from this place. You've gotta be getting stir crazy by now.

"Oh God, you wouldn't believe, how bad!" Nodding her head in delight, jumping up and down splashing him with mud all over his leg. He pinched her cheek trying to bring her out of her child like state. She felt the sting all the way to her pussy. Sophie let out a low moan. "How about we drive to Crave County? It's about a two hour drive from here. We can stop on the way for some breakfast. Then we can head up to my cabin. We can stay there for the weekend."

"Love to."

Sophie hadn't showed any type of spark in the past month. Feeling frisky, she loved to play games as a child, especially ones that involved running. Tag was one of her favorites; she knew she could outrun most boys. She wasn't quite sure about Kyle but no time like the present to find out. With a slap on his bare chest, she yelled "Tag you're it." She ran as fast as she could and headed for the house.

Enjoying the drops of rain hitting her skin, Sophie felt alive. Coming up fast on her heels, she felt Kyle's breath hit the back of her neck as her tackled her to the ground. The two rolled around, laughing and giggling as Kyle tickled Sophie's side.

Feeling like a weight had been lifted off her shoulders, the two kissed. She heard Kyle growl into her ear, "Now I caught you, and I'm never letting you go." She was totally in bliss hearing those words come from his mouth.

Chapter Thirteen

After getting breakfast in a quaint little diner, just outside of Crave County, the two had one more stop to make. Over breakfast each wrote done on separate napkins a shopping list. Sophie was put in charge of food items, while Kyle wrote down different kinky implements that could be picked up at the local store... Not giving any hints to what he wrote on his napkin he folded it up and placed it in his pocket.

Once the two entered into the mini mart they separated and took care of their shopping lists. He told Sophie to take her time; he didn't want her wearing herself out. She was to text him once she had completed her list.

Kyle dashed down the aisles as if he was on fire; he found the small crock-pot, candles, oils, and tarp. Checking off the items on his list one by one, had been easier than what he thought it would be. With time to spare, he noticed a little liquor store next to the mini mart when they pulled up.

A nice bottle of wine and six-pack of beer would relax my girl even more.

He even picked up a lovely bouquet of flowers on his way to the register. Paid for his cart of stuff, loaded it into his Range Rover and made his way over to the liquor store, picked up the libations in just enough time to get a text from Sophie saying her list was completed.

"Done."

Sophie wasn't the great outdoorsy type of girl, a true city slicker, feeling the excitement brew up inside of her was just like a kid going to the candy store to pick out a new treat. This was no different.

Having all the excitement in the world was worth it, she just had to have her man by her side. Pulling up to the cabin, Sophie squealed in exhilaration. Just seeing the huge log cabin had Sophie thinking back to when she and her brother had a set of Lincoln logs, which they would build and build log structures for hours. Their houses looked just like Kyle's cabin does.

Kyle grabbed their overnight bags and told Sophie to leave the groceries; he would take care of them once he showed her around. Kyle explained to her how his father acquired the property back in the late 70's during a poker game, and when his father left he was given the cabin.

They walked in and all she could do was gasp at how gorgeous the inside was. Knowing that Kyle brought her parents here to protect them, brought tears to her eyes. "Omg… this is beautiful Kyle. I thought you were taking me to a dark old structure that didn't have modern amenities. I feel like I'm at the Hilton."

"I've had a few upgrades done over the years.

My father used the lodge for his clients who were visiting from other countries. He felt it was better to give them a homely feel versus a stuffy hotel. That's one thing I did inherit from my father his love of the great outdoors.

He'd bring Derek and me up here for a long weekend, and we'd run around in the woods pretending to be cowboys and Indians. When it came time to pack up on Sunday night, we both found reasons to stall, trying to get dad to give in just a little bit longer. Mom on the other hand never liked this place at all. She'd keep Piper in the city with her and Carmela would always come to the cabin with the guys. Sophie got a strange feeling when Kyle mentioned Carmela; she wasn't sure why, but she did.

Touring the large cabin, being shown around room by room, and the long drive wore Sophie out. She yawned a few times, trying to shake the cobwebs from her brain, but it wasn't working.

She was exhausted. She hadn't wanted to admit it to her guy. How could she be so tired from riding in the car and talking with Kyle? It struck her that she hadn't thought about being shot all day, which was a great sign.

Knowing that look in Kyle's eyes, she let him take her hand, guide her to the master bedroom, help her slip out of her clothes, and tuck her under the covers. He told her to sleep. He told her over and over the past few weeks he would take care of her and by God that is just what he was doing. He saw she was worn out. She didn't even question his decision, and she snuggled under the covers, closed her eyes and feel asleep.

After putting his girl to bed for a much needed nap, Kyle knew she would be out for at least a couple of hours. Putting all the groceries away, he went to the one area of the cabin which was not on the tour. Taking the key from his pocket, he opened the door to the away from home dungeon.

Some of his favorite BDSM toys lined the dark black walls. Several kinds of floggers hung off a pegboard. Next to them were several different sizes of leather wrist cuffs along with ankle cuffs. In the corner of the room was a king size bed with overstuffed pillows.

Hanging from a beam in the ceiling were two long chains. Directly underneath the chains and jutting from the floor were bolts with rings attached to them. Off in the other corner of the room stood a St. Andrews cross, and in a stand next to the cross stood multiple wooden, lexan and delrin canes.

Just looking at his collection, Kyle had an instant hard on. He couldn't wait to bring his girl to this room after she woke up from her nap. Spreading out one of the plastic tarps on the ground, he then pulled out the massage table, and set it up on top of the tarp.

Next to it, he set up a small metal table. Placing the new crock-pot on top, he checked his phone to see what the proper mixture of wax to oil was. He set the correct temperature for melting wax. It had been a while since he last played with wax, and he sure didn't want to burn his girl.

Getting everything set up took him no time at all. He walked over to a cabinet which held all of his rope. He pulled out several bundles and placed them on top of the metal table. The only thing he needed now was his pretty slave to wake up.

Not wanting to risk any complications with Sophie's healing, he dialed Gail to make sure he wasn't going to cause any setbacks. He pushed her number, and while he waited for her to pick up his call, he stared at everything he set out.

"Hello, how's our patient doing?"

"She's taking a nap. I decided she needed a change of scenery for a couple of days, so I brought her up to Crave County."

"Planning on scening with her are you?"

"How did you guess?"

"Your girl called me about two hours ago. I'm guessing for the same reason you're calling me. Am I correct?"

"Yup, so she called you, hmmm? I'm proud of her for stepping up."

"You should be. Like I told her, as long as she's not short of breath, and you are not suspending her by her arm, she should be just fine. She'll need another month or two before you can hang her from the rafters."

Both of them laughed at the same time. "Good to know, Gail. I'll keep that in mind. I've been thinking about taking her out of the country for a mini vacation, do you think she's up to a four hour plane ride?"

"With your luxury jet and staff pampering her? How could I say no? Plus, she hasn't taken a damn vacation in years. Do yourself a favor... Just put her ass on the plane, so she can't come up with an excuse. By the way, when are you coming back to The Cellar? I have some business to propose to you."

"Not quite sure yet, just playing things by ear with Sophie. I haven't wanted to leave her yet. Why don't you stop by the house on Tuesday, and bring your slave with you? I'm sure Sophie would love to have company over."

"No, Kyle, I want you to come to the club. Sophie needs you to push back just a little, give her some breathing room. The hardest part is over. Now is the time for the two of you to start putting your lives back together."

"I'm hearing you loud and clear."

"Oh, by the way, have you put a collar around her neck yet? You know what you owe me when you do." Chuckling aloud, Kyle didn't respond to Gail's last question, but instead he said, "I'll see you at the club on Tuesday night at seven," and hung up.

He hadn't given any thought recently to putting a collar around Sophie's neck. Instead, all he could think about was keeping her from running. Now, that he had put his mind at ease, he'd set up a meeting with his jeweler and have something custom made. Checking the time on his phone, he realized his girl had only been sleeping for an hour.

Random thoughts crossed his mind now that Sophie was cleared to travel. He had to settle his own problem...Daniel Zeller. As Kyle hit the programmed number for Master Sergeant, all he could think about was facing his demons with his father.

"I was wondering how you and your sub are doing."

"Much better. It was touch and go for a little while, but now she's on the road to recovery. We happen to be up at Crave County visiting the cabin for a few days."

"Sounds like your little filly is doing a whole lot better."

"Yeah, she really is. That brings me to why I'm calling, Sarge."

"Go on son, spill it."

After a long pause, "I need to get back to Puerto Rico, next week, perhaps Wednesday if possible. It'll give me and Sophie another day up here. I can get her back home for a couple of days of some rest, and then she'll be up to traveling again."

"You think that's wise son? You bringing her into a hostile situation with your father?"

Kyle thought for a few seconds. "Sarge, I need to go at this in a different way than before. I was going to storm his house and force him talk to me; I realize that's not going to work. I've come up with another plan. I'll be posing as a businessman who wants to expand his business in Puerto Rico. I've already set up a shell company."

"You've been busy, haven't you?"

"Since I've had some down time while Sophie's been home recuperating, I did my homework. I've been in contact with my father's secretary a few times by email and once last week by phone. I told her that I needed a few more weeks before I could make the trip. She told me to give her a few days' notice to clear her bosses calendar. I think I can contact her and tell her my plans have changed."

"Did you cover up your tracks?"

"I did; I just sent you an email with all the new files."

"Give me until tomorrow to review everything. I have a pain slut who needs a session with my signal tail."

"I have my own plans to attend to as well. I'll call you tomorrow."

Waiting for his girl to wake up gave Kyle enough time to marinate the steaks Sophie picked out at the mini mart. Tossing the bag salad in a bowel took no time at all. Beer chilled in the fridge, strawberries washed and sliced, grill ready to be lit.

He didn't expect her to need as much sleep as she did, but he didn't mind as long as she woke up without having any pain.

Kyle checked the crock-pot again, making sure the wax had started to melt. Shutting the door to his dungeon. He heard the wood floor creak. His girl was up and moving. He'd give her a few minutes to get herself together.

It was close to three in the afternoon when Sophie finally made her way down the staircase. She looked more radiant than before taking her nap. She took his breath away just by watching her descend the stairs. Kyle met her at the bottom of the staircase.

"You look well rested, my darling."

"I feel wonderful. I can't believe I slept so long."

"You thirsty, baby girl?"

"Parched."

"How about we grab a couple water bottles? We can hit some of the trails, and take in the scenery while it's still light out."

"Sounds like a plan to me."

"Good, but before I let you go I need to have your sweet juicy lips pressed up against mine. Kiss me baby, I missed you."

"Gee I only took a nap, buddy."

"Oh, my girl's got her sass going on."

After exploring several of the trails, Kyle showed her some of his best hiding spots. Bringing back old memories of his happy childhood made him look at Sophie in a different way. She was his future. He would do everything in his power to keep her by his side.

Eventually everything that was his would be theirs, including the lodge. He would need to tell her about all of his businesses, properties, and net worth. He'd spend the next few days breaking everything down for Sophie, hoping that it didn't overwhelm her.

The two held hands all the way back to the cabin, just like any couple would do. Once they reached the cabin, Kyle had Sophie take a bath while he grilled the steaks.

During dinner, Kyle pulled out a marble notebook. He placed it in the center of the table, letting Sophie stare at it all during dinner. She asked several times what the book was for, but Kyle told her she had to wait until after dinner to find out. He used his favorite statement. "Be patient. my dear."

Once dinner was finished, Kyle had Sophie clean up the dishes as part of her therapy for the day. She needed to get back her dexterity before she could go back to being a surgeon. Kyle had come up with small jobs over the past few weeks. Nothing big. Just things that made her use her right arm more and more each day.

While Sophie cleaned up the kitchen, Kyle used that time to go and take a quick shower. But before he went upstairs, Kyle went back to the dungeon and checked the wax one more time. He needed it to be perfectly melted, before he could use it on her body.

The blank notebook sat in the center of the table. Sophie had no idea what it would be used for. All she knew was Kyle told her to be patient, he would explain after dinner. Feeling excitement bubble up inside her belly, she waited for Kyle to return from his shower.

To kill some of the time, she pulled her cell phone out of her purse, she hadn't checked in with her mom today. So before the National Guard was put on high alert, Sophie felt it was best to give her mom a quick ring.

It had become a daily ritual for the two women to talk. Sophie at first felt her mother was prying with all of her questions about Kyle, but as the weeks pushed past, Sophie's mother just wanted to make sure she was happy. Before hanging up with her mother, she reminded her to tell her dad she was coming over on Tuesday for lunch.

Looking around the big open living room gave Sophie a sense of happiness, comfort and love. A vibrant multicolored patch quilt was draped on the back of the sofa. Taking a day trip, Sophie once traveled to an Amish market in Pennsylvania a few years back. After talking to the store owner's wife, she found out that the quilts were made using the technology of 150 years ago, stitch by stitch, or as the women called it "hand by hand."

Most quilts were given to a newlywed couple as wedding presents, or after the birth of a child. Each quilt could take a female over a year to finish, depending on the intricate pattern. Sophie remembered the women saying, quilts last for generations to generations. She'd need to ask if this quilt had any significant meaning or if it was purchased for decoration. Knowing Kyle and his family background, it most likely had been given as a wedding present to his grandparents.

Sophie had been given several family heirlooms from her parents. She cherished a porcelain tea set that was once her great-great-grandmother's. Every morning she would steep her favorite tea. Never meeting her great-great–grandparents, she only had photos to reminisce over.

Sophie had often day-dreamed about starting her own family. She wondered what Kyle's take on raising a family would be. Somehow, she would need to bring that up in a conversation.

Placed strategically around the room were small knickknacks. Everything seemed to have its own place; or rather, nothing looked out of place. Several photos sat atop the rustic cedar fireplace mantel. One that caught her eye was a large golden photo frame in the center of the mantel. Sophie looked intently at the photo; it was a picture of a teenager who most likely was Kyle, Derek and infant girl Piper. Kyle was holding Piper, and Derek was sitting on the floor petting a brown dog.

Each one had a smile plastered across their faces. It was easy to tell they were siblings by their vibrant blue eyes.

She couldn't wait to get to know them all better. Both of Kyle's siblings had come to the hospital several times to sit with Kyle during Sophie's hospitalization. It was Piper who had touched Sophie's heart, though.

Piper knew just how to cheer a girl up. She buttered Sophie up by bringing her chocolate. Piper made killer chocolate brownies, and what better to help an injured girl?

Piper reminded Sophie of her little sister, Laura. Both girls were flakey, or better yet, lost in the world. Neither one had found their purpose in life yet. Sophie hoped in time, she could get the two girls together for some good old fashion girl's time.

Just like Piper, Derek too visited Sophie, but his visits were more for Kyle. It would take her some time to get used to Derek, because he scared her in a way, She wasn't sure why, but he did. Derek had all the charm and charisma, but something told Sophie he was nothing like Kyle.

Derek was half owner of The Cellar so in Kyle's absence Derek stepped up and did his share plus Kyle's share. That's what family was for Derek had told her many times as she tried to thank him.

Both Kyle and Derek had striking facial features that showed a likeness to their father. Kyle didn't display photos of his father, but kept them in a drawer that was easily accessible. Kyle pulled out several family albums during the past few weeks. Retelling stories of his childhood years. Never had Kyle talked bad about his father, but constantly said he needed to get to the bottom of why he up and left his family.

❤

Kyle finished up his shower, making sure he had washed away all the crud from his earlier hike. Nothing like being stinky; that could really ruin the mood. Number one rule he taught all new Doms was to take a shower before entering into a play scene because there was nothing worse than being all smelly and stinky. "You'll never play with that person ever again," he told them.

Before joining Sophie in the living room, he went back to the play room, checked to make sure the wax had melted and was at the correct temperature. Once he was sure everything was set to his liking, he closed the door ever so lightly.

As he made his way back into the living room he watched from a distance as Sophie stared at the picture on the mantel. He wondered what was going through her mind. She had a fairly intent look. She always looked as if she was dissecting something. Maybe that had to do something with her love of the beating heart.

Kyle held the notebook that had been sitting on the dining room table. He walked over to the sofa, where Sophie was now sitting.

He watched her eyes as they traced down to his hand that was holding the book. She saw her pulse speed up in her neck. He loved watching her work herself up, for his pleasure.

Kyle scooped Sophie up in his arms and sat her rump on top of his thigh and handed her the marble notebook.

"Pet, I see your mind is working over time trying to figure out why I have given you this book."

"You're correct. I've come up with a dozen different ideas, but I'm pretty sure I'm going to be writing in it. Am I at least close?"

"You're such a smart girl. Have you ever kept a journal?"

"Are you talking about a diary?"

"No. I said journal, not diary."

"Aren't they the same?"

"No baby girl, a diary is usually your private thoughts written for only your eyes to see, whereas a journal is not private. Your thoughts are shared or opened for others to view."

"Oh, I get it now."

"Good. I know a few Doms require their slaves/submissives to keep a journal. I've given great thoughts about the pros and cons of keeping one and I think keeping a line of open communication between the two of us is very important."

Sophie nodded her head in agreement.

"Sometimes, timing plays a big part of our being able to communicate. Journals are often kept so that the slave/sub can freely write down anything that bothers her or him about their relationship with their partner. Some people can't express their feelings face to face, so this gives the s/type a way of communicating without clamming up. Not all the time, but more often than not, the s/types learn more and more about themselves as they write in their journals."

Sophie looked a little confused.

"Sophie baby, I want you to write things in your journal that you might be afraid to tell me, things that embarrass you, things you find enjoyable, things you hate. I want you to write something in your journal daily. It can be one word or a million that is all up to you.

The next part of this scenario is a protocol that I would like to introduce at the same time. You remember what protocols are, Pet?"

"Yes Master. You already have a couple of protocols set in place; I can't wear clothes to bed, except for when I have my period, or if I'm sick. "

"That's correct, baby girl."

"Oh, and a morning kiss before I get out of bed."

"You got it, baby girl. As time goes on, I'll add even more protocols. Just like I'm going to do now." Kyle kissed the top of her head as he stroked up and down her injured shoulder. He felt her shutter as his fingers grazed the wound.

You're to kneel naked at the foot of my bed nightly. I know. Don't look so concerned. You're to have your journal entry done for the day by the time you're ready for bed. If you don't obey, you'll be punished. Do I make myself clear?"

"Yes, Sir."

"You'll hand over your journal, and I will release you from your kneeling position, where you'll join me in bed. Questions?"

Kyle watched as Sophie closed her eyes. He had taught her how to center her thoughts and watched as she took in a cleansing breath, slowly letting the air come back out through her mouth. Kyle felt her stiffen up in his lap. "What if I write something that is not pleasing about you Sir? What happens then?"

"We are adults, Sophie. You're not a puppet. You don't have strings attached to your arms. I don't want you to write things that please me or stroke my ego. I expect you to be honest and true to yourself first. As long as you write things from your heart, I will not be offended."

He watched as she started to settle more comfortably in his lap. She no longer felt stiff as a board. "It's my job as your Master to guide you through your journey, not hamper it. The sky's the limit with your journal. Nothing is off limits."

"When do we start, Master?"

"Mmm let me think for just a second. I have a special treat for my slave for the rest of the night. How about I give you the next ten minutes to write in your journal, while I go lock up? Will that give you enough time, baby girl?"

With a slightly sneaky laugh, Sophie jumped off Kyle's lap and ran towards the kitchen. "I can handle that, Sir. Just need to get a pen from my purse."

Kyle loved Sophie's girlish spark. Every day she accepted new challenges that he proposed to her, and she hadn't questioned his authority since being shot. Yes, she was a true submissive, through and through.

Chapter Fourteen

Kyle did a final walk-through of the cabin. He glanced over his shoulder looking at his beautiful girl as she wrote in her journal, and she looked content making her entry. Kyle strolled over to the front door, locking it. The ten minutes he had allotted for Sophie's journal entry went by like a flash. "Times up, baby."

"I didn't finish, Master."

"That's okay, Pet. Tonight was just to get your creative juices flowing. You'll be your own timekeeper in the future. You'll take time out during the day that fits your schedule. You'll just need to have it ready by bedtime.

Now, take your journal upstairs and put it on my pillow, go to the bathroom, and take care of any needs you have, then meet me back here when you're done." He watched Sophie stand up. As she crossed in front of him he swatted her ass.

Sophie yelped, "OUCH!"

"Get your ass moving. Your Master doesn't like waiting. It makes him impatient. Now go!"

She did just as he told her to. He watched her skip across the floor until she made her way to the large spiral staircase. She blew a kiss to him once she started up the steps, taking two steps at a time until she reached the top.

Yep, he definitely saw the playful side of Sophie, and he fucking loved it.

After a few minutes, Sophie finally made her way back to the living room. Kyle had planned the perfect scene for his slave tonight.

"Undress, for me Pet." Without even thinking, Sophie began to shuck her clothing off. Kyle already felt his cock hardening as he watched his girl strip for him. He loved that fact, that Sophie loved to be watched as she took off her clothes. *She going to love being on display at the club. That would be his next step in her training… taking her back to the club.* Maybe next weekend with a little more prep she'll be perfect. *Hell she was already perfect for him, what was he thinking?*

Kyle took Sophie's hands and pinned them behind her back. Nothing he would do tonight would cause pain; everything he'd do would send her soaring higher than she ever had. "Pet I want to show you my playroom." Kyle watched her facial expression. Her cheeks had turned a light shade of pink. I can already tell you want to without you even muttering a single word.

"How's that so, Master?"

"Your cheeks give you away every time, baby girl."

"Well I guess I can't hide my feelings from you, can I?"

"Nope, baby girl, your body gives you away every time. Kyle unlocked the door to the playroom. He watched as Sophie scanned the entire room. She had seen a lot of the BDSM equipment already at the Cellar, but had not yet experienced anything on any of the equipment.

"What's going on in that pretty little head of yours, baby girl?"

"Mmm," sucking in as much as air she could, "I'm excited beyond my wildest dreams, but at the same time I'm scared."

"Thank you, darling for being honest. That pleases your Master to know you trusted him with your thoughts."

"I do trust you, Sir. I never expected you to have so much stuff here in the cabin. I didn't even know this part existed. You wouldn't even know the panel I put the key into was a door if you didn't know what you were looking for."

"Makes a lot of sense to me. Can I ask you a question?"

"Yes of course, you might not get an answer you like but ask away, my dear."

"Do you have one of these back home?" Kyle let out a loud chuckle, "Yup, why do you ask?"

"Just wondering that's all."

"Tell me what you're thinking, Sophie."

"Um, um."

"Just say it Sophie, now."

"Have you played with anyone here or at the house?"

"No one at my house, I never felt anyone was worth bringing home, until now." He watched as Sophie started to relax. She had gone all tense asking her questions. "Baby, here's a different story. I've hosted play parties for a few of my friends. We'd have long extended weekends up here entertaining. I can tell you my heart only belongs to you now. No one else. Hopefully we can entertain our friends in the near future here and at The Cellar."

"I don't know why I became so overly jealous, but I did. I think it's going to take me some time to get used to having such a popular Dom in my life. You're the jock that every girl fantasizes about. That's all."

"Well, lucky for you, Sophie, I have the most beautiful sub to show off from now on. I'll be beating the other Doms with a cane if they come close to you."

Sophie let a giggle. "Promise?"

"Promise."

"You better now, baby?"

"Couldn't be any more perfect than I am right now."

"Good, what's your safe-word?"

"Crash, Sir."

"Excellent, I want you to hop up on the massage bed." Without any hesitation, he watched as Sophie jumped up on the bed.

"You marked wax play as a no limit. We're going to have a good time with that tonight."

"I'm so excited, Master. I saw some beautiful pictures on the internet when I was doing my research."

"That's what I love about you, Sophie. You saw the beauty of the pictures. Most people don't see that. So that my canvas doesn't move I'm going to bind your arms lightly with some rope. At any time you feel pain in your right shoulder, I want you to say the word "shoulder" for me. You good with that baby?"

"A ok."

"Lie back for me."

Taking one of the four hanks of jute rope from the table Kyle began to secure her ankles to the rings at the bottom of the bed. He spread her legs wide open, leaving her pussy fully exposed, and she was already wet. "You really want this, don't you baby?"

"Oh God, yes! I love being bound."

"Good because I can tell you it's one of my favorite kinks to see you bound for my pleasure." He also realized she got more into headspace when he brought out his dominance. She loved it when he talked dirty and sexual to her.

He grabbed the third hank of jute he twisted the rope around her left wrist, wrapping it up to her armpit in a diamond pattern. He took the final hank of jute knowing her shoulder couldn't be extended above her head yet. He opted just to put a wrist cuff around her wrist with nothing fancy.

It still gave the feel of being bound. He could quickly release her wrist if needed. Once he was done, he bent forward to gain control of her mouth. He heard her moan into his kiss, making his cock jump even more.

Kyle stepped back and just stared at his canvas. "Such a beautiful girl. I'm going to put a blind fold over your eyes, baby. You ready?"

"Yes, Master. Make your sub beautiful."

"No, baby, my sub is already beautiful. I'm just opening up her world to color." Kyle slowly covered her eyes with a fur lined eye mask. Darkness covered Sophie's world now. Her senses would soon be on over load. "Baby, you doing ok?"

"Yes, Master. A-Ok." Reaching for the remote control for the sound system Kyle had already preprogrammed the music for tonight's scene. Triple drums began to play softly through the stereo. Kyle told Sophie to take in a deep breath. Watching her chest rise and fall was just beautiful. She responded to his touch and voice perfectly.

Kyle watched her purse her lips in pleasure. *She is fucking gorgeous and she is all mine.* He was getting an erection that stiffened up against his zipper. He hadn't even put a drop of wax on her yet.

"Tonight is all about sensation. You might perceive the heat from the wax as pain, but not to worry, I'll take care of you. Since I'm not sure what your pain receptors are like, we'll work together until we come up with a happy medium. You're to trust me, Sophie. You're not too lose your voice. I need for you to communicate to me. This doesn't make it any less of a scene. You're to be respectful with your tongue, no crude remarks. Got it?" He could tell Sophie was getting into a comfortable state of mind, as she moaned out her response, "Yes." He had to be the luckiest bastard in the world, to have such a willing sub lying nude, bound and her sight taken from her.

Kyle poured coconut oil in a bowl, even though the coconut oil was at room temperature it would still feel cold on Sophie's skin. Slicking up his hands with the exotic oil had the room smelling like the islands.

With his girl bound and blindfolded, he started massaging her toes, one hand on each foot. He called it double team work.

Rubbing the oils in and around each joint on her feet, he heard Sophie let out slight moans. "My baby likes her feet being massaged, doesn't she?" "Oh yes, Sir. I can't tell you how good that feels."

"Good, baby, that's exactly what I want you to do.. feel. He moved slowly up to her ankles, then to her calves rubbing and smoothing the oil all over her skin. He knew bringing the blood to the surface of her skin would heighten the feel of the hot wax hitting her skin.

Making his way to her upper thighs, he had a direct view of her now glistening pussy. She was wet for sure. Lightly he spread coconut oil on her labia, feeling tiny shutters coming from Sophie's legs told him she was coming close to exploding.

"Baby, I want you to hold off from coming. I want you begging me for your release." Kyle waited for a response but got none, so he slapped her thigh. He knew that would bring her out of subspace fast. "Ouch!"

"You back with me, baby?"

"Yes, Sir."

"Now where was I? Yes, I was exploring my pretty pink pussy."

"Oh God, Sir, you're driving me crazy with your fingers. I don't know how much longer I can hold out."

"Oh my Pet we just started, we have a long night ahead of us."

"Sweet baby Jesus!" Kyle slowly pushed one finger inside of her hot soaking wet cunt, and she sucked his finger in like a vice grip. Massaging her insides he pushed in a second finger and then a third. Working his way until he reached her g-spot. He had already made her squirt once before, and tonight he would again, but that would be later.

Now he needed to concentrate on his canvas. It was naked, and needed color. Slowly he pulled out of her cunt. Sophie gave a couple complaining moans as he released his fingers from inside of her. "Hold on, baby girl. That was only a little tease to get you started."

Kyle made his way up to her tight stomach. Sophie had been clenching her stomach muscles when Kyle worked her pussy over with his fingers. He knew she was getting hypersensitive which would make the wax even more delicious.

Her nipples were already the size of eraser tips. *God would I love to use clamps on her now, but that would surely send her over.* Instead, he took his mouth and sucked her left nipple into his hot wet mouth.

Bringing the blood to the surface had Sophie screaming out her enjoyment. He just listened to her babble. At some point, he was sure she asked him to fuck her, but that to would have to wait.

Kyle went back to applying the coconut oil all over Sophie's chest. He watched as her breathing became more erratic with his touch.

Kyle looked one more time at where she had been shot making sure her wound was completely sealed.

She had a large scar that ran from the top of her right shoulder down to just above her right breast. The way her scar traversed across her tight shoulder, he could see the pattern of a cherry blossom branch running across her chest to her shoulder. Maybe she would be interested in getting a tattoo in the future to hide the scar.

Kyle had only one tattoo located on his upper right shoulder. He'd been drunk one night and a bunch of the guys from his unit had gone to a tattoo parlor. They all had the same designed etched onto their shoulder.

It was the American Flag all decked out with red, white, and blue. A black skull that had two long swords underneath it. Their unit number was etched into the blades of the swords. It looked badass when he was wearing a tank top.

Every time he saw his tattoo he thought back to the grueling days and nights of his service. He would definitely bring up the subject of getting a tattoo to Sophie.

He had been very careful in the past few weeks to make sure Sophie was kept as comfortable as possible. She still had a long road to recovery ahead of her, but at least the worst was behind them.

After making sure all of her skin was coated with a light coating of coconut oil, Kyle took a ladle full of the hot wax, he dropped a couple drops from about two feet above his forearm, then from one foot, making sure it wasn't too hot. Yes, it had a bit of pain, but nothing his girl couldn't handle.

He started with her toes, taking a ladle full of hot wax, dropping it from about two feet above her, he watched for her reaction. She slowly blew out a breath and shuttered just a bit, but nothing that said she couldn't handle the heat from the wax.

Kyle repeated the process all the way up her legs. She moaned and groaned during the entire time.

Kyle knew that as he got closer to her pussy she would be screaming. Changing his tactics, he left her pussy open for his view and went for her breast. Before ladling the wax on her breast, he sucked her nipple into his mouth, he bit down sending her to a deeper level of subspace.

He added a drop of red food coloring to the wax in the ladle. Turning the wax to a deep dark red. He couldn't wait to remove the blindfold from Sophie's eyes so she could see his beautiful canvas. He still had a ways to go to finish, though.

Sophie let out moans and groans each time Kyle splattered her body with the wax. She thrashed around just a bit, but Kyle had secured her to the massage table. She had nowhere to go.

"How do you feel, baby girl?"

"Warm and tingling, Master, and in a good way."

"You're about to even feel more, baby girl. I want you to fight the urges to come. Got it?"

"Yes, Master."

Kyle parted her pussy lips as wide as he could with his hand, and dipped his tongue directly onto her clit. He felt Sophie squirm about and removed his mouth from her clit, then slapped her pussy with his hand sending her higher and higher.

"Lay still, no moving. You'll beg me to come."

"Moaning her response, Sophie could no longer form words. Her clit had swelled just from his touch. With her pussy lips spread open, Kyle took a ladle full of wax and added a drop of blue dye. Holding the ladle at about two feet above her body, he tipped the ladle and watched the wax coat her pussy. As the hot wax hit her flesh, Sophie yelled out, "Master I don't think I can hold out much longer, The sensation is overwhelming. Oh God, please let me come."

Kyle took another ladle full of wax added another drop of blue dye, this time he lowered the ladle to about six inches above her already covered pussy. As he tilted the ladle, he watched her slowly calm down, and as she did, he splattered her pussy again with the wax. "Come now for your Master." As the wax hit her sex, she screamed, "Yes, Oh Yes, Yeeessss, I'm coming." He watched her body ride out the enormous wave of pleasure that had swept through her entire body.

Watching his girl come just about sent his throbbing cock through his zipper. He had to have his release. Now. He shed his jeans, toeing off his shoes and jumped up onto the massage table. He touched Sophie's lips with his fingertips. "Open baby girl, I'm going to feed you my cock. I want you to suck me off. I need to fill you with my come."

Still in a foggy daze, Kyle helped Sophie open her lips as he fed her his cock. Inch by inch she took him in. All the way down to his balls. He started out slowly by pumping into her mouth, but by the forth pump he was feeling his balls squeezing out his come. Kyle closed his eyes as he felt his release, groaning out in a primal moan he yelled. "MINE!"

She sucked every last drop out of his shaft. When she was done she said to him in a low voice. "MINE."

Chapter Fifteen

After experiencing the most amazing orgasm from Kyle, Sophie started coming back to earth. She was most sure she had just had an out of body experience. She saw flashes of vibrant colors of light as her orgasm took over her entire body. It opened up heart to a new level of trust.

She felt Kyle remove the blindfold from her eyes. "Open your eyes slowly, baby girl. Even though I have the lights down in the room, you'll need time to adjust." She began to blink as the light hit her eyes. She couldn't move. She was still bound to the table. Kyle still straddled her chest. His cock was now flaccid. He had sweat covering his upper torso. She could lick the sweat from his chest, but unfortunately for her, both of her hands were bound.

Glancing down she finally took in Kyle's beautiful work. Her shoulders were the color of alabaster. Her breasts were the color of blood. "I can't believe you did all this with the wax, you made me beautiful."

Tears began to trickle down her cheeks. "No, baby. You're beautiful without the wax. That's what makes me love you so much."

"Thank you for opening up my eyes. I've been so sheltered and closed off to the world, I lost track of who I really was. You bring the brightness out of me."

She watched Kyle slip off the table. He picked up a blade, which looked just like a surgical scalpel. She took in a deep breath as he came closer to her body with the blade. Jokingly, Sophie said, "Now you're a surgeon, hmmm?"

"I'm a Jack of all trades. I need you to stay perfectly still. I'm not finished with my art project."

"So you're an artist to boot."

"Flattery will get you everywhere with me, baby, now lay still or I'm going to punish you."

"Yes, Sir."

Sophie did just as he asked and lay as still as possible her mind full of pleasantries. *Would this be her future?* A burst of energy shot through her as Kyle placed the cold scalpel against her skin. He had to wedge his fingers in between the wax and her skin. Feeling the wax pull from her skin sent shivers up and down her spine.

The contrast of the cold hitting her skin was as if he had just touched her with an ice cube. She hadn't seen Kyle dip the scalpel in a glass of ice. The steel against her skin was shocking. It sent sparks all the way to her clit. *How can I be reacting to such stimulation when I had just had a mind-blowing orgasm a few minutes ago? Must be my inner bad girl coming out. I never had an inner bad girl.* Such a happy thought.

She wasn't the only who had that same thought, she looked over at Kyle's cock. It now was as hard as a rock. Her mouth began to water, just by the sight of his cock. She hoped he would fuck her once he was done removing her body armor of wax.

"I can see the wheels in your head turning, baby girl. Tell me what you're thinking." Feeling a little silly, she blurted out, "I hope you fuck my pussy with your cock when you're done."

"Would you like that?"

"Oh, God yes!"

"So since you didn't hesitate with your answer. Your wish is my command."

She watched as Kyle worked feverishly to get every bit of the wax off her skin. It helped that he had applied a thick layer of coconut first. She could just image what it would have felt like without having that barrier.

Kyle held up a wax mold of her entire body. She was amazed at how skilled he was with not only the scalpel, but also the creativity he displayed by applying the different colors of the wax to her intimate body parts. He even fucked her pussy until she came another two times before he carried her limp body up to his bed.

After such a wonderful time at the cabin over the weekend, Sophie hated to leave her newfound love of nature. She made a silent wish that she would return to the cabin sometime in the near future.

Sophie had several things to accomplish in the upcoming weeks. The first on her checklist was to have the durable medical supply company come and pick up the rented hospital bed. She no longer needed to sleep solo. Kyle took one of the sex tantric foam wedges from the dungeon and Jimmy rigged it in his bed to elevate Sophie so she didn't have a lot of pressure pushing on her chest or her shoulder. She didn't mind it as much so long as he was lying next to her and she could feel the warmth of his body.

After a long discussion on their way home from the cabin, Kyle finally agreed to go back to work starting on Monday for a few hours a day. Sophie knew it was now or never to push him out the door. To make the transition easier, Sophie would make damn sure, she would be up and dressed an hour before Kyle even stirred awake.

The aroma of fresh brewed coffee wafted throughout the house, even though Sophie never acquired the taste, she didn't mind the smell. *I must get to the apartment and bring back my favorite tea set. Maybe I can learn how to serve tea Japanese style to Master.*

Today she would be spending the day all to herself without the man who had opened her eyes to a new life.

Feeling hyped up from the weekend and their love making session last night, she knew she was running on pure adrenaline.

Getting back to some kind of routine was still not going to happen today, but it was in the future. No time like the present to make plans for the next couple of weeks. Sophie pulled out her phone and glanced over her calendar. Today she had therapy for three hours. Tuesday therapy in the morning, then lunch with her father. Wednesday nothing. Thursday therapy. Friday therapy. A large chunk of her calendar was filled with her therapy schedule, nothing fun. She was going to change that.

She'd planned on talking to her therapist today about arranging for one day a week going to the therapy center. Hopefully, if she got it approved with the therapist first, Kyle would surely agree.

Still unable to drive, Kyle had already insisted that Jake be her driver and security when he wasn't available. One of Volkov security would be stationed at the house any time Kyle was not present.

Sophie did the wise thing; she didn't throw a royal fit. Kyle made his claim on her and that required her to obey his rules. He made it very clear to her that if she didn't obey his rules, she would not sit down for at least a week, if not longer.

Looking back at her calendar, she still had three weeks to plan Kyle's birthday party. That's what she would speed her down time doing. She would need the help of a few close friends to execute everything, including getting help from Kyle's brother, Derek.

Before she could make any plans, she needed to send her Master to work. A little nervous, Sophie paced the kitchen, waiting for her Master to enter.

Daisy being the thoughtful sub, and knowing that Sophie wasn't the best cook in the world, prepared a few quick dishes for Sophie. Everything was labeled and stacked neatly in the fridge. She also left a list taped to the fridge of supplies she needed to purchase from the store. Sophie pulled out the container she had labeled for breakfast. Nothing too hard to put together. Scramble eggs, sausage links, fruit already sliced and diced. Everything looked easy to assemble. Nothing to cause the house to burn down.

Headphones in her ears, sausage cooking on the stovetop, Sophie was in her own little world. Kyle snuck up behind her, sliding his arms around her waist and sending her into a frenzy.

Sophie screamed as if she was being attacked. Luckily for Kyle, he just held her tighter; it was only after he removed the ear buds from her ears that she calmed down. Finally her heartbeat went back to normal.

"Shit, you scared the crap out of me."

"I see that, baby. You ok?"

"Yeah, just give me a minute to catch my breath. You're lucky I didn't pick up this hot skillet and let you have it with scalding grease."

"That's two of us. Does this have anything with me going to work?"

"Are you good with me going to work today?"

"Oh God no, don't do that. You just startled me that's all. I happened to be in my own world when you snuck up on me."

"Are you good with me leaving you today? If you're not, I can always have my clients come to the house instead."

"Really Kyle, I already have stuff to do. Breakfast will be done in just a minute. Do you want me to set the table or would you like to have breakfast out on the deck? It's not too hot out yet."

"Deck's fine with me."

After breakfast was done, Sophie pushed her guy out the door just like an old married couple. She had daydreamed about being married. It thrilled her just to have that vision. What thrilled her even more was raising little Kyles and little Sophies. Kyle had already told her he wanted children in the future. Hopefully, that would be with her.

She needed to have Meghan, her sister-in-law, and Gabby, her niece, come over and have a play date. Now that she had so much free time, she'd fill her days with fun stuff. That sounded so odd for Sophie, because her days were always filled with hospital stuff.

As a last minute effort, Sophie called Lexi to see if she was up to a mani/pedi. Every time Lexi came over in the last two weeks, there had always been at least one other person with her, and she needed to have some alone time with her best friend.

Kyle had already given Sophie the rules of having Jake with her at all times, before leaving this morning. No, ifs and or buts, but she had to clear everything with Jake. He told her wherever she wanted to go was fine with him.

Since Kyle had splurged for her last day spa trip and she really liked the service at the facility, she gave them a ring to make sure they had an opening for the two them. She was resolved to giving into all of her pleasures, and even new ones she didn't even know she had. That was the new Sophie now.

Instead of making Lexi meet them at the spa, Jake swung by her apartment. Just being with her friend had Sophie all giddy.

Lexi had fully healed from being shot and had no residual effects from it. All she truly wished was that Sophie had finally seen the light.

Sophie, never liked having her feet touched, but when it came to having a pedicure, she felt all the stress drain from her body when she got one. That's just another one of life's indulgences that she would be happily enjoying now. The spa attendant brought both girls a glass of wine, just to relax them even more. *Nothing like being pampered.*

Sophie had to recruit the help of as many of Kyle's friends as she could, so why not start out with her friends Lexi and Bryce?

"Kyle's birthday is in three weeks, since you've known him longer than I have, I need your help with planning a party."

"What are you thinking? Family and friends or something over the top?"

"Well, I hadn't given it much thought. I think maybe over the top sounds... Perfect. Will you help me?"

"Is the sun shining outside?"

"Yeah."

"What do you think dip-shit, that I'd leave my BFF out to hang herself?" Both girls laughed until the nail technicians told them they needed to sit still or both would have painted feet.

Sophie knew she could count on Lexi to help her out, but what she didn't know was whether she could get the Club for the party. "What about having the party at the club; do you think that will be a problem, since I'm really not a member?"

"What are you talking about Sophie? You're the girlfriend of the owner. You need to use your connections."

"I want the party to be a surprise for Kyle. So I'm going to rely totally on you. I was thinking about asking Candy and Orja to help too. What do you think?"

Sophie watched Lexi's reaction to the last two names.

"Love the idea of having them help. A thought just popped into my head, though. Why don't I book the club the same night as Justine's baby shower? Do you remember me talking about the slave from Crave County?"

"Is she the one who married three brothers?"

"Yup, she's having triplets too."

"She married the Murray brothers a year ago. They're big time billionaires who run the largest cattle ranch in Crave County. I give Justine all the credit in the world; she has three very dominant men. A couple of us were going to get together to throw her a small impromptu get together just to give her presents for the babies. Hold on for a second; let me give her a call."

Sophie listened as Lexi talked to Justine.

"Hey Miss Prego, how are you and the aliens invading your body doing?" Great to hear. You coming into town tomorrow for your ob appointment? Ok how about we meet up at Sophie and Kyle's house? We girls have some planning to do. Ok, three sounds perfect. If anything changes, I'll give you a buzz."

Sophie heard everything. She was totally going to need the help of everyone she could get. She knew putting Lexi in charge would result in the perfect party. Sophie can hang tomorrow with the girls after her lunch date with her dad. Everything was lining up just perfectly for Sophie. She saw her life having meaning, and it all had to do with her man.

Kyle hated being away from Sophie, but he knew that in order for her to adjust, he needed to give her some breathing room. Gail had told him that just a couple days ago. He felt like a parent sending his child out into the world for the first time.

Just like a parent, he made sure that her every needs were taken care of, even down to having Jake take her anywhere she wanted to go.

Trying not to be away from her this first week was going to be tougher than what he thought. His partner had called out sick this morning, which freed up the office even more, but what that also did was make Kyle realize how much he had neglected his duties in the office.

Meeting with his secretary Maria first thing this morning, she had everything laid out in plies. Important, not so important, and the final pile of crap that could wait.

Kyle had set aside a few hours to be away from Sophie, but when he got her call that she was going to get a pedicure and manicure with Lexi, he knew he could spend more time at the office sorting through stuff.

Kyle checked in with Jake several times making sure his girl was safe. He needed that reassurance; he had almost lost her once. There was no way he would do that again.

Kyle felt his phone buzz with an incoming text.

Sophie: What color should I get on my fingers & toes?

Kyle: Get something tropical.

Sophie: This place has a gazillion colors.

Kyle: Anything you pick I'm going to love. Got to go baby, my client just go here.

Sophie: see you @ home later.

Kyle needed to get through this session, so that he could give Master Sergeant a call. Kyle kept glancing at his phone the entire session. No word from his father's company in Puerto Rico. He was trying to be professional, but his mind was just too pre-occupied.

He'd been keeping his eyes wide open for the past few weeks while staying low on the radar, so to speak. All he needed to do now was to secure the meeting for Thursday morning. And if Thursday didn't work, he would shoot for Friday.

Setting up a shell company was easy for Kyle. He planned to blindside his father when he walked into his office. Just seeing the look on his face after all these years would be priceless especially since Kyle had already spent a small fortune trying to locate him.

Finally finishing up his last session of the day was music to his ears. Never before did he have a purpose to escape his mundane duties at work. He did now and she waited for him at home.

He still hadn't heard from Master Sergeant yet, but knowing him, he probably was working out the final details of the trip.

After having her pedicure/manicure, Sophie had Jake take her back to Kyle's house.

Sophie had a few calls to make. She pulled out the card Gail had given her a few days ago. She dialed the number and was surprised when a bubbly young woman answered the phone.

"Good afternoon. Lisa Phillips. How may I help you?"

Sophie drew in a deep breath, thinking she was just going to leave a message on the counselor's recorder, she spoke shakily at first. "Hi, I'm Sophie Spencer. I was given your card by my doctor, Gail Cunningham."

"I was expecting your call Sophie, Gail already filled me in. It's ok to call you Sophie?"

"Oh, yeah."

"So what can I do for you?"

"Well I was wondering if you had any openings sometime this week."

"You happen to be in luck, what are you doing in an hour? My office is about fifteen minutes from Kyle's house. Either I could come to you, or you could come to my office. I have to warn you, I work out of my house most of the time, and have a dozen or so animals running around. So if you have allergies or have a problem with my zoo, we can always meet somewhere neutral."

"I don't have any allergies at all, so that's not a problem. I can come to your place."

Sophie quickly jotted down the address and access code to the gate, and she ended the call and sent a quick text to Jake asking if he could take her to her appointment.

The drive to the therapist's office was quiet. She felt an uneasy feeling talking to someone she didn't know. She hadn't had a session in almost six months. She felt weak when having to tell someone else her problems. She was damn good at hiding her own emotions, especially her true deep down feelings.

She couldn't have others seeing her as weak; she hid everything under her imaginary Superwoman cape. She had bottled up so much shit in the past two years; she was surprised she hadn't already been committed to the funny farm.

She needed to feel whole again. Not this shell of a broken down woman. Jake pulled the car up to a large black metal rod iron gate.

A small sign read: 'Our wounds are often the openings into the best and most beautiful parts of us.'

She watched as Jake punched in the code that Lisa had provided over the phone. Sophie took in the neatly manicured lawn; multiple flowerbeds lined the entire front of the house. Every imaginable color in the color wheel was represented in the flowerbeds. Hundreds of butterflies fluttered around the buds of the plants.

She remembered how she had seen several butterflies in the past few weeks. She felt she always had one at her side. *My guardian angel.* Was her guardian angel guiding her along today?

Making her walk from the car to the front door, she felt like she had cement shoes on. Her legs were heavy; she almost stumbled when she felt Jake wrap his arm around her forearm.

"I know you're scared, but Sophie you need to fight whatever is locked deep down in your heart. Don't let your pride stand in your way. There's no shame in talking to someone about your problems. Hell, when I came back from the war, I had PTSD so bad after the shit I saw over there, I had to get it off my chest before I could function without going gun crazy and killing innocent people."

"Really? I knew it was bad over there, but I had no idea how bad, though." With a sigh, she nodded, lifted her shaking hand and rang the doorbell.

A tall Asian woman in her late fifties answered the door. She had the shiniest black long hair Sophie had ever seen. The woman wore a Japanese Kimono covered with dark magenta flowers. The pattern against her fair skin brought out her green emerald eyes.

"Hi, you must be Sophie; I'm Kora, Lisa's partner. Come on in, Lisa is finishing up in her office. I have a few forms for you to fill out.

"Sure no problem." Sophie watched as Jake took a seat on one of the black leather sofas.

Lisa hadn't been joking when she asked if Sophie had any problems with animals. A beautiful Siamese cat strolled over to Sophie; she rubbed her body up and down Sophie's legs, purring and sniffing the entire time, laying her scent. Sophie realized pretty fast that the cat was just trying to soften up Sophie's mixed emotions.

She glanced around the room, until she spotted a large fish tank with large white angle fish, swimming peaceful around a pirate chest filled with gold. Just hearing the tiny bubbles from the air tank slowed down Sophie's heartbeat.

A large chocolate lab slept on top of an even larger golden lab. Lisa wasn't lying when she said they had a zoo full of animals.

Her last therapist's office was nothing like this one. The room was already filled with so much color, Sophie felt like she was walking into an art studio. Nothing like the boring neutral tones of color that covered the walls at the other office, the walls here had splashes of blue, yellow, greens, pinks and red. A true painters dream.

She already felt more at ease just having the small comforts of candles flickering throughout the room, which had Sophie's nose already trying to figure out the aroma that filled the room. She knew it had to be something exotic.

She saw things that helped center her inner soul. Out of one of the large picture windows, Sophie caught a view of the back of the property. A large pond filled her vision; it was lined with large floating lily pads. She thought she saw a fish splash out of the water but wasn't sure if her eyes were playing tricks on her. She heard birds chirping in the distance.

What she didn't hear was the hustling and bustling of cars. Sophie sat down next to Jake she began filling out the necessary forms. She watched him play his favorite game, Candy Crush. He said he played the game to ease his mind.

Sophie jumped when a door behind her opened. She turned slightly on the sofa. A tiny Asian woman appeared in a similar kimono as Kora. Her skin was just a tad lighter than Kora's; they had the same slant to their eyes. The women who stood in front of her had hair slightly thicker and a darker black then Kora's, much like a charcoal briquette color, and much longer. It went straight down her spine until it touched her butt cheeks.

But what really caught Sophie's attention were the bright gorgeous tattoos covering both of her arms. A large blue dragon wrapped around her arm. Five long claws on each foot looked as if it pierced her small bicep. Coming from the dragon's mouth was a long tongue that crawled up just peeking out and touching her neck, while licking the Triskele symbol.

On her left arm were flames of bright, red, blue, and orange that swirled around her arm. Sophie's attention was drawn to how Kora's facial expression lit up when Lisa entered the room. It showed that she was not only her business partner but she was also her bed partner and lover.

"Hello, you must be Sophie. My name is Lisa Phillips." She extended her hand towards Sophie. The instant they touched, she felt the energy flow from Lisa's hand to hers. It sent a warm feeling through Sophie's entire body.

"It's nice meeting you, Sophie."

Instantly, Sophie relaxed hearing her calming voice. Lisa looked, nor sounded anything like her other therapists. He was a staunch, old crotchety man, who smelled like he hadn't bathed in a month. Lisa on the other hand smelled of jasmine, and honey.

"I see you met my partner Kora, she happens to be the other half of my life. If you every need anything and I'm not available, you can always communicate with her. She knows how to get me immediately."

"Ok thanks, I'll remember that."

"Let's go into my office where we can sit and chat for a while." Lisa escorted Sophie into her office; again, Sophie was surprised at what she saw. Two small cushions sat on top of bamboo matts. No sofas, chairs, desk or anything that you would normally see in a doctor's office. No stacks of charts, no books, no pens, no computer. Just the two cushions, a teapot and teacups. Off in the corner of the room, Sophie noticed a small bucket that looked like an old time milk pal.

"Pick your cushion Sophie." Surprised that she was given the choice, Sophie thought for a second. *Either I can pick the thicker, plusher cushion one that has the moons and stars pattern or I can choose the cherry blossom pattern that had the winding veins.* After giving it much thought, Sophie chose the cherry blossom. She felt the veins most likely represented her life at this moment. She had so many veins running in every which way, and she prayed that one day they would point her in the correct direction of life.

Both women sat down on their cushions. Unlike what Sophie originally thought about the cushion not being very supportive, she actually sank down to a comfortable Indian style position. Not uncomfortable at all.

"Before we start, I'd like to share a cup of tea with you. It's a tradition when you come to a Japanese house, you cleanse your palate with a nice cup of tea. Since I'm the

Mistress of this dojo, it would please me if you partake in my traditions."

"I would love to honor your tradition. It pleases me to know you would include me in such an honor."

She watched Lisa pour the tea with expertise, not spilling a single drop over the side of the teapot when she tilted it. She noticed as Lisa mouthed a few things in Japanese as she began to pour the contents from the pot.

"The traditional Japanese tea has become lost in some households but not in ours, it's more of a spiritual experience for Kora and me. The tea embodies harmony, respect, purity and tranquility."

Sophie took the small cup; she swirled it first, then lifted it to her mouth. She closed her eyes and as she swallowed down the warm liquid, she felt as the tea was cleansing her soul.

"This is so good. I have so many flavors bursting in my mouth all at once."

"I can see you're a true lover of tea."

"How did you guess?" "I have my ways of seeing the whole person not the person on the outside.

"When your cup is empty, please help yourself to more."

Lisa was making this so much more enjoyable than she first imagined. She just hoped it stayed that way.

"So tell me Sophie, what brings you here today?"

Lisa watched as Sophie shifted on her cushion until she settled back down. On a large window sill behind Lisa sat a few objects, but she couldn't see them clearly. Sophie felt a sense of emptiness just thinking about why she was here.

Tears began to stream down her cheeks, as she pictured her life. Helpless, powerless, weak, broken. Lisa walked over to the sill, which held a box of tissues and a small tray that held a long incense stick. Handing her the box, Sophie blew into the tissues, then wiped away the wet spots on her cheeks.

She watched as Lisa lit the incense, as Sophie took in the scent she smelled a deep earthy aroma, not a sweet smelling flower as she thought would be coming from the stick.

"What variety is the incense?

"It's an agarwood stick, it's used as a form of meditation, and I can tell you're having difficulty expressing yourself. My question sent you into a not so pleasant place. Japanese custom uses many different scents from the earth that recenter your moods."

Sophie took a deep breath and breathed in the aroma. She was starting to feel a little calmer.

"I'm here because my doctor feels like I need to talk to someone about things I tend to bottle up inside myself."

Sophie took another drink of her tea.

"Ok, but that's not the question I asked you."

Sophie shifted on the cushion trying to figure out what Lisa was actually saying to her.

"Let me rephrase my question to you. Are you here for something you want to work on, or because someone else wants you to be here?

Sophie twisted her hands in her lap trying to be brave. "I'm broken, and I need to understand why. It was only after Gail gave me your card that I realized that my friends saw something that I wasn't seeing.

A couple of years ago, my husband was killed in a car accident. I was the only survivor. I couldn't save his life, and from that day on, my life changed. I've suffered from depression, so deeply that I wished I had died during the accident. A part of me still feels that way. I feel trapped with no way of moving forward.

I struggled for the longest time even to make it to work. Don't get me wrong I love being a surgeon but seeing death day after day. It somehow brings me back to the day my sorrow began. I'd have panic attacks so bad that my previous therapist keep me so medicated. Most of the time, I was a walking zombie.

If it hadn't been for my friends, I would be still in the same sad sorry state. They really did do a number on me to help bring me out of the depression. Each one of them played an important role in my life before my husband died; I know they did it to save me from doing something stupid.

I met Kyle that same weekend. I had promised my best friend that I would try something new. Lexi challenged me to go to a BDSM club with her, but me being me, I jumped the gun and went by myself. Again, I was feeling like I had nowhere or no one to turn to, so I did what I knew was best. I researched the club, put my big girl panties on and went out by myself. Not knowing what I was doing, I sort of winged it. That's where I met Kyle.

I was ready to come out of my pent up shell. Seeing Kyle for the first time, I knew we were meant for each other; we had a connection that I can't explain. It feels like Kyle was sent to me to be the next chapter of my life. We instantly clicked, I didn't even have that reaction to my husband, and it scares me to say the least.

Only after being with Kyle a few days I knew more about myself then what I did in the previous 29 years. I opened up to him in so many ways that I never dreamed that I could. I feel a sense of having power that I haven't felt in a long time.

I guess with power comes a false sense of hope, because it was when I let my guard down that I was shot by a gang member who had been stalking me. I've never felt so helpless in my whole life. I've always been a very strong person, never having anyone doing things for me. I find it as a sign of weakness in my character to reach out to anyone for help.

The newest problem that I have since being shot. I keep having the same nightmare night after night. Sort of like the movie 'Ground Hog Day', where Bill Murray keeps reliving ground hog day over and over, each time remembering something new each time. Well that's exactly what's happening every night. I have the same dream about being in the car accident with my husband. I wake up staring at my dead husband."

Sophie reached for her tea, she realized that she had drank it all and reached for the teapot. She gestured to Lisa if she could refill her cup. She watched as Lisa nodded her head in acceptance. Sophie sat with a peaceful look across her face. She had just been truthful and honest about everything leading up to her walking in the therapist's office. She felt a large tug on her heart as she spoke the truth to Lisa.

"Ok, so let me recap for you. You suffer from depression, panic attacks, you're flawed, weak, struggle for perfection, and you're afraid of opening yourself up to others, to ask for help of any kind, and suffer from nightmares. Ok, I'd say we have our work cut out for us. I'm hoping in our sessions we can start to work on why you're feeling the way you do.

The most important thing for you Sophie is to be honest with yourself and me. You need to feel that anything you say in our sessions is private. I won't judge you for any of your reasons or problems."

"Can I ask you a question?"

"Sure, go ahead."

"Does that include talking about lifestyle issues?"

"Any issues you have are to be expressed to me or we can't work on them. I'm not a mind reader; I don't have a crystal ball that can tell the future. I only can give you suggestions to work through your issues."

Sophie nodded her head up and down as she registered everything that Lisa was saying to her. "Wow I never knew how much I needed this until you put it that way."

"Sophie, your heart needs time to heal, and you need to make the effort. Once you do, things usually fall in line. I always look at things a little differently from most therapists. Not everything has a specific meaning of who, what, when or why things happen to us. Instead, I look at how once something happens, how you can overcome them and keep from letting them happen again. No one is ever cured 100%. Remember, it's how you chose to deal with your issues, not how you react. Does your family know that you suffer from the things you've expressed to me?" "My dad, is the best man I've ever known. He's what I would call the ideal husband that every girl looks for in a guy."

"So you two are very close."

"Very. Does he know you struggle with depression?"

Looking more ashamed then ever Sophie answered her question with her head tilted down. "Yes."

"Sophie, don't look down when I ask you a question. I don't want you feeling ashamed, and looking down at the floor is something you should only do at your Master's request. I'm not your Master. I'm your therapist. Get it?"

"Got it."

"Good, now continue on."

"My dad took me to and from my other therapists after the car accident. I never made a big deal about having to go; I didn't want him constantly worrying about me, so he was basically my taxi cab driver."

"Did you ever share anything about your sessions with your parents?"

"No, I keep everything to myself. Even the part about taking medications for panic attacks. In a way I know it was wrong but I just couldn't let them she me that way."

"What about your mom, what's your relationship with her?"

"My mom was the typical stay at home mom, she did everything and anything. She raised three children, ran a house, and kept my dad happy."

"The way you say that Sophie, it's like she did something not to your liking."

"We really never connected like a mother and daughter should. I compared my friend Lexi and her relationship with her mother to mine, and they were constantly doing the mother daughter things. Shopping, getting their nails done, roller skating, horseback riding, they did the fun things together. My mom and I did the necessary things to just get by."

"Do you resent her?"

"It's not resent, I just wished it was different, that's all. Don't get me wrong. My mom had three kids to raise all by herself while my dad was working."

"Fill me in on what you did if you didn't do it with your mom."

"I knew at a fairly young age that I wanted to be a doctor, so I pushed myself by studying when it came to fun things. My mother kept that dream alive for me when she enrolled me in every advanced program for gifted children. I was often told she couldn't bear to see me flounder my life away. In her eyes, if I wasn't perfect at everything I did, then I wasn't anything in her eyes. She forced me to be perfect; she'd push and push until I isolated myself by her need for me to be perfect. I was living through her wishes and dreams."

"Were there ever outward signs of love or affection shown from your mother?"

"She said the words, but I always felt I needed to do more. Unlike my mother, my dad saw me slipping further and further away. He made it his job to pull me back to reality every now and then. I'd change for a bit, but would soon feel the pressure from my mother and I would slip back down the same path."

Instantly, a sick feeling swirled in side Sophie's gut. *Will I be the same way with raising my children? Just like my mother, striving for only perfection, or would it be ok for my children to get average grades in school, go to a junior college, not an Ivy League college as she did?* She had never thought about these things before. Until now. She wondered why. *Would Kyle have any apprehensions about raising children? Would his issues of being abandoned as a child make him a better or worse father? Would he suddenly disappear just like his father?*

"Sophie our time is just about up for today."

Sophie hadn't realized how fast the last hour had gone by. Never had she ever felt this good about a session. Yeah a lot of questions were raised, things she had to figure out, but knowing that Lisa was going to work with her made Sophie feel stronger than what she had before, almost as if she had a soul cleansing. "Now for the part I think you were expecting. You have homework."

"I had a feeling I wasn't going to walk out of here without doing some soul searching."

"Has your Master had you keep a journal yet?"

"Yes, I started one over the weekend, I write in it daily, and then give it to him nightly."

"I had a feeling he would do that with you. Once a Dom, always a Dom."

It hit Sophie that Lisa had to be the Dom in her relationship; she oozed the same characteristics as Kyle. She had given Sophie an order and Sophie obeyed immediately.

"I'd like you to write a letter to your mother, telling her how you feel about how she raised you. Your dislikes and likes about her. I don't want you to send it to her, though. You'll bring it with you, when you return next week for your next session."

"Why am I writing specifically to my mother?"

"You'll find when you're honest with yourself, most of your problems started way before your marriage ended. Trust me when I tell you that you are a very strong person deep inside. It's just been locked away for so long. Your soul told you to make the phone call to me today for a reason, and I bet once you unlock that part of you, you'll see it stems from your mother. Sometimes it's much easier to write things down. Most people have a harder time with expression of speech. You must be honest with yourself first; you hold the key to your happiness. This exercise is just the beginning of many more that I have in store for you. Any questions?"

Sophie shifted once again on the cushion, a chime sounded in the distance.

"No, I understand my mission."

"Great, before you go, I do need to tell you something. Both women stood at the same time. It took a lot of courage for you to make the call to me today. You should walk out of here feeling like you've accomplished something.

Feel free to contact me day or night. I always have my phone on. If by chance I don't pick up, leave a message or text me. I'll get back with you ASAP. If for some reason I'm out of town Kora is also available for emergency calls, she is also a therapist, and even though she primarily deals with children she is also licensed to treat adults."

"That's great to know. I can't tell you how much better I feel about coming today. I was really worried at first, feeling your energy has sparked something in me that I don't know how to express yet, but I'm sure you already know that."

"I see you, Sophie, as who you are. You're a strong woman who has amazing qualities that are locked down, but with time, I'm hoping those qualities shine. Just like your beautiful eyes. How would you feel if we extended a few of your sessions to include Kyle?"

"I'm fine with that."

"When can I come back to see you again?"

"Now that's music to my ears. How about next Wednesday, same time as today?"

"Shouldn't be a problem. I'll check with Kyle and Jake to make sure their schedules are cleared."

"If you can't make the appointment, I realize things pop up at the last minute, just drop me a text, I'll get you in ASAP."

Sophie left Lisa's office feeling like a different person. She now had some questions she had to work out in her head. Things she had locked away for a long time.

Seeing Candy in the kitchen starting dinner gave Sophie a huge idea. *Who better to give her cooking lessons?* "Hi there, something smells delicious."

"I thought I'd change up the menu for tonight. Chicken Marsala over some egg noodles. I hope you don't mind."

"Not at all. I'm just happy you know how to cook. Dropping her purse on the counter, Sophie made her way over to the fridge.

"Would you like a glass of wine?"

"Sure, as long as you're going to join me."

"Red ok with you?"

"Great."

Sophie only had a few girlfriends growing up, one of whom happened to be Lexi. Most were obsessed with which football player was going to ask them out. Even in college, most of her sorority sisters went to frat parties while Sophie had her nose buried in a textbook. She had no room for friends back them. Now was a different story.

Her goal was to change her social status. Starting today, that would all change. Pouring the two of them a glass of wine. It was now or never to get their friendship going.

"So, I was wondering if you could teach me how to cook. It's one thing to boil water, but it's a whole new ball game to prepare a meal."

"Sure, what do ya want to know?"

"Everything if that makes any sense."

"Why don't you pull up a stool?"

The two girls giggled, drank an entire bottle of wine, and laughed for over an hour. It wasn't until Sophie heard the sound of a car driving up on the gravel road that she realized how much time had passed.

Feeling like a weight had been lifted off her shoulders, she gave Candy all the credit in the world.

Candy had to grow up under deplorable circumstances. Her mother was a crack whore, and her father was nowhere to be found. Candy had to raise her younger brother from the time she was eight. After hearing Candy's story, Sophie had a better understanding of who Candy was and what she had to do to survive, hence her love of cooking.

Both girls shared stories about growing up. Each one had come from totally opposite sides of the fence. Sophie was raised in a two parent, loving household, whereas Candy was 'raised' by a low income, single parent, crack whore who did just about anything and everything not to raise her children. They both were submissive and loved to serve. Even though they were from a different social status, that didn't make any difference in Sophie's eyes. She saw Candy as her equal.

Bumbling around the kitchen with only one hand brought a disadvantage to Sophie as far as chopping, slicing and dicing went, especially. Candy made a deal with Sophie. Sophie would plan the meals for now, and with the help of Candy, the two would prepare meals that would knock the socks off of Kyle and any guest of his choice.

Sophie had nothing but happiness filling her today. *Would she feel this way in a week, a month, or even a year from now?*

Candy finished showing Sophie how to arrange a meal planner, and where to find recipes on the internet when Kyle walked into the kitchen. His tie was undone from around his neck, suit jacket slung over his shoulder, brief case in his left hand, and a bundle of deep red roses in his right hand.

He looked amazing in Sophie's eyes. Her heart started to speed up as he made his way over to her. She loved how responsive her body had become. He made her heart feel so alive.

Handing over the roses to her, Kyle had only given her roses one other time and that was when they were staying at the condo. She loved getting fresh flowers, watching the tiny rose bud fully open was a sign of life in Sophie's mind. Even when the rose petals fell off the stem Sophie loved to store them in glass jars around her apartment. It saddened her when she'd see her neighbors throwing away the dried up petals in the trash. She often would remove them and add them to her jars.

She watched as Candy walked out of the kitchen, Sophie assumed it was to give her and Kyle some privacy.

"They're beautiful. Thank you."

Kyle dropped his brief case on the marble island. Not knowing what to do, Sophie brought the flowers up to her nose. Smelling the bouquet opened up her lungs with a sweet aroma.

"How's your arm doing today?"

"I'm starting to get some feeling back in my pinky finger and I have more movement than what I did last week. George the therapist told me he thinks my nerve endings are starting to heal."

"How can he tell?"

"He brought a portable ultrasound machine, I watched as he scanned up and down my arm showing me the new sprouts that had grown. It was amazing to watch. I wish you could have been here to see it."

Kyle stroked the top of her head, just having his hands caressing her hair sent shivers up and down her spine. It didn't take Kyle long at all to possess her lips with his. She really did miss him throughout the day. She felt it was better to keep herself busy versus giving her mind time to think.

"I hope you're hungry. Candy's been cooking up a storm."

"I'm hungry, but it's not food I want."

She saw the devilish look on Kyle's face. Sophie swatted at Kyle's chest in a playful manner.

"Do you always have sex on the brain?"

"Baby, that's what you do to me." Sophie blushed; her cheeks turned a nice color of pink. It's only been eight and half hours since we last had sex. You'd think that would I have been satisfied for today."

"I could be inside you all day long and still not get my sweet fill of you. She loved it when he talked sexy and dirty to her. Now kiss me woman, like you missed me."

Kyle was surprised to find Sophie's hospital bed was gone from the master bedroom, even after their wonderful weekend at Crave County Kyle had insisted she sleep there; she had slept just last night in the hospital bed. She had baulked at first, but when he gave her a stern Dom face, she forced herself to climb into the hospital bed, but being under his spell, she did it gracefully.

"Where's the hospital bed, Sophie?"

"I had the company come and get it this morning after you left for work. Before you get all crazy and mad, I called Gail this morning to make sure it was ok with her. I explained to her what you made for me while we were away. She told me that was fine, but she insisted that I have a therapeutic wedge. So when the company picked up the bed, they brought over the wedge at the same time."

"Are you sure baby? You know I'm not a still sleeper. I roll all over the bed. What if I accidentally roll over on you in the middle of the night?"

"So, you'll wake me up that's all. I'll wince in pain for a second or two then I'll roll over and go back to sleep. Kyle, I need you holding me at night. It's one thing to know you're in the same room, but it's another thing to have your body touching mine. I feel protected when you're holding me. I feel like you own me, possess me. I've never had that feeling before."

"Sophie, I'm so glad to hear those words coming from your mouth. You've gotta promise me no matter what, if I hurt you in any way, you must be honest with me and tell me. I'm not a mind reader. Our relationship is built on trust between us."

"Yes, Sir I've had this remarkable revelation over the past few weeks. I've finally realized I can't be a one-woman show; it takes two to be whole. I'm so glad you stuck by me through the bad times, now I wish we only have good times ahead of us."

"Sophie I can't promise to solve all of your problems, but I can promise you that you won't have to face them alone anymore."

"Well that brings me to a little surprise I planned for the two of us."

Sophie had a puzzled look on her face as she listened to Kyle.

"What do you mean?"

"The night you left, I know I told you, I hopped on my plan with a few men from Volkov Security in search of my father. Come to find out he's in Puerto Rico under the name of Matthew Hendrich."

Sophie still didn't know what this had to do with her but she sat on the edge of the bed and listened as Kyle explained to her.

Kyle proceeded to tell her, how he had found his father, but never got the chance to see him face to face. He went over the new plan, on how they would pose as business partners, starting up a new company. The fake shell company he had set up was already operating wonderfully. The only thing he needed was her by his side.

Sophie had always been adventurous before the car accident, but had become reserved in the past two years. She kept telling herself for the past week or so, she needed to reignite her old self. This was exactly what she needed. She needed to add adventure, thrill, and a vacation to boot.

Even after her session today with Lisa, she knew she had to stop being so withdrawn and reserved; she had to live life to the fullest. Going on vacation was another way of living life. She would also be standing by her man in his time of need. She felt a slight tingle of excitement in her chest. She loved the way her body reacted to Kyle's charm and charisma.

"So when are we leaving for Puerto Rico?"

Kyle pulled her into his arms and vowed he would protect her from this day forward. It turned Sophie on when he talked all romantic about her. It had been a while since anyone was willing to protect her, it made her feel wanted again. She finally felt whole again.

"Is two days enough time for you to get packed?"

"Well let me think for a second." She now showed the excitement of a bouncing baby. "I guess that's why you said to get something tropical on my fingers and toes."

"Guilty as charged, Baby. So that you're not overwhelmed, I have the owner of Delilah's boutique coming over later tonight with some of her latest fashions."

"Kyle I don't need any new clothes. I already have plenty."

"One thing you'll need to get used to is my obsession to give you the world. It's my job as your boyfriend and Master to shower you with pleasures."

"But Kyle…you do know I have money, maybe not as much as you have…"

She felt Kyle's large hands grip her ass. "Let me just set you straight before we go any further." She loved it when he became demanding, he squeezed her ass cheeks, she let out a soft moan as he squeezed her even harder.

"I don't care how much or how little money you have, you could be the richest woman in the world, but when I say I want to buy you something, you nod your head like a good girl and say 'thank you, Master.' No fighting me, Sophie. Remember as your Master, I have needs and this is one that I need you to fulfill for me. Now let me hear you say it." He gripped her ass even harder.

"Thank you Master."

"Now that we have that settled, tell me all about your day, baby."

Sophie filled him in on everything she had done. When she got to the part about going to Lisa Phillips' office, she saw the surprised look in his eyes. She explained to him the differences between her old therapists to how Lisa ran her practice. She actually didn't even feel like she was a patient. She felt more like she was discussing her problems with a friend.

She even asked if he could go with her next week to her session. Needing Kyle's support was the key to helping Sophie face and conquer her challenges, she was extremely happy when she asked him for his help by attending a few of her sessions with her. She was surprised that Kyle hadn't forced her to make the call. She thought he would have, but it was music to her ears when he didn't even bring it up in any of their conversations.

She was so pleased when he told her that he would support her in any means that he could, and if that meant he would attend her sessions with her, then he would be at her side. Sophie knew he meant every word. She was falling deeper in love with him every minute she spent with him. She just wished and hoped that nothing would happen to disturb her newfound love for him. She wasn't sure how she would survive if something bad happened to him. She had already lost one man in her life.

Chapter Sixteen

It had been several years since Sophie had set foot on Gunpowder Gun Range, although she been trained by the Maryland State Police to carry a gun. Sophie made the decision after being shot that she needed to sharpen up her skills. Another one of her newfound freedoms. She pre-arranged with the range to have two lanes reserved for her and her father. Surprised when she set up the lunch date with her father, he hadn't questioned her choice for lunch. He'd soon find out what Sophie was really up to anyway. It was better to have her father on her side.

Being around guns was not unusual for Sophie because she had been around them her whole life. Coston Spencer, Sophie's father, made sure all of his children were trained and knowledgeable about gun safety. He made a point in saying it doesn't hurt to know how to use a gun, but hopefully you'll never have to use it in self-defense.

Knowing someday she would be returning to the hospital, she had the right to protect herself in any way she chose. Before leaving the house she pulled out her Maryland State Handgun Wear and Carry Permit and noticed it was going to expire next month. She quickly went online and completed the renewal application. All she needed to do now was get a few practice rounds in and she'd be good to go. Never had she dreamed she would need to carry her Smith & Wesson .380 pistol, but times were a changing.

Her pistol was small and fit perfectly in her purse. She had been surprised when her father gave her the gun as a graduation present from medical school. She asked Jake to drive by her apartment before going to the range. She hadn't taken her gun with her to Kyle's house, but after today, it would be always be with her.

Surprised to see her dad already waiting for her, she ran over just as she had done when she was a child. She saw his face light up, just like it was Christmas morning. She was super excited to see her dad. She had so much to talk to him about; getting his advice meant the world to Sophie.

"Hi, Dad. I'm so glad I could steal you away from mom for the afternoon."

"I bet you are. How's my girl doing? You look radiant, and well rested; you must be feeling better."

"Dad I feel so much better it's hard to even describe." Sophie motioned over to the waiter that they were ready to be seated. "I have so much to tell you. I'm not sure where to begin." Just like an anxious child Sophie she shimmied into the booth across from father.

Sophie looked around the restaurant, taking in everyone in the room. She felt relaxed in the presence of her father. "Dad, you know how you said if I ever needed anything you'd help?"

"Yeah."

"I need to brush up on my shooting skills."

"Did you bring your gun?"

"I did; it's in my purse."

"Let's eat and talk first."

"Sounds like a plan."

"So tell me what's really going on…why the sudden urge to brush up on your gun skills?"

Sophie took a deep breath, feeling her pulse raise slightly, "I was foolish for running from Kyle's house the night I got shot. I didn't really think I was in any danger. I thought Kyle was overreacting to the news about a nurse who had been attacked the week before."

"Sophie, what does that have to do with you carrying your gun?"

"I don't want to ever be in a situation that I can't defend myself again."

"I see. How's your range of motion?"

"Each day it's getting better. I'm nowhere near where I was before getting shot, so that's why I thought I'd like to switch to being a left-handed shooter."

"I see, but what about your right hand? Don't you want to try shooting with that hand?"

Sophie had been sipping water the entire time she and her father were talking. She really could use a stiff drink right about now, but she didn't think that would help her to shoot any better.

"How much pain are you in when you use your right shoulder?"

"As long as I stretch before doing anything I can handle the pain. If I just wing it and try to do something, the pain sends me to my knees. My therapist comes to the house daily, though. He keeps telling me to hang in there, and I'm truly trying, but some days I can barely lift my arm, while other days I'm fine.

You probably think I'm whining but dad, I need to be able to protect myself when the men in my life, especially you can't protect me. There's going to be a day when I go back to work, Kyle can't be with me 24/7 and I don't expect him to be either. I need to be strong for myself. This whole ordeal has been a big wake up call for me."

"What's happening with the gang members who shot you?"

"I met with the state's attorney last week. They have enough evidence to convict the younger boy, he's the one who actually did the shooting, and the other boy was on lookout duty." Coston reached across the table and took Sophie's hand in his.

"Dad, can you believe it? He's only fourteen, and it doesn't seem right to send a boy who had a shitty upbringing to jail for twenty years. Literally his parents were killed when he was eight; his sister was thirteen and practically raised the boy. The way they survived was despicable. No one should have to grow up that way. The only way they survived..." Sophie had to choke back the tears that were forming. "The sister hooked up with one of the local gang members and they took them in. In return, they were grooming the boy the last six years to be a full member of the gang. Supposedly once he shot me, he would be initiated into the gang. Sadly enough he pulled my name. I was his target."

"What's your heart saying to you? I can see you're struggling with something weighing you down."

"I've been toying with a couple different scenarios. I'm not sure which outcome will be my final decision. My heart tells me one thing, but my gut is telling me something different. Just so you know I haven't said anything to anybody yet. You're the first person I've talked to, Dad, that's including Kyle; he has no clue. What would you think if I took the house that Carl had built for us, and turned it into a boys' home?"

She felt her father glaring at her. He didn't have a stoic face, but it was one that gave her great concern. She knew she had to pitch it to her dad first and once he was on board, everyone else would go with it.

"Orphaned kids often become wards of the state, some are mistreated and some are just plain forgotten about." She knew this from watching kids come in through the ER.

"Dad, giving an orphaned boy a second chance in life, a place where he can be safe, be given good nutritious meals, and an education, is my main goal. Maybe just maybe, I can prevent a boy from getting involved with gang crap, and then I know I could be satisfied."

"Are you sure this is something you want to do?"

"I do, Dad. My only problem, well not my only problem, but I'm not sure where to start. That's where I need your help. You have all the business smarts. Remember I'm the girl who fixes sick organs." She had giggled more in the last few weeks than she had in the last year. "I want to learn everything there is so I can fix broken children.

When it comes to zoning, permits, and the legal stuff, I'm lost. I need someone I can trust to guide me in doing what is right. I never spent a dime of Carl's money after his death. It's still sitting in an account our lawyer set up for me. I think it's time that money gets put to good use."

She knew she was getting somewhere with her father, because he had a different look on his face now.

"When do you plan on talking to Kyle about your project?"

"We're going away for a mini vacation the day after tomorrow. I was thinking about pitching it to him while were away. The house is fully paid for. It's just sitting vacant; before Carl even started the construction, he made sure we would never have a house payment. You know what?"

"What sweet heart?"

"I've never been back to the house. Did Bryce give you the keys?"

"Yeah, they're hanging on the hook in the kitchen, you know the one I'm talking about. Yup. All you need to do is drop by the house and pick them up."

"I'm not sure I can go by myself yet." Sophie stared out into space. She thought about finally being able to walk into the house, but walking in without her husband still scared the shit out of her. She thought about the children they would never have, the parties that would never be enjoyed with their friends.

No, I'm not going to do this to myself. I need to put on my big girl pants and fight the urge to head back into a depression, when I have so much to look forward to. I can still have those dreams it's just going to be with someone else in a different home. This home is going to give dreams and hope to unfortunate boys. She knew she couldn't do it alone. She was going to need all the support she could get.

She felt her dad stroking her hand. It brought her back to the present. "Can you believe Carl's death benefits were over three million dollars? That's not including Volkov Construction stocks, which I now own. Thank goodness Bryce stepped up when Kyle died."

"That's one thing I had to give to Carl, he was excellent with his business skills. He made sure his family would never suffer for anything. He was ruthless in the boardroom. That's why he put his all into the business and he's been missed by all of his colleagues, including his family. I must admit, I see a change in everyone at Volkov Construction. Everyone seems to be moving forward, which is a great sign for business. I even see it in you too sweet pea."

"Dad, I think I have a meaning in life, a new purpose that I didn't have before, and it's all because of Carl. Honoring Carl's memory by doing something good with the money he left me, gives me hope that his legacy will always live on. I wouldn't have come to you if I didn't think it would work."

"Well it looks like we have a lot of work in the next couple of months. I caution you up front; we're going to run up against obstacles at times; your most important job at all times is to stay focused. You're never to give up hope. If you do those two things, I can guarantee your boys' home will be a success."

Sophie had tears running down her cheeks, not of sadness, but rather of hope, love, and a new beginning.

Something she hadn't had in a long time. After shooting a few rounds on the range with her father's guidance, Sophie had to call it quits. Her arm just hurt too fucking bad. She'd work a little harder with the therapist in the upcoming weeks to gain more flexibility and better range of motion before she'd tackle coming back to the range.

She left the range with a sense of confidence she hadn't had when she walked in. She had a purpose, her new boys' home. Now she needed to plan a kick-ass birthday party for the man she loved.

A new type of excitement bubbled inside of Sophie. Her sexual desires no longer had an off switch; her batteries had been sparked to life and showed no signs of a power shortage. No off switch for the seeable future.

Sophie was grateful that Lexi and Justine had no problems meeting back at Kyle's home after Justine's OB appointment. She prearranged for Candy to be at the house for cooking lesson number two. Sophie picked an easy dish for tonight's dinner, something that everyone could enjoy.

Kyle had informed Sophie that he had some important business at the club that needed his attention. Sophie wondered if it was really club business or if it had anything to do with the trip to Puerto Rico.

She did feel a little uneasy about the whole situation with Kyle's father but she knew once Kyle had it in his head to do something a certain way, his mind couldn't be changed. Kyle consoled her that it could be a long night ahead of him at the club; this would be her first real night alone by herself in the house.

He told her it was nights like these he would just spend at the city condo and wouldn't come home. She tried to reassure him that she would be just fine all by herself. She was a big girl. Kyle told her that come hell or high water he would make it home to her. She even tried to push the subject by telling him she could have a girls sleep over with

Lexi and Candy. He wasn't ready to be without her even for one night.

He put his foot down, by saying to her that he would come home from work, changes his clothes, have dinner with her and the girls, head out to the club, have his meeting, then return back home, and he better find his pretty sub tucked into bed.

Again, with his No. Ifs ANDS or BUTS policy.

Sophie said, "Yes, Sir" and that was the end of that conversation. He had pulled his dominance card once again and she was left with surrendering.

Sophie pulled out her sling; she had only worn it when she absolutely had to. After her time at the range, her arm was more sore than ever. Her motto was no pain, no gain and boy was she feeling the pain tonight.

Sophie was grateful for having Candy to help her with all of the cooking, cleaning, and household chores. She didn't know how she would have done it otherwise. Candy explained how to prepare the pork chops. Sophie was amazed when she learned the secret tip to making the coating on the outside thick and crispy.

All it took was soaking the chops in milk for five minutes before dunking them in an egg yolk batter, then dredging them in a mixture of Italian breadcrumbs. Having her skillet scorching hot was another tip Candy let her in on.

Sophie watched as Candy placed the chops in the sizzling skillet. Good thing she had an apron on. Having the grease splatter up on Candy's pretty tank top, it would have been sinful to ruin such a pretty top.

Sophie smelled the aroma as it quickly filled the kitchen. She remembered these smells coming from her own mother's kitchen as a girl. She now wished she had spent more time learning how to cook from her mother's hand, rather than Candy.

She missed a lot of years' worth of bonding with her mother while she spent the time with her nose in a book, striving to be perfect in her mother's eyes. She would have rather had the useful skills of cooking, but she couldn't travel back in time; she could only go forward.

She could ask her mother for some of her family recipes that Sophie loved as a child. She remembered her mother making Sunday pot roast for supper, and the vegetables melted in her mouth. Her mother made fresh biscuits or bread every day, and in the summertime, her mother was known for making jellies and jams that lasted them all winter long.

It was these things Sophie needed to learn. She'd someday have children of her own and would need to teach her daughter or son how to survive. Sophie had survived on Ramen noodles while in college. Even up to four weeks ago Ramen was her go to food.

Having dinner almost done, she was wondering what was taking Lexi, and Justine so long to get to the house. Sophie sent Lexi a text.

Sophie: What's your ETA?

Lexi: 2 min. Justine had to pee every 5min.

Sophie: gotcha.

Sophie met the girls the door, Not knowing Justine put Sophie at a slight disadvantage. Aside from being a bundle of nerves, she already had a trying day at the gun range when she couldn't really shoot her pistol. So adding more excitement on top of that was surely to set Sophie off.

Lexi was known for being a little rough around the edges until you got to know her, that's why Sophie and she had become BFFs so many years ago. Lexi was the bad girl and Sophie was the good girl, when you put the two together they were like a volcano ready to erupt. Now they were about to add, two more girls to the mix.

Sophie already had the pleasure of bonding with Candy for the past few weeks. She too had the good girl attitude just like Sophie. Candy had a true desire to serve. She didn't care who she served. Sophie believed that is why her and

Candy had hit it off from the very first time they met at the club, everything Candy did was done out of love.

What would Justine bring to the mix? All Sophie knew about her was she'd married three brothers from Crave County, which wasn't uncommon for that town, was pregnant with triplets, submissive to the bone, and without a doubt Lexi raved about her kick ass party planning skills. After all, if Candy, Lexi and Justine were all friends, that meant Justine couldn't be all that bad. Or could she?

Justine waddled in as Sophie greeted both women with hugs. Even though Justine was carrying triplets, Sophie could barely tell she was seven and half months pregnant. Justine's petite structure made her small in comparison to Sophie's size. She had long wavy, red hair, a light complexion, and the cutest little dimples that made a person want to stick their fingers in them.

The first words that came barking out of Justine's mouth were, "bathroom now, my three hellions are playing kick ball with my bladder. All I seemed to do it pee every few seconds." Sophie pointed and said third door on the left down the hall.

The two girls watched as Justine waddled down the hall. It had only been yesterday that Lexi, and Sophie had a chance to see each other. But any day that Sophie got to spend time with her BFF was a good day.

"You're going to love Justine. She is such a hoot once you get to know her. Wait until you meet her three smoking-hot husbands." Sophie watched as Lexi fanned herself, pretending like she was on fire. "All three of them are Doms to the core. Each one has his own special skills. That drives poor little Justine crazy."

"I can't image three husbands. God how do they all fit?"

"You'd be surprised when they play at the club. Everyone stops and watches their scenes. I could come just by watching them." Both girls began to giggle when Justine made her way back to the living room.

"Dinner will be done in about a half hour. Candy is in the kitchen finishing up. I figure we can start planning the party, but I have a request, when Kyle gets home we talk about the baby shower or something else. I want this to be a surprise."

"I totally understand, Sophie. If it were my guys, I'd want the same thing. Plus it's the biggest kick to watch their faces when you shock them. Ok, I don't know about you guys, but I need to get off my swollen gorilla feet."

"You're so funny Justine, you don't have gorillas, and they look like ballerina feet."

"Girl are you blind or just being nice? These babies have me hopping and they haven't even shown me their darling little faces yet."

"Does your OB expect you to go full term?"

"Yeah, but I already have a plan for that too. My guys have given me, the no touch my couch with their penises policy starting last weekend, saying they were going to give the demons brain damage by hitting their tiny heads with their penises. So basically my hole is closed for business until my little darlings stop taking up residence in my womb."

"Oh god you poor thing." Lexi reached out and stroked her arm. "Does that include oral sex too?"

"Not sure, David put on Pretty Woman for the hundredth time. I swear he knows that movie makes me horny. He started rubbing my swollen toes. I'm most sure I could have come just by his touch. But, no, Mr. Sadist himself carried me off to bed, tucked me in like I was some kind of cripple. I must have fallen asleep before my two other Neanderthals, short for Lee and Hugh, joined us. I woke up this morning all horny, ready to go out of mind when all three of them carried me to the shower. Each one had a morning hard on that made my mouth water. But no,

I wasn't even allowed to give them a blowjob. Lee did tell me to check with Dr. Sully, if I got permission from her to have orgasms, he would see what he could do when I got home tonight. So you know what I did, I had her call my cavemen. She told each one of them, she was prescribing orgasms for the next few weeks at least.

She told them that women can have sex up to an hour before going into labor and that doesn't hurt the babies at all. "Just because a girl's having three torpedoes for babies doesn't mean she's off limits until after the babies are born. I'll be humping the bedpost by the time these three are born, if I leave it up to the three of them."

Sophie hadn't expected Justine to be so funny or as open as she was about her personal life. Justine pulled out her party planner calendar from her briefcase, Sophie told her the date of the party. She wanted to have it on Kyle's actual birthday, which happened to fall on a Friday. She watched as Justine leafed through the pages. Candy had finally made her way into the living room with a tray full of drinks for the girls. In big bold letters Justine blocked out *Friday, August 26, Baby Shower for the Demons.*

Hosted by Lexi, Candy and Sophie.

Time: 7-10 pm.

Location: The Cellar.

"Is it common to have a baby shower at the club? Do you think Kyle will be suspicious at all?"

"You leave all the worry to me. All you have to do is be a beautiful hostess."

"Wow, wait a minute. I don't know any of Kyle's friends."

"No problem at all. It's already an open play night so any member who has full privileges will be on the RSVP list. We just won't have any potential new members that night. Candy, can you handle putting together a menu with Sophie? Whatever the two of you come up with, I'll even make sure you can use the restaurant kitchen the day before to prep everything." Both girls nodded their heads in unison.

"Lexi your job's going to be sending out invitations. You know all of Kyle's friends anyway, and you have all of their info. As long as you don't object Sophie, I'll get the final ok from Master Derek to put the baby shower down on the club's general calendar. If it's ok with you."

"That's good with me."

"So what else is there to do? I'll have a couple of the subs from our slave/sub group decorate the day of the party. If I remember Master Derek and Master Kyle both love to play golf, I'll arrange for Master Derek to take him golfing in the afternoon."

"How about I ask Julia if she can have Kyle over for a family birthday dinner. That should keep him busy spending family time with them. I can leave him there and maybe Derek can bring him by the club to pick me up."

"I love how you think Sophie; you're one step ahead of my planning. This is going to be so much fun."

"Are you sure this isn't too much for you to handle. Justine? I don't want you overdoing it."

"Girl, my only worry right about now is whether I'm going to get laid tonight. Who's going to hoist this girl out of this comfy recliner? Demons are kicking my bladder again. I'm sure your Master doesn't want a stain on his lovely leather chair."

Both Candy and Lexi went over and helped Justine shimmy out of the chair.

While Justine was off doing what most pregnant women do the most, pee, Sophie had the most amazing thought. "Lexi when you had your nipples pierced, did it hurt a whole lot?" "What are you thinking Sophie? Tell us please."

"Well Kyle keeps telling me how he'd loved to pierce my nipples when I'm a little further along in my healing. But

I was thinking, if I got Gail to give the all clear I could, how to say this?"

"Just say it, Sophie. We're all friends here. Nothing's going to shock us."

"I'm thinking birthday present."

"Gotcha, I think he'd love that."

Just as she finished saying he'd love that Kyle opened the front door. "What am I going to love?"

Sophie had to think fast. "I hope you love the way the pork chops are cooked. Candy showed me an easy way to keep the breading on them today."

"You know I love everything you've cooked so far, baby girl."

"Let me think. The only thing I've made so far has been eggs, sausage and coffee."

"Well at least the smoke detectors didn't go off."

She just shook her head, letting him know he was so full of himself.

"Get over here and greet your Master properly. You're looking healthy, Lexi. Your Master taking care of you?"

"Of course, Master Kyle, I'm all cleared from my injury. Good as new. Thanks for everything."

"You bet. Anything you need, you let your Master know, okay?"

Sophie loved the way Lexi and Kyle interacted. Kyle whispered into Sophie's ear. "Meet me upstairs in five minutes." He wrapped his arms around her, as he kissed her lips. She melted into his clutches.

Just as the two were done kissing, Justine made her way back in the living room. She cleared her throat, "Babies in the room, they can hear everything you two are doing."

"Good to see you, Justine. You're looking radiant today. How's your three tiny Martians doing?

"Kicking up a storm, I think they might be playing kick ball with my bladder."

"Any names yet."

"No, not yet. We don't even know the sex of the babies yet. My Masters said as long as they're healthy, they don't care what we call them."

"Makes sense Justine. I'm going to leave you girls to discuss girl stuff as you call it and go freshen up before dinner."

The girls watched as Kyle made his way upstairs before they started to giggle. "What's so funny?"

"Good thing I'm already collared, married and knocked up, because if I wasn't I'd be falling all over him like a horny dog. God he's got a fine ass."

"Jesus, Justine, you need to get fucked by your Masters," Lexi squealed.

"Yup you said it. Maybe you can put in a good word for me when Leeland comes to pick me up later."

"Sure thing what are sisters for? I've got your back covered."

"Can you guys think of anything else we need to do? Justine, we need to exchange our contact info." Each of the girls took out their phones and programed the others' numbers in.

"Nope I think that about covers everything. Let me go and check on dinner. I already have the table set. I just need to pull the trays out of the oven. Who wants to help me?" Candy said. Both Lexi and Justine raised their hands at the same time.

"I'm going to check on Kyle to see if he needs anything."

"Hey you better not come back smelling like sex, because if you do, I'm liable to attack you once he leaves."

"Funny Ha, Ha. You're right Lexi, I really do like her."

"Told ya."

It had only been six weeks since she had been shot, but it felt like a lifetime ago. She hadn't had another nightmare since they returned from Crave County, which was a relief to Sophie. She was living life to the fullest. She had to tell

Kyle about her new plans for the boys' home, but tonight wasn't the correct time.

She made her way up to the master suite, just as Kyle had instructed her to. She heard water running, which meant Kyle was most likely already taking his steamy, hot shower. The door was left open for a reason. She made her way into the bathroom and pulled herself up on top of the long countertop. She picked up his towel and pressed it up against her nose. It smelled just like a bouquet of spring flowers. Never in a bazillion years did she ever think she would be sitting on her lover's counter, sniffing his towel waiting for him to get out of the shower.

Chapter Seventeen

Sophie couldn't believe how her life had done a complete three sixty turn. It had been only six weeks since the shooting. She had gone from being a depressed, widowed cardiologist who loved her job, but not her life, went to a BDSM club by herself for the first time, being stalked by the local gang members, to meeting a guy who she was falling in love with, was shot by a teenage gang member, which could have possibly changed her career from a budding Cardiothoracic surgeon to not being able to use her hand.

She had set the plans in motion to throw her hunk of a boyfriend a birthday bash at the BDSM club. Wow, that was enough to make her dizzy when she actually thought about her life. On top of all that, she was going to branch out into the business world by opening up a boys' home. Her life had most certainly changed for the better.

For such a long time, Sophie could barely drag her sorry ass out of bed in the mornings to go to work; now, she no longer felt the pressure of being perfect. She just wanted to be herself: Sophie, Kyle's submissive, girlfriend, and lover. She heard the water turn off, seeing her man stand in front of her dripping wet, made her sex tighten. She could stare at him forever.

Sophie noticed two packages lying on the bed. She watched as Kyle strolled over to the bed with just his towel wrapped around his hips. He picked the first one up and handed it to her. Acting just like a child opening up her Christmas present, she tore the wrapping off, and threw the shreds of paper from it on the bed. Lifting the box lid, she gasped when she saw the new Louis Vuitton Cappuccinos bag that she had been talking to Lexi about. Sophie let out a loud squeal when she took it out of the box.

She stroked the luscious leather, just as if she were stroking Kyle's cock. She ran her finger over the flowery gold button and feeling the cold metal under her finger sent a shiver up her spine.

"I love it, but how did you know I was looking at this very one?"

"You left your iPad on the table over the weekend with this on the screen. So I had it shipped from Paris on Sunday."

"I can't believe you bought this for me."

"The light rose color will complement the new suite for our trip."

"I can't wait to show the girls down stairs. Lexi's going to flip out." Sophie opened the beauty flap, revealing what set inside. A matching new wallet and passport holder all done in the same pattern as her purse. "Oh my God. This is so beautiful, but you shouldn't have."

"What…" before Kyle could get another word out of his mouth, Sophie dropped the purse on the bed, and jumped up into his arms. She's lucky that Kyle had no problem picking her up.

"I meant to say, thank you, Master. I love my purse." She felt his cock twitch as she said Master. She took her mouth and placed her lips over his. Forcing him to open to her. She had never been this forward or demanding before with Kyle. She was about to show her man, just how much he meant to her.

She broke off the kiss with a loud pop. Slowly she slid down his chest just like a sneaky cat, scooting her body down his, kissing and nipping as she descended to the floor. She gracefully knelt down at his feet, with her head bowed down towards the floor.

Sophie's adrenaline was building inside of her at a rapid pace. She wasn't sure how long it would take Kyle to release her to return to her friends; she hoped it wouldn't be too long. She waited until he gave her the signal to proceed. She felt Kyle's finger tap her on her shoulder.

"Master, your slave would, like to serve your needs." She loved saying the word slave. It gave her a sense of his ownership. She belonged to him and him only. To do as he pleased.

"What does my beautiful slave have in mind?"

"Let me show you Master" She watched as he shook his head. She could see the bulge of his cock pushing up against the terry cloth towel that was wrapped around his waist. She wasted no time at all. She reached up and undid the towel from around his waist, letting it drop to the floor.

Sophie licked her lips. She had already become breathless just by staring at his enormous cock.

"You're driving me crazy my little slave girl. Can you see how you make me hard as a rock by just being in the same room?"

"Yes, Master. I'm so glad that I have that effect on you."

"Your sassy mouth better get a move on it or our guests will think you abandoned them. Go ahead baby, take what you want."

She rubbed up the sides of his exquisite thighs; she had to hold on to him so that she didn't lose her balance, what better place to hold than his ass cheeks. She loved how he had a smattering patch of hair just under his belly button that ran down to the base of his cock. She wanted to take her time to explore him but she already knew that wasn't going to happen, especially since the girls waited for them downstairs.

She looked at his turgid cock and licked her lips. She wrapped her tiny hands around his already large shaft, tightened her grip and began stroking him up and downward. She used her right hand for the first few strokes until she started getting pain shooting up her arm.

Quickly she changed hands, pulling on his foreskin she licked under the cap down the large vein that was beginning to bulge. The first few drops of pre-come escaped from the head of his cock. His cock was now a dark shade of purple, she loved that she turned him on in this manner. She tightened her grip and she saw the color get even darker. She heard Kyle grunt out low moans as she closed her lips down the over the head of his cock.

She loved the taste of her man. Eagerly, she lapped up the tasty treat that he was giving her. It pleased her inner soul that he was giving her a part of him. Sliding her tongue down his entire shaft, she wet him with a mixture of his and her juices that escaped her mouth. She cupped his large sagging balls a few times,. then lowered her and sucked in one of his balls into her mouth. Her mouth wasn't big enough to take both of his balls in at one time, so she switched the first ball out for the second one and did the same.

She felt him twitch as she sucked on his ball. She squeezed his shaft with her hand until she held it as tight as she could without letting go of his cock. Releasing his ball from her mouth, she had to have him seated fully in her hot wet mouth.

She slowly eased his cock in her mouth taking him inch by inch down her throat. She had gotten much better at giving him a blowjob.

At first she could only take him in a few inches before she began to gag, but with him talking to her, she eased him in her mouth, as he told her to breath in and out of her nose instead of trying to breath out of her mouth.

All of his coaching really did help her; she used all of his encouraging words to relax her throat as much as possible, which allowed her to take him down even further.

Sophie felt herself start to gag and pulled back just a little bit, giving her mouth time to adjust to his enormous size. She sank back down onto more of his cock and felt Kyle's hand on the back of her head.

Sophie pushed down on his shaft as he slowly stroked her hair. She heard Kyle coaching her to take him deeper, at a certain point Sophie had slid into subspace; she closed everything off around her. She no longer had not a care in the world except to service her man. He could have been talking to her in tongues for all she knew. It was nothing but gibberish to her. She was so in tuned to what she was doing for him, she hoped it was as good for him.

She tightened her lips around him and swallowed him even deeper than she had ever done before. She felt the beginnings of him start to twitch in her mouth. Kyle's hips began to move more erratically back and forth. He was finally letting himself go in her mouth.

Yes, he was face fucking her. She felt the first squirt of his hot come hit the back of her throat. She swallowed several more times as his seed squirted across her tongue. Her mouth was filled with his fluids and she loved the taste of him. She moaned as she swallowed him down. Cleaning up and down his shaft and getting every last drop of his goodness set Sophie's mind into orbit. She had serviced her man, which pleased her inner soul.

As she finished, she bent down and kissed both of his feet. Keeping her head bowed down, she waited again until he released her from her slave position. She felt her heartbeat begin to slow. She had never had this many emotions running through her at one time. She realized her passion had always been to please others, before she pleased herself. It felt good to have these kinds of feelings swirling around in her mind.

Kyle slowly bent down lifting her head up. She had tears streaming down her cheeks, knowing that she touched his soul also. She felt Kyle's tongue licking up the side of her cheek. She opened her eyes as he began to lick up the side of her other cheek. "Tell me why you're crying, baby."

"I have so many things running through my mind all at once. It's a little scary to think that I could please you. I mean really please you. You had a look in your eyes that touched my heart. When I sank down on my knees, I suddenly felt whole again. I haven't felt that way in a long time. I felt like I had surrendered to you in a way that I have never done before. I wasn't being forced to surrender, but I was surrendering because I had a need. Something inside of me burst at the same time."

"Sophie, you please me more than you know. That's why I love you so much. I'm not just saying the words to say them. I'm saying them because I feel it deep down in my heart." She watched as Kyle took her hand and placed it over his heart.

She felt his strong heart beating under her hand. She took his hand and did the same to her heart. The connection that the two had just experienced was earth shattering. His heart beat for her, and her heart beat for him. Two lovers who had been given a second chance at love.

"You need to rejoin our guests downstairs."

"I know. I just need another minute with you holding me."

"You have me forever Sophie, but your job as a hostess is not to give our guests idle gossip."

"But isn't it good gossip, when they're talking about sex?"

"You're such a brat. Now go get your other present while I get dressed"

Sophie scooted over to the bed; she joyfully opened up her second present. She looked inside this box, with a puzzled look on face she took out the horseshoe device. She turned it around several times, trying to figure out what it was.

Still intrigued she pulled out the package insert. On the front of the brochure, read We-Vibe 4 Plus. Not knowing what this device was she kept reading on.

'Share the control and come together for more pleasure than you've ever felt before. The We-Vibe 4 plus is the world's slimmest, strongest, couple's vibrator.' Sophie felt her cheeks start to warm up just reading the package and she was sure that her face was already red; she continued to read the insert about the vibrator.

'Designed to be worn inside the vagina and against the clit during sex.' *Oh yay this was for the both of them, Kyle could be inside of her at the same time. Boy was that going to be a tight fit.* 'The new We-Vibe 4 plus gives you expert G-Spot and clitoral stimulation and shares the vibrations for satisfaction you'll both love, and with the We-vibe Plus free app, We Connect app, you can now customize the vibrations or share control with your lover from anywhere in the world. Play with your We-Vibe 4 plus while one of you is across the room or across the globe.' Sophie let out a giggle as she finished up reading the rest of the brochure.

Kyle sat down with her on the bed, stroking her shoulders as she inspected the tiny vibrator.

Kyle pulled out his cell phone and hit the app on his phone, startling Sophie when the vibrator started to vibrate in her hand. "Omg, this is amazing, I can't believe how much technology has advanced in the past few years."

"This is my gift to you baby. I can now give you orgasms from anywhere, at any time during the day, as long as you have this baby inside you."

Sophie shivered at the idea. "What if I'm shopping and you decide to turn it on."

"Well I guess you better be quiet or I think you'll be sounding like the girl from *When Harry met Sally*. I think she was pretty vocal having her orgasm. Like I told you before, your orgasms are at my control not yours. This is my way of surprising you.

Thankfully, I already took the liberty of charging up the battery for the recommended five hours. Now, pull down your panties, lie back on the bed, spread your pretty legs and show me your beautiful pussy."

Sophie did exactly as she was commanded. Kyle took the vibrator from her and inserted it directly into her vagina. She squirmed just a bit as he seated it directly up against her clit.

"Baby, I'm going to turn it on low, just relax and feel the vibrations."

Sophie slowly closed her eyes, letting the first wave of vibrations pulse on top of her clit, and then she felt the next set inside her vagina hitting up against her G-spot. She let a moan escape her mouth.

"Wow, I can't believe you only have that on low."

"I thought you'd enjoy my present baby." She watched as he hit the button to increase the speed, as soon as the intensity hit her clit Sophie began to moan even more. She felt her heart begin to pound in her chest at the same time the sensation to her clit began to intensify. "Oh God, that feels amazing."

"I bet it does, so that's why I'm going to love playing with the buttons. Remember baby, you must ask for permission to come. Therefore, if I'm not here with you, you'll need to text me and ask for permission to come. If you come without permission, you'll be punished. When we're in public together, you can either ask or you use hand signals. You can cross both of your fingers over like this." She watched as he showed her the signal he wanted her to use. I love the fact that all your orgasms are controlled by my hand Sophie. You don't know how much this adds to feeding my desires for you."

Instantly she felt the small vibrator stop. As fast as her clit had been brought to life, that fast the throbbing stopped. "I'm glad you like your new toy. Tomorrow were going to start training your beautiful ass, to take my cock. That means more coconut oil and a shiny new butt plug. Get yourself together baby girl, we've got guests waiting for us downstairs."

She wasn't sure how this was going to work, now that she had a vibrator up her crotch and tomorrow she'd have a butt plug stuck up her ass. Just the thought had her clinching her legs together.

She wasn't sure what excited her more, knowing that Kyle would be controlling her orgasms or sticking his large cock up her ass. Sitting at the dinner table would be certainly a challenge. Hopefully, she wouldn't embarrass herself or Kyle. Somehow, she knew she would survive.

For the rest of the evening, Kyle had turned the new vibe on several times but had only left it on for short intervals at a time, nothing that would cause Sophie actually to have an orgasm. She breathed a sigh of relief after everyone had left for the night. Kyle had sent her a text saying that he had made it to the club and would be starting his meeting shortly. She was surprised when she felt the vibrator come to life between her legs; she wasn't sure if he would let her ride out her orgasm.

Luckily, for her, Kyle switched the vibrator up to level three and she felt the speed and intensity kick up even more. Her clit was extremely sensitive because of all of the stopping and starting and stopping all night. Quickly, she sent Kyle a text.

Sophie: Master, may I have permission to come?

Kyle: Yes baby girl, I'm so proud of you. Come for your Master.

Sophie felt the big wave go through her entire body. It started deep down at first then made its way up to her heart. She felt her legs tremble from the way the vibrator rocked her world. After gathering her wits, Sophie picked up her cell phone and sent a quick text to Kyle.

Sophie: That was spectacular. My legs are still shaking. Thank you, Master

Kyle: Next time I'll have you Skype me while you come.

Sophie: Such a wicked dirty man.

Kyle: You haven't seen anything yet.

Sophie: Promises. Promises

Kyle: No need for you to stay awake. Go ahead and get in bed. Baby girl, I'll be late

Sophie: Ok, wake me when you come home. I love you.

Kyle: I love you too.

Sophie meant the words she typed. She did really love Kyle. It was finally a relief for her to say she loved him.

The weather had taken a turn for the worse as they started out for the evening. The skies grew dark, the wind began to blow, and large drops of rain hit the windshield. Hating to drive in bad weather, Sophie wiggled back and forth in the passenger seat, looking out the window. The long winding roads gave Sophie the willies; she wasn't sure how she was going to handle the roads when she had to commute back and forth to work. No taking these roads at high speeds when running late. That was for sure.

The storm didn't look like it was letting up anytime soon. Crackling sounds of Lightning bolts lit up the evening skies. The deep rumbling of thunder was heard in the distance with frequent crashes indicating the storm was getting closer and closer.

Sophie had stopped making small talk a few miles back when the road narrowed just a bit. Kyle needed to concentrate on driving. Fidgeting in her seat, Sophie no longer could keep quiet, "Only a few more minutes until we arrive. I hope we get there soon, before it gets any worse." Kyle just nodded back at Sophie saying, "Yup" It was nights like this she'd rather be at home cuddled up on the sofa with popcorn watching a horror movie with Kyle at her side.

As Kyle made the last turn onto the country rode, seeing out the front windshield had become almost impossible. The windows had fogged up, most likely from Sophie's heavy breathing. Kyle tried to reassure her by signing along with the song that played on the radio, but all Sophie heard was the rain, lightening, and thunder.

The rain hit the window even harder; Sophie had a white knuckle grip around the door handle, all she could think now was hopefully they would get to the new house...Kyle drove the small sport car on rare occasions. He handled it like a race car driver, and she loved how he could look so damn sexy behind the wheel of any vehicle.

The car picked up speed as it went around a windy curve in the road. She looked over at Kyle. He loved taking some of the turns just a little faster than what Sophie liked. He would hit a certain crest in the road making the car go a little airborne just to get a rise out of Sophie. Feeling her stomach jump up into her throat always gave Sophie a big thrill but tonight she just wasn't feeling it. Knowing that Kyle would never put either one of them in danger. Sophie scooted as far back in the seat as possible, and closed her eyes, wishing they would get to the house soon.

Steering down the narrow country road, trying to slow the speed of the car down, Sophie saw the panic displayed all over Kyle's face. Blinking back fear Sophie asked Kyle what was the matter, as he tried to slow the car down to a more controlled speed. He finally yelled out to her "No brakes, baby, brace yourself."

"Please, don't leave me. I can't lose you too."

Sophie thrashed around in the bed for a few seconds, until she finally woke up from the horrible dream. She was drenched, from head to toe with her own perspiration. She sat up, reaching for the lamp on her side table, and glanced over at the clock. It read 2:00 am. She looked back over to the opposite side of the bed, still no Kyle. *God, did I just dream that Kyle and I were in the car accident instead of Carl. Shit has something happened to him?* Sophie felt her entire body start to shake as she reached for her phone. No text, or missed calls from Kyle.

Trying to settle herself down, Sophie did the only thing that she knew to do. She dialed Kyle's phone. Her heart began to speed up, as she hit send. It only took Kyle two rings before Sophie heard his sexy voice on the other end.

"Sophie, what's the matter?"

"I just got worried when I woke up and you still weren't home. I just needed to hear your voice to make sure you're okay."

"Baby, I'm just finishing up my meeting. I'll be home in thirty minutes. Go make yourself a cup of hot tea, by the time I get home, you'll be ready to fall back to sleep."

"Just promise me you'll drive safely coming home."

"Did something happen? Are you okay?"

"I'm good, just come home safe, ok?"

"Ok baby, do this for me then, stay on the phone; go ahead down to the kitchen. Start the water for your tea.

Sophie heard the click of his Italian loafers on the hardwood floors at the club, she also heard the sound of a beating drum in the distance. "Baby, hold on for a second."

"Okay." She heard Kyle say good night to Paul one of the bartenders, then she heard the rustling and rattling of his keys. She needed to pull herself together before he reached home, or she had a feeling he would never leave her alone again.

She knew that wasn't a good solution to her problems. Figuring out a way to control her anxiety would be a new challenge that Sophie needed to overcome. She couldn't have this controlling her life. She had to take off her rose-colored glasses and figure out what was truly causing her this much anguish in her life.

Sipping on her tea, did calm her down enough that when Kyle blew into the bedroom she wasn't a blubbering mess. Their eyes met as he took off his shirt, and threw it on the chair that sat next to the bed; he quickly removed his slacks, socks and shoes. Sophie wasn't sure why she suddenly felt extremely dizzy, but she did. Trying not to act too concerned about the sudden wave of nausea Sophie took another long sip of tea. She hoped it was just from getting herself upset.

"Baby, tell me what's going on."

"I just had another nightmare, that's all. And when I woke up, and you weren't home yet, I got a little scared." She prayed he did ask her about her nightmare, because she wasn't sure what effect it had on her yet. All she knew the nightmares were happening more and more frequently. She remembered when she was a kid, she had the same dream about a scary clown who lived under her bed. It took her over a year to come to the realization that the only thing that lived under her bed were her shoes and dust bunnies.

Out of sheer desperation, she took her mattress off the frame, put it on the floor and slept like that for years, all because she needed to see under her bed every night. It wasn't until her friend Lexi had come over for a sleep over, that she convinced her she couldn't let her fears get the best of her.

Lexi her BFF had ways been her partner in crime, Sophie would refer to their relationship as *Thelma and Louise*. With Lexi being wild and crazy like Thelma and her being, more like Louise. Lexi never let her fears get the best of her. Sophie needed to do the same thing about her anxiety over her nightmares. She had to face them, but tonight she just needed the secure feeling of her man holding her. She needed to soak up the protection that he was willing to give her.

She felt the bed dip as she watched him slip in under the covers. She instantly felt his large arms pull her closer to him. She could stay like this forever. She felt like she had just dodged another bullet when Kyle didn't ask her any more questions, but instead stroked her shoulders until exhaustion took over her body.

Chapter Eighteen

Yawning and trying to shake the cobwebs from her brain, Sophie made her way over to the bathroom. She had only been able to fall back to sleep for three more hours until Kyle had his way with her. She loved being woken up with him already using her. Afterwards he told her to go back to sleep for a little while longer.

After stuffing her suitcases with tons and tons of new clothes, Sophie did a mental checklist of everything she needed to pack. Kyle insisted that whatever she didn't have, he would just buy it for her once they arrived. She still didn't feel a hundred percent herself this morning, but she had so much to do.

She noticed on several occasions now that her ability to feel safe without having Kyle around was beginning to be more of a problem than what she first was willing to admit. Somehow, she had to regain that part of herself.

She still didn't know how it was going to work for her. Kyle had a few hours of work to do at his office this morning, which left Sophie to get ready for their trip.

Keeping her mind off of her current insecurity was going to be her plan of action for today. Sophie went back over all the information that Kyle had given her about the shell company. She had to give it to her man; he was one thorough businessman when it came to his business sense.

She panned through the pictures in the portfolio. She wasn't all that surprised when she saw a recent photo of Kyle's father. He was a middle-aged gentleman with strong facial features face just like Kyle's. Majestic blue eyes were the classic feature that all of the Zellar's children had, after looking over the photos she saw those same eyes staring back at her on the photos. They had definitely inherited that trait from their father for sure.

She wondered if in thirty years or so, would Kyle be a carbon copy of his father. Would he up and leave her just as his father had done to his mother. Shaking her head, she knew Kyle once he set his mind to something, would never do that to another person. He hated the fact that his father had up and left him and his family.

Giving the photos one final glance, she focused on something she wondered if anyone else had noticed. Nowhere in any of the personal information had she remembered reading if Mr. Zellar had remarried. She pulled out the packet and reread it. *Nope nothing about a recent wife, kids or any anything that would say he was ever married. Strange, hum...* She scanned the photos one more time. In every one, he was definitely wearing a wedding ring on his left hand.

She needed to mention that finding to Kyle when he got home. *Maybe that was his wedding ring from Kyle's mother.* She always thought she could be the next Nancy Drew. If anyone could solve a mystery, her childhood fictional character could; she just needed to snoop a little more. Sophie even pulled out her iPad and did a google search on Matthew Hendricks. Everything that was on the portfolio was also listed on the internet.

Listed was a telephone number on the top of the letterhead. Sophie came up with a great idea. She pulled out her cell phone and dialed the company number. *Yep, Nancy Drew would totally be doing her homework, and so would I.*

"Good afternoon, Henderick's and Associates, Alice speaking. How I may direct your call?" Sophie had to come up with something and something fast. "Good morning Alice, this is Ms. Jackson, my partner Mr. Champion and I will be flying in tomorrow for a business conference with Mr. Hendricks."

"I have you guys on our schedule. Would you like to speak with Mr. Hendricks?"

"Well maybe you can help me with a little personal question."

"Sure, Ms. Jackson I would be happy to help you if I can." Sophie knew she was on a roll now. Alice was her ticket to the truth. "I'd like to bring something special for Mr. and Mrs. Hendricks from our wonderful state of Pennsylvania. I was wondering if the missus was a modern type of woman or was she more country style."

"I've only been to their house a few times, but from what I remember, everything had a Hispanic theme. We love our bright colors. So if anything, I would say Ida would love something with bright colors."

That answered Sophie's question. There is a Mrs. Hendricks. "Well Alice you've have been a huge help. I have the perfect idea in mind."

"Great, if you or Mr. Champion need anything during your stay, please feel free to ask me. I've worked for Mr. Hendricks for many years now. I have no problem with giving you touristy type stuff to do while you're here."

"I'll keep that in mind, but I think Mr. Champion already has a full itinerary set up. All work and no play. Both girls giggled as Sophie thought about what she had just said. She already knew they would have mostly play, and no work. I'll let you know if our plans change. See ya soon."

Anxiety filled Sophie veins as she hung up with Alice, she now have another piece of the mystery pie. Her big question, why hadn't anyone else picked up on the fact that there was an actual Mrs. Hendricks? Did Kyle already know this or was it new information. None of his intel said his dad was remarried. Thinking like a detective Sophie sent a quick text to Kyle

Sophie: Hi, babe, hope I'm not interrupting? Within a few seconds, she heard her phone pinged.

Kyle: No, baby I have a few minutes free... What's up?

Sophie: looking over Intel, is your dad married?

Kyle: No, why?

Sophie: just wondering. Trying to do a little snooping, that's all.

Kyle: Ok, be home in two hours. Sophie had to change the subject fast.

Sophie: Can't wait to see the beaches.

Kyle: Me too, baby. Now the mystery pot was boiling for Sophie she had uncovered something important. Kyle probably wouldn't be happy knowing his father had left his mother for another woman. Something just didn't add up in Sophie's mind. Obviously, a lot of this mess didn't add up in a lot of people's minds.

Her only concern was for her man, would he be able to face the consequences of what the truth really was? They would sure find out soon enough.

She wondered how Piper would take finding out that her dad had a whole separate life going on in a different Country. She remembered talking to Piper just recently about growing up with just her two brothers and mother. She didn't even remember her father. She had blocked him from her memory. She often said that sometimes it's better to block out the bad stuff in your life and replace it with only things that matter. Obviously, her father didn't matter to her at all.

Sophie pitter-pattered around the house gathering up odds and ends that she thought would be useful during the trip. She made sure she had all the charging cables to all of her electronic devices; hell, she needed a separate suitcase just for those items. Kyle had told her not to worry about packing his stuff; he would take care of that when he came home later.

As the time ticked off the clock, so did her thoughts. She slowly stopped thinking about being alone. Her boys' home came popping up in her vision. She hadn't spoken to her father since she proposed her business plan to him. She had this burning desire to know what he had come up with so far. Luckily, for Sophie, her dad loved being challenged with new business ideas.

She glanced down at her watch she knew he would most likely be in the office at Coston Construction. Curiosity was taking its toll on Sophie, so she did what any anxious person would do.

After an hour-long conversation with her father, Sophie could have been jumping up and down just like a child when her dad said everything was going as planned so far. What surprised her even more was he had submitted all her permits and hoped they would be stamped with the City's approval by late next week.

This gave her plenty of time to tell Kyle her wonderful plan. She just hoped that everything worked out for Kyle and his father. Then she could tell him her news.

Everything had been working in Sophie's favor, the boys' home was looking more and more like a positive thing. Kyle's birthday party had over a hundred and fifty guests on the list as of today.

She hoped that Justine didn't go into labor early with her triplets. Sophie was really counting on her skills to throw one kick ass party. Lexi had given her the name and number for a specialist jewelry who dealt with designing unique body piercing jewelry for people in the lifestyle. After a couple of conversations with several designers, Sophie finally chose a local guy.

He gave her several references, some name she recognized from Kyle mentioning them, and some she was already friends with. Maxwell told her that whatever design she came up with he was sure he could reproduce for her. She surfed his website until she found exactly what she was looking for. She was amazed that he was able to change up the design. He even sent her a picture of what she wanted down to every last detail. Maxwell assured Sophie that he would have them ready in a little over a week, which gave her enough time even if he ran over by a couple of days. Life surely was looking up for Sophie, and it showed by the happy glow she sported. Excitement brewed deep in Sophie's stomach at the fact they would be leaving in less than an hour for the airport. Her nerves did kick in after she had physically checked her luggage several times. Finally, being the Dom that he was, Kyle took matters in his own hands by removing her luggage out to the SUV so that Sophie could no longer obsess over them. In a way, she loved when he went all Dom on her, it eased her mind knowing that he took charge and she only had to obey.

Kyle managed to calm Sophie's nerves just a bit by having her insert the We-Vibe 4 into her vagina. He zapped her a few times as she was walking around the house. He loved knowing that he could bring her to sexual peak without even touching her. He mentioned several times to her he couldn't wait to sink a butt plug in her. He watched as her face turned bright red whenever he talked about her ass.

Having all of his things packed and ready to go, Kyle called the club and spoke to his brother.

One, he needed to make sure that whatever he found out about his father, his brother was going to support Kyle's decision, even though they'd had years of conversations over the possible reasons why their father up and left them, they both needed closure.

Hell, they all needed closure. Kyle often wondered why his mother never understood why they needed closure.

She'd change the subject whenever Kyle mentioned his father's name in conversation.

Two, he needed to make sure that the club was fully staffed for the next few days. After their board meeting two nights ago, things had been stirred up just a bit and Kyle needed to make sure that his brother could handle the new responsibilities he had been given.

Kyle took pride in everything that he did for and with the club. It still made him a little nervous knowing that if anything went wrong at the club he would still be held responsible.

The drive from the house to the airport only took about a half hour. Kyle concentrated on finally coming face to face to his father after all these years. No matter how many times he looked over the portfolio that Master Sargent had given him a few weeks ago, he recognized the man in the picture but he had obviously aged in the last few years.

Hopefully tomorrow all of his questions would be answered, and once they were, he could move on with his life. He had already made his mind up that even if the outcome wasn't to his liking, he was still ready to make that commitment to Sophie. She was the only one for him.

She made his heart zing just by her being in the same room as him. She brought out the best in him. She made him look at his life in so many different ways. Not just as the Dom but also as the man he knew he could be. That's the provider, lover, and husband she deserved.

He was prepared to share the good times, bad times, and the ups and downs with her as long as she would have him. That's why he knew she was the one. She made his whole life feel so good when he was having the not-so-perfect day. Just her smile would make the sadness go away. He may have had a fucked up childhood, but when their time came to have children, he would be the best father in the world.

Occasionally, he stroked the side of Sophie's leg. He felt her shiver from his touch. He watched as Sophie stared out the passenger's side window. When they didn't take the departing flight exit for BWI, he wondered if Sophie even noticed they weren't going to the normal check in area. He never told her that they wouldn't be taking a regular commercial flight to Puerto Rico. Boy did he have a surprise waiting for her on the tarmac. He loved when her eyes lit up from the smallest surprises; he was going to love spoiling his girl.

He had the logo on the side of the jet changed to Champion Enterprise for this trip, and this trip only to Puerto Rico. He had to keep up the impression that he was the CEO of Champion Enterprise. Once he concluded his business in Puerto Rico, he would have his company's logo reattached.

As he drove up to the security check in, he watched Sophie twist and turn in her seat. The entire drive from the house she hadn't said a word. She just stared out the window. He wondered if she was having second thoughts about going.

"Baby, you've been awful quiet is everything ok?"

"I'm just a little nervous, that's all."

"Baby, why didn't you say something?"

"I felt like a jerk telling you that I don't like to fly."

"Well hopefully I can change that for you."

"What do you have up your sleeve for me today, Master?" He loved when she called him Master. He felt his cock twitch in his pants. *No, I can't get a hard on walking onto the jet, because I have to wait until we get in flight to fuck her brains out. She'll never be afraid to fly again if I have anything to do with it.*

After passing through the security, Kyle pulled the car under a carport that was directly next to a large building, and stopped the car. He took Sophie's hand and brought it to his lips. He couldn't believe how scared his girl really was, but he knew once they were up in the air, she would be taken care of fully.

"Baby, you ready to go?"

"I need a minute to call my parents if you don't mind."

"Sure thing, do you need some privacy?"

"Oh, God no. I just need to tell them that I love them, that's all."

Just listening to Sophie's conversation with her parents, telling them how much she loved them and how she would miss them, almost made Kyle's heart ache for that kind of relationship with his own parents.

He swore silently to himself once his business was settled with his father he hoped for that same kind of relationship. He knew Sophie had issues with her mother, but that still didn't stop her from loving her.

"I'm ready. I'm all yours. Take me to paradise."

"You're chariot awaits you."

Briskly, Kyle jumped out of the vehicle, went over to the passenger side door, and helped Sophie get out the car, just as any gentleman would do. The two of them walked over to where three gentlemen stood.

As they approached the men, Kyle felt Sophie's grip tighten on his hand, "Baby just relax. I want to introduce you to Captain Jackson Terrance, otherwise known as Captain Jack. He watched as Sophie slid her hand over to shake the captain's hand. Sophie, he happens to be my cousin. Seeing how anxious you are about flying I thought it was better to have a formal introduction to the man who I trust with my life and yours. He will safely get us to our destination."

"Nice to meet you, Sir; I feel like such a baby for being scared."

"Ah no worries Ms. Spencer. I used to feel the same way before I got my pilot's license. Now it's like driving my truck back and forth on the highway, except without all the congestion to deal with."

"Does that mean we're not taking a commercial flight to Puerto Rico?"

"I'll let Kyle explained that to you, I need to go and finish up with the final inspection. See you once you board, Ms. Spencer." Sophie let out a slight giggle when he said it that way.

"Sophie, I'd like to introduce you to Master Sargent Marco Pearce, he was my guiding force while I was in the military. He happens to be the best private investigator that I know."

"Now, son you know I hate when you go all sappy on me, but Sophie it is a pleasure to finally meet the woman who has captured the heart of one of my soldiers."

"It's a pleasure to meet you too, Sir. I wasn't aware you were coming along with us. I thought we were posing as possible business partners to the Hendricks Company."

"That's the plan so far. I promised Kyle that I would see him through this ordeal and felt I needed to be with you guys every step of the way just in case something was to happen."

"Sophie, so that you're not surprised, Jake is also on his way. Just like at home he'll be your security guard when I'm not with you."

"Kyle why would I need security in Puerto Rico? The gang members don't know that I'm going on vacation."

"Baby I know that, but I'm not sure what kind of man my father has turned out to be. For all I know, he could be the worst criminal in the world and I'm not willing to take any chances with your safety. Plus it makes you look important when you arrive with your own security team."

"I'll remember that. Do you have someone protecting you?"

"I do. You'll meet them shortly. They might even already be on board."

The three of them walked out from under the covered carport, onto the actual tarmac. The sun was starting to burn through the morning clouds and sitting in front of them was a Bombardier Learjet 75 with Champion Enterprise written across the belly of the jet. .

"OMG, are we flying to Puerto Rico in that?"

"Why? Don't you like it?"

"I've never been on something that small before?"

"Ah, your all about size, are you my little minx?"

"I thought you would have controlled your Pet by now, Kyle."

"Well Sarge, she just might need to have her ass paddled before we take off. Don't look so surprised, Sophie. Sarge is in the lifestyle too; nothing I say or do to you will shock Sarge. He taught me everything there is to know about the lifestyle." He watched as Sophie turned as red as a tomato. "See Pet, it helps to have your friends and family close to you at all times."

"You...wouldn't really paddle my ass, would you?"

"Try me."

Kyle heard her snicker under her breath, he knew a little teasing would take her mind off the flight and put her in the proper headspace. She had the cutest twinkle in her eyes, when she let herself fully submit to Kyle's wishes.

He escorted Sophie onto the jet. She took several small deep breaths as they climbed the stairs together. He felt her palms begin to sweat. "Baby, just relax as soon as we get on board I'll get you something to calm your nerves." She just nodded her head.

"Good morning, Mr. Zellar. Welcome back. I have everything you requested already waiting for you."

"Good morning, Darlene, how's my favorite stewardess doing on this fine day?"

"Wonderful, Sir. Looking forward to spending a few days at the beach once we land."

"Darlene, this is Ms. Spencer, my submissive, anything that Ms. Spencer needs I expect you'll get for her."

"Why of course, Mr. Zellar. Good morning, Ms. Spencer. My name is Darlene. I happen to be Mr. Zellar's personal flight attendant. Anything that you need, don't hesitate to use the call button."

"Nice meeting you Darlene."

"I need your passports, so that I can get you guys checked in with immigration."

"Don't we have to do that?"

"No sweetie, when you're on a private charter, my job is to see to all those little things."

"Oh, ok. I'm a virgin at this. I'll follow your lead if that's alright with you."

"After today, I bet we'll be seeing you more often."

"Not too sure about that; I much prefer to have my feet on the ground versus up in the air." Both girls just giggled. Kyle was truly blessed to have such wonderful friends and family members who worked for him. He really did appreciate everything they did for him and his company.

Once everyone was settled in, Kyle instructed Darlene to bring them a stiff Mimosa. He knew Sophie loved to sip on her favorite cocktail; this would surely relax her for the rest of the flight. He watched her down the entire champagne flute. *She must have needed that drink bad.*

Just like a kid would react, Sophie squealed as the jet took off. Once the jet had reached its cruising altitude, Jackson gave the all clear.

"Would my girl like to take a tour?"

"There's more to see than just this?"

"You haven't seen anything yet."

"You're not going to take me up front where the captain's flying, are you?'

"If you want I can make that happen."

"No, I think it's best to stay back here. He needs to concentrate on flying, not giving me a tour."

"If you change your mind." Sophie swatted at Kyle's arm, making an awful face. "Lead the way, Master."

Kyle pulled her from the seat and kissed her on the top of the head, "Now that's my girl talking."

Kyle walked her back to the Master bedroom. Sophie was amazed by the size of the bed that was centered in the middle of the room. "You have extravagant taste, Mr. Champion." She had practiced calling him by his made up business name for the past twenty-four hours. They needed his father's staff to believe they were posing as a couple who was expanding their business in Ceiba, Puerto Rico, hence the name change.

"I can't believe you have a complete bedroom on the plane."

"No, Ms. Jackson, this is not a plane. It's a corporate jet."

"Ok, Mr. Showoff corporate jet guy, isn't this just a little bit extravagant? I know we need to pretend about having wealth but don't you think this is a little over the top?"

Kyle burst out laughing.

"What's so funny?"

"No baby, this is really my jet." Sophie stared at him; she wasn't sure what he was saying. "I made enough money in the early stages of my business, once I was able to afford luxury items, this was my first big purchase. Even before I had the house built, I bought the jet."

Before she could ask any questions, he leaned in and kissed her. He traced her lips with his tongue. She wrapped her arms around his neck. She felt her toes curl in her sandals. Her skin tingled from just his kiss. When he released her, she felt her pulse suddenly start to race.

"Baby, are you a member of the Mile High Club?"

Sophie let out a giggle, "No Sir, but I think I might be up for being inducted as a new member."

Kyle loved how she joked back and forth. "Maybe I'll become a frequent flyer pretty soon."

"You're funny, baby. That's what I love about you. You say the craziest things. You're my sunshine on a cloudy day."

"Isn't that a song?"

"Yup," he pulled her in closer and kissed her again. As their tongues did a dance in and out of her mouth, she repeated his words over and over in her head. Sophie felt her body temperature rise. She was boiling hot for her Master. Kyle started to untie the flimsy little strap that held the sundress around her neck. She wasn't wearing a bra or panties, as part of her Master's wishes.

Lowering the dress to the floor, Sophie stood before him completely nude.

"You're beautiful, Sophie. I'm the luckiest man in the world." He bent down, and began to kiss her neck, trailing his lips down to her right breast. He took her nipple in his mouth, swirling it around, until he captured it between his teeth.

The pressure he built up in her breast gave her a sense he was never going to let go. Just as a baby would when suckling on his mother's breast. She felt a deep vibration down in her clit. It began to throb with such intensity.

She could feel her orgasm just below the surface. She already knew she needed to ask permission to come and if she didn't, she would be punished. Kyle knew her body completely; he could tell if she was close, or if she came without permission.

Not wanting to blow her adventure with a punishment and a sore ass, Sophie yelled, "Master, Oh god that feels so, Oh Master, may I have permission to come?"

"No, you may not sweetheart. I want you to hold out a little longer. You need to learn how to control your urges; we've been working on this."

Sophie had been told no more times in the past week than she ever had been in her life. She was starting to hate the word no.

"I want you to undress me first." Oh God, she took her shaking hands and ran them up and under his bright blue polo shirt. Just having her hands on him pulled her thoughts from having an orgasm.

Kyle released her nipple just long enough for her to lift the shirt up and over his head. Once his shirt was removed, he latched onto her other nipple. Sophie let out a loud moan when Kyle started sucking, kissing, and licking her already hard nipple. There was no way she would be able to last for much longer, and he knew that.

"Master, mmm. I need to touch you too. May I, please?"

Kyle released her nipple from his mouth with a loud pop, "My body is your body, baby."

Sophie took her hands and ran them up and down his chiseled chest. She lowered her mouth over his nipple, capturing his nipple in her mouth, just as he had done to her. "Oh baby that feels so good.

"I see why you like having your nipples sucked on. Just imagine how more erotic it's going to feel after I pierce these beauties." Kyle had a hold of both her breasts in his hands. He massaged both of them at the same intensity and speed. "You're about to drive me insane with your newfound desires."

Sophie released her mouth from around his nipple. "How about I let you pierce my nipples, if you let me pierce yours. Staring into his eyes, she waited to see how he would react to her question.

What is fair for one is fair for the other she thought. But knowing him, he probably wouldn't go with it. "Baby, I trust your skilled surgeon hands. I would be delighted to have you mark me as yours." Almost jumping for joy, Sophie pulled herself up into his arms.

"I can't wait to get the feeling back in my hand, and when I do you'll make me the happiest girl in the world."

"Just like I said, Sophie. I trust you."

He picked her up and carried her over to the large king size bed and lowered her onto the white lacy down comforter. Kyle went over to one of the windows, pulled the curtain open so that the morning sun could shine on his beautiful woman. Her skin glowed from head to toe, just from the beams of light hitting her body.

She watched as Kyle removed his khakis. Today he was dressed a little different from his usual three-piece business suit. He felt it was important to travel in comfort, not in high fashion.

Sophie lay across the bed and was completely under his control. Kyle climbed on top of her just as a lion climbing on top of his lionesses. He ran his hands up and down her sides causing her to shiver. She needed him inside of her in the worst way.

Sophie had already been told she had free rein of using her hands in any way she wanted. She reached around, grabbed both of his ass cheeks and squeezed them in her hands. She heard him moan in her ear, "You're bringing out a side I never thought you had in you, and it's making my cock hard for you.

All of her senses were lit up, just from hearing his words of dominance. She removed her hands from his ass, grabbed a handful of his long hair and tugged it back from his head. She was sure he could feel it deep down in his scalp. He often told her he loved that she too had the power to control him for her desires.

He gave her everything and in return, he expected the same from her. "I think my girl, has a wild streak in her today."

"I do and I love the way you let me explore my sexuality with you."

"Baby, there'll be times when I give you total control, but you'll have to earn that from me. Today I'm feeling generous. Your body is perfect. I could never get my fill of you." Sophie felt Kyle's thick hard cock pressing against her pelvis. Pre-come seeped onto her skin. Her pussy was dripping wet; her juices covered the insides of her thighs. She was more than ready to take her Master.

"I need you Kyle, inside of me so bad. I'm burning up with need and desire."

"Baby, I need you too." Her heart started to flutter with his choice of words. Without any hesitation he aligned his cock up to her entrance. He had full intentions of making slow love to his woman, but once desire and lust hit his soul, a feral need came over him. He no longer could hold himself back, he covered her entire body just as a lion covering up his prey.

"I'm not going to be gentle. My primal side tells me I must have you now. I intend to take you hard and fast."

And so he did. He plunged deep inside of her pussy. Her eyes closed as he rocked his pelvis against hers. She felt Kyle's cock hit up against her cervix and she moaned in pleasure. Sophie was repelled deep into subspace. She loved the out of body experience she felt when she hit subspace. She began speaking words that Kyle could no longer understand. She was praying to God, loving life, and shouting out expletives.

"Oh God you feel so hot deep down in your pussy. Its feels like you're sucking the life out of my cock" he said.

"Fuck me, Master. Fuck me hard. I need to feel I belong to you."

"You only belong to me, and no one else, forever you're mine only Sophie."

"Master, I need to come. I can't hold back any longer."

"Come with me Sophie," and as his words left his mouth, Sophie screamed out in ecstasy. Kyle took her nipple into his mouth and bit down as he released his seed deep down in her womb, He knew she was his forever, and she knew he was hers forever. The two fell peacefully asleep for the remainder of the trip to Puerto Rico wrapped in each other's arm.

Chapter Nineteen

Almost three hours later, Kyle caressed the tops of Sophie's thighs to wake her up. He knew his girl was happily sated before falling to sleep. He wanted her to watch as they landed. Gently he started whispering into her ear to wake up for him. She looked just like a sleeping angel all sprawled out on the large bed.

"Wake up sleepy head, or you're going to miss watching us land." He already knew Sophie wasn't nice when he woke her up. Normally if she wasn't woken up by him going down on her, she was a bear. Maybe that is why she was acting the way she did before the flight. He'd remember that for the trip home. Leave as late in the day as possible, no early morning flights for his girl. "What time is it?"

"9 am Puerto Rico Time."

"Shit I slept through the entire flight.

"Yup, but so did I. We must have needed it."

"No, I think I wore you out sexually with my body." Kyle pulled back the covers exposing her naked body. He swatted her on the ass, leaving a bright red imprint of his hand, hearing Sophie yelp sent his cock into over drive. *He had no time for that.* "Maybe so baby, go freshen up in the bathroom and then meet back up with the rest of the team."

"I can't believe how green everything is," Sophie said as she felt the jet descend lower to the ground.

"I know," Kyle agreed. "It's almost as it's a completely different shade of green than we have back home, bright and cheery colors."

"My thoughts exactly."

"Once we're cleared by customs, our driver will take us to the cottage."

"Is everyone staying at the same cottage?"

"No baby, the guys have the cottage next to ours. I have you all to myself." Sophie definitely liked the sound of that. She didn't mind sharing the cottage but when it came to Kyle's kinky ways, she didn't want to be the entertainment.

Kyle spared no expense and had a limo waiting for them once they departed the jet. Luckily for Sophie, only she and Kyle were put into the limo. The rest of the team had separate transportation. The countryside of Ceiba was breathtaking. The lush green landscape, contrasted against the beautiful blue sea, which glistened.

The lavish cottage that Kyle rented sat up against a large rock cliff. Multiple types of tropical plants surrounded the entire house. You would have thought that either a rich fancy movie star or royalty owned this type of estate. This wasn't your typical rental that Joe blow rented for a family vacation. Sophie had seen pictures on the internet of the house, but was surprised that the pictures didn't do it any justice.

The keys for the rental were given to Kyle from the limo driver. Luckily for them, the house had been fully stocked with food and beverages. Kyle hired a maid and a cook so that they could totally relax. No hassle, no fuss was his motto.

The maid opened the door when Kyle started to put the key in the slot. "Hola, Senor Champion, bienvenida Puerto Rico. Soy el ama de llaves Rosa."

"Gracias Senora Rosa. Hobla usted Ingles?"

"Si senor. This is Ms. Johnson, Rosa."

"How do you do Ms. Rosa?"

"Welcome, my dear."

Rosa took them on a grand tour of the house. The rooms consisted of the highest quality furniture. Each room out did the last, with authentic Puerto Rican culture scattered throughout the place. Sophie was amazed when she stepped into the master bedroom. The bed was big enough to sleep a family of five. She had never seen such a bed. There were four large pillars, two at the head of the bed and two at the foot of the bed. An ornate carving was etched in each of the pillars; it reminded her of a Paul Bunyan bed. The decorative bed covers had a geometric design made out of bright color squares, almost like the Amish quilt that was on the sofa at Crave County.

Kyle lugged the luggage up to the master bedroom, they unpacked, changed into exercise clothing, and decided to explore the beach. Kyle had reminded Sophie that she still needed to do her daily exercise routine, not wanting her to fall back on her schedule. She had already advanced so much.

Once the two reached the beach, Sophie began to jog along the surf, and Kyle followed along. Neither one lacked for physical exercise, but after being on the flight they both had pent up energy that needed to be burned off.

After running for about two miles, Sophie felt her mind release everything that had been locked up. Hearing the waves hit the beach, the crunch of the sand under their feet, the sun beating down on her body, and the cool ocean breeze stroking her hair, everything that had been building up in her heart released. She had no fears, worries or cares. She radiated her own beam of light. The only thing that mattered was the here and now. Nothing else.

Finally, the two returned to the house. They both showered, had a bite to eat and Kyle reviewed the portfolio again with Sophie. She still hadn't said anything to him yet about knowing his father had apparently remarried. She needed to talk to Master Sergeant first to see if his was aware of her findings. Her inner Nancy Drew was now working overtime. She just had to figure out a way to get in touch with him.

"Master, when will be meeting up with the team?"

"Why do you ask Pet?"

"I didn't know if we would be meeting up with them tonight, or if they were just going to meet us at Hendricks and Associates tomorrow morning."

"Everyone should be over shortly. Last minute, Intel sharing Ms. Johnson, you'll find that I'm all about being prepared when going in for a mission."

"Sounds like you have everything all worked out, Mr. Champion."

Making her way over to the kitchen, Sophie practically bounced like a bunny rabbit, showing more joy in her step, than she had in quite a while. She hadn't felt this alive in a long time.

Rosa had already prepared several trays of appetizers. Since Sophie really didn't know the men on Kyle's team she made sure there was beer chilled in the fridge, along with soft drinks. Hopefully without Kyle noticing, she could pull the Sarge off to the side, she had to fill him in on what she'd discovered while playing Nancy Drew.

Maybe it was nothing, but to her it was a lot.

Sophie counted to ten before entering the living where everyone sat eating and drinking. Kyle motioned for her to come over to him. He patted his knee, signaling her to pop a squat. Everyone had their portfolio out, Kyle held his out sharing the documents with Sophie.

She still didn't understand why Kyle needed a security team; she hadn't read anything about his father being a threat to anyone. The room was filled with male testosterone; she could just about taste it. All of them had the same dominant characteristics as her Master has, which when she thought about it wasn't a bad thing at all. They all told her that they would protect her during this trip.

A short time later, after being briefed again for the hundredth time, Sophie started daydreaming about setting up house with Kyle, not only as his submissive but also as his wife, and the mother of his children. Seeing him play with their son and daughter almost brought tears to her eyes when she really thought about her actual future.

She knew she was falling deeper in love with Kyle, she just hoped that whatever happens tomorrow doesn't change Kyle's outlook on having a family. Hopefully it would be with her.

She felt herself start to stir on her Masters lap, but she had to redirect her thoughts to something more meaningful, and that didn't mean sex. What that meant was she had to figure out how to get Master Sergeant in the kitchen.

Thinking quickly, Sophie went to scoot off Kyle's lap when it hit her. Bending down, she went to pick up the tray of uneaten appetizers, when suddenly her right arm dropped the entire tray on master Sergeant lap. "Holy shit, Marco. I'm so sorry." Sophie had to lay the shit on thick. She started shaking like a leaf in front of all of the men. She immediately started picking up the spilled food from Master Sergeants lap.

He used the tray to scoop up the tiny sandwiches that now covered him.

"Please forgive me, Sir."

"Sophie, don't worry it's just a few sandwiches that's all."

"I know but look at this mess all over you."

"No need to beat yourself up over a few dropped pieces of food," Master Sergeant said to her.

"God, I feel like I have a case of the dropsy."

"Sweetheart, are you sure that's all it is? Is your arm bothering you again?"

"No Sir, I don't think I got a good grip on the tray, that's all. I need to get Marco into the kitchen before the mustard sets in as a stain. I have a stain stick in my purse." She knew she was acting like she was in a Broadway show. She even had tears to show for her performance.

This was her chance to get Master Sergeant into the kitchen. She walked over to the sink dropping the tray of smashed sandwiches. She was so thankful that Master Sergeant followed her. The rest of the men did stay in the living room. Not wanting to bring attention to herself she asked Master Sergeant to come over to the sink, that way she could keep an eye on the entranceway from the living room.

"I'm really sorry for doing what I had to do, to get you by yourself but I have to ask you something in private without Kyle hearing our conversation." Being the girl that she was, Sophie pulled out the stain stick from her purse just like she said.

"Go on Sophie, what do you need to ask me?"

"Did you know that Kyle's dad is remarried?"

"How did you find that out?"

"Well I'll take that as a yes."

"Does Kyle know you know?"

"No, I figured it out yesterday. I happened to be staring at the photos when I noticed a wedding ring, which I thought was a little odd. Especially when he supposedly left his wife. No, man wears a wedding ring after they dump their family."

"Go on."

"So I called Hendricks secretary yesterday, and I asked her what Mrs. Hendricks would like from Pennsylvania. That's when she told me all about Ida Hendricks."

Sophie watched as Master Sergeant wiped the stain stick over the mustard spot. "Does he know about her yet?"

"No, Sophie, I thought I could talk him out of confronting his father, but Kyle being pig headed wouldn't let it go. He keeps saying he needs closure, and the only way in his stubborn head is to do that face to face. I'm here for damage control, to make sure Kyle doesn't go off the deep end."

"Why, has he done something bad before?"

"When it comes to one of my soldiers, who have seen and done a lot while in combat, I tend to stay close by until all the demons of their past are unlocked. The last thing I want to see is for Kyle to do something stupid and have to pay for his father's mistakes for the rest of his life."

"Do you think he'll do something wrong?"

"Deep down in my heart? No. But sometimes soldiers just snap. I want to make sure my soldier stays intact."

Trying to turn off her overreacting brain, Sophie knew she had a job to do, not only as Kyle's submissive, but as his future. "I need to tell him what I've uncovered. Its best I get this over with tonight, versus waiting until tomorrow when it's too late."

"I see why he loves you so much."

Sophie knew it was better to do this in front of everyone instead of waiting for them to leave. She knew Kyle would only be calling them back over after she disclosed her findings.

Sophie carried a bottle of Kyle's favorite scotch and four glasses. She felt it was better to have some liquid courage just in case Kyle went ballistic in front of everyone.

As, she walked back into the living room with the tray of drinks, she listened to the guys shooting the shit. Jake was talking about how he had been unsuccessful with finding a submissive. Kyle had given him some names of potential submissives that were currently un-collared. Sophie's ears perked up when she heard Kyle mention Candy's name as a potential partner.

Pouring each person a nice shot of scotch, Sophie placed the drinks in front of each person. "Thank you baby, you must have known that I needed a drink." Sophie watched as Kyle sipped his scotch. It was now or never, feeling like she might chicken out, Master Sarge gave her a slight nod indicating she needed to speak her peace.

"Master Kyle, I need to ask you a question." Sophie was now sitting on Kyle's lap.

"Yeah baby, what is that you need to ask me?"

"I noticed something when going through the information about your father."

She felt Kyle's body stiffen up. He didn't say anything. The next few seconds seemed like days.

"Baby, what's wrong?"

Sophie picked up the first photo instead of saying what she needed, she pointed to exact spot on the picture indicating his ring finger.

She felt Kyle's thighs harden under her ass. "Sarge were you aware of this finding?"   Sarge ran his fingers through his thick, black hair. The look in his eyes said that he already knew who she was.

"Son, I asked you a few weeks ago if you really wanted to delve into this situation fully."

"What's that have to do with knowing whether he's married or not? I just need to know why he left us. I don't give a shit who he's screwing. I'm gathering that you two know who she is by the look on your faces."

"Master, I only know her name, that's all. I couldn't find any other information about her."

"What about you, Sarge, do you know who she is?"

"No, like Sophie the only thing I could find on her was her name. Your little detective there has a real knack for being a good snooper. Her name is Ida Ramirez-Hendricks; they've been married for ten years, and have two children. One boy ten-years-old and a daughter eight- years-old. I couldn't find any pictures of any of them anywhere."

"Master, are you ok?"

"I knew by finding him that things would be unlocked about his life that could be unpleasant. All I'm looking for is some kind of closure." Sophie reached up and stroked the side of his face, just touching him she felt so connected to him.

"I'm here for you, Master. You can lean on me for support. Just like I lean on you for support. We're a team, nothing is going to break our bond that we currently have, no matter what happens tomorrow, I will stand by your side"

"Baby, I needed to hear you say those words. The dominant side of me is burning up inside because I'm dragging you through this mess, but my heart is telling me that I need you by my side more than you'll ever know."

After everyone had left for the night, Sophie felt that her conscience had been wiped clean. The only thing left to tell Kyle was her plans to open her boys' house. That could wait until after tomorrow's meeting.

Chapter Twenty

Kyle had been awake for several hours. The sun hadn't even come up yet. Not wanting to wake up Sophie, he had taken her every way possible, except her ass he was saving that until he collared her.

Hopefully, that would be in the near future. Hearing her tell him that she was standing by his side, deepened the connection the two had for each other He knew that she was his. He had already contacted his personal jeweler to have her engagement ring and collar made. They would be ready for his birthday.

He loved that she had no problem fully submitting to his every command. Last night was no exception. Taking her in his primal state fueled her to a deeper subspace than she had ever experienced before.

Pushing his physical stamina, Kyle took a long run along the beach, and felt his muscles burn from the amount of energy he exerted. He needed this type of release from time to time. It helped recenter him. Once he reached his euphoria cleansing, concluding his business transaction with his father could be an obtainable goal.

He knew now that Sophie was totally committed to their relationship. Cleaning up the shit with his father, couldn't take that long, he hoped. He had researched the island on different places to visit; he planned on spending the rest of the vacation showing his girl the best time of her life.

Finally, when he reached the beach house he found Sophie already showered, dressed and set to go meet his father. She even had Rosa make breakfast for the two of them. Sophie had set the table perfectly for the two of them.

He noticed that she learned a lot from Candy about formal and informal service already. He loved seeing her shine when it came to serving him in the manner he loved. As she expanded her training, he was sure that they would host many parties in the future.

Two hours later, Kyle was ready to tackle the obstacle that brought them to Puerto Rico. He would be at the top of his game when meeting with his father.

Sitting in the waiting room of Hendricks Associates, even though the air conditioning was on, Kyle felt like he had sweat running down his back. Darlene, the perky secretary, greeted all of them, welcoming them to Puerto Rico, and Hendricks Associates.

After taking their seats, Kyle went into an op mode. He made sure he had an exit plan in place if things got out of hand. He made sure his phone was connected to Jake and the Sarge's phone. He wasn't sure how his father was going to react being face to face after all these years. He needed to make sure Sophie wasn't in any kind of danger. Positing himself next to Sophie on the sofa, Jake stood behind Sophie and The Sarge stood closest to the door.

Time seemed to stand still, as they waited. He felt Sophie's hand caress his fingers, she had a way of soothing him when he needed her touch. Having her by his side was all he needed to get through this.

He heard the intercom at Darlene's desk ring. He knew it was show time. No turning back at this point. Sophie whispered into his ear when she felt him tense up.

"Master, I'm here for you. I love you, no matter what happens."

He saw the love in her eyes and it touched him in a way that was breathtaking. "I love you, Sophie. Thank you for being by my side." He reached down and tilted her chin up, not wanting to break that connection; he took his lips and gently kissed hers. The power exchange that was given between the two of them was electrifying.

"Mr. Champion, Ms. Johnson, Mr. Hendricks will see the two of you now." Kyle stood, being the gentleman and helped Sophie to a standing position. He ran his hands down his Armani suit making sure he looked his best. He had come a long way from the boy he used to be.

When his father last saw him, he was just a teenager, who didn't know what he was doing with his life. He was the menacing boy that liked to get in trouble with his cousins. Playing pranks, hooking classes, underage drinking the normal things that most teenagers did Kyle did ten times better. At least once a month, Kyle's father was called to the principal's office for something Kyle had done.

Focusing on the here and now, Kyle squared his shoulders back, and walked into his father's office. Holding Sophie's hand, he felt her give him a squeeze as they entered.

Seeing his father's face for the first time in many years, Kyle felt his stomach churn. "Welcome Mr. Cham... Holy shit what are you doing here?"

"Is that the best you can do? Not even a 'hello son'?" Daniel Zellar looked like he had just seen a ghost. No, it wasn't a ghost. He hadn't seen his adult son since the age of thirteen.

At first the pain in Kyle stomach was an unpleasant feeling, but fighting through it, suddenly the pain eased up. Realizing he had surprised the shit out of his father. Kyle suddenly felt larger than life. He finally found the man he once called father. Now he had to find out why his father abandoned him.

"Well, Father, you look like you've seen a ghost. Let me assure you, I'm not a ghost but rather I'm one of your children that you chose to abandon years ago."

"Kyle, that's not really what happened."

"So do tell. What really happened that dreadful morning. Before you answer my question, I'd like to introduce you to my girlfriend, Dr. Sophie Spencer."

"Hello, Ms. Spencer. Wouldn't you be more comfortable if you waited out in the waiting area? I think I need a few moments alone with my son."

Before Sophie could answer that question, Kyle said, "No, she's not going anywhere. Whatever you have to say to me, you can say in front of Sophie. Consider her part of the family."

"Miss Spencer, please, make yourself comfortable. Can I have my secretary get you something to eat or drink?"

"No, Sir I'm fine, but thank you."

"Kyle are you sure Miss Spencer needs to be present? Can't we discuss family business just you and me?"

"Like I said to you before, Sophie will be staying by my side. Now, where were we? You were about to tell me why you left us."

Feeling like all the air was being sucked from the room, Kyle started to pace about the room. Waiting for the answer to his question, he took his hands and brushed his hands through his hair. The torment that his father had caused against their family had almost forced his mother to lose everything that meant anything to her.

He remembered hearing his mother cry for hours upon hours, sometimes for days, weeks, and months. Until one day she stopped crying. She told Kyle that she was no longer a weak woman. She had three young children to raise, and that no man was worth her tears, especially not a man that up and left them.

Cold, hard, facts were that his mother overcame her feelings of loneliness by surrounding herself with women who were less fortunate then she was. She raised herself to the powerful woman she was today. Yes, she did it all out of love for her children. Kyle now waited to hear his father's side on why he left them.

"Kyle, there's no easy way to tell you how sorry I've felt. I've lived hating the decision that I had to make, but I did what I did to protect all of you." Having to force himself to stay in full control of his anger, Kyle looked around the room, trying to find answers to many questions that filled his now pounding head.

On the corner of Daniel's desk sat a picture frame of two young children, a boy and a girl sitting at the beach building a sand castle. Kyle presumed this must be his half brother and sister, but did not say a word.

Just hearing his father's voice almost made Kyle's stomach lurch, knowing whatever his father said would most definitely open wounds that never got a chance to heal.

"How does getting up one morning, being a happy family equate to by lunchtime you're long gone? Dropped off the face of the earth, nowhere to be found. How does that result in protecting us? I just don't get it. When someone says they're protecting themselves, they do just that. They don't get up and run."

"Kyle, I had no choice. Either I stayed and watched the people I loved get hurt, or I did the most unthinkable thing. I left."

"But why?"

"Like I said, I had to. It's as simple as that. I protected my family by leaving. I know it wasn't the easiest thing I ever did, but it saved all of you from being harmed."

"You're not making any sense. How where we going to be harmed and by whom?"

"I got involved with the wrong people. My business was going to shit, and at the same time I was being watched by the government. Take a seat Kyle, you're driving me crazy pacing back and forth. If you must know everything, I will tell you."

Sophie patted the sofa that she was now sitting on. It wasn't like Kyle was nervous or anything he just wanted answers from his father. He wasn't here to try and build a relationship with his father. He never saw that in his future, he just wanted answers, so that he could move on with his life.

"Back when I started Zellar & Styles Corporation in the late seventies, my late partner Michael Styles got greedy. He made our company soar in less than two years' time. All because he needed to be the best of the best. He was a wiz at getting new clients and having them invest without even questioning his ethics.

What he was doing was robbing Peter to pay Paul. That seemed to work for years before anyone caught on to his strange business deals. I met a few of the big wigs who invested a shit ton of money, but never really knew who they were. I had no idea what was going on. I used my marketing skills to draw potential money making deals to get products shipped to the US.

It was only when one of the crime family heads came to visit me on the golf course, looking for his share that was owed to him. I had no idea what he was talking about; he laid everything out for me. How much he put in and how much he was owed. What was even more shocking was when he showed me what other mafia families' investors had put in and they were all going to come collecting. Still being left out in the dark, I was shocked to find that after ten years of being in business, my friend and partner could have made such deals with criminals.

There was no way Zellar & Styles was worth anything. All the books had been doctored to look like we were a fortune five hundred company, but that wasn't the truth."

Kyle looked at his father as he continued to tell his story, and at some point Sophie held his hand in hers stroking his fingers. That always seemed to calm down Kyle. She touched his heart by the slightest touches, and this one was his favorite one.

He watched as Sophie just sat and listened, she was like a quiet little mouse, taking in everything. She sat by his side just as she said she would, knowing that she was his lifeline. He wondered if his father's problems with the mafia would be a trigger for Sophie. He'd need to watch her closely, to look for signs of any problems. His main concern now was being the protector, lover, supporter, and future husband to her.

Kyle watched as Daniel picked up the phone. "Darlene, please bring in some coffee and tea for our visitors, and when Ida arrives please buzz me right away."

"Sure thing, Mr. Hendricks."

"Now where was I?"

"You were just about to tell me why you left. Which it seems like your just stalling, I don't really care about how your business, was successful or even failed. I just need to know why. What was so important that you couldn't stay?"

Hearing the desperation in Kyle's voice must have somehow scared Sophie because he felt her stiffen. "Baby, are you alright?" She now had a look on her face that told Kyle she was fighting her inner emotions.

"I'm good, don't mind me."

"Baby, at any time you want to leave you just say the word. I'll have Jake stay with you."

"No, Kyle, please. I can handle this as long as I'm with you."

"Okay."

The door to the office opened and Darlene came in carrying a tray with three mugs, a carafe of coffee, and a second carafe of hot water. A small wooden box sat next to the carafe's along with a small bowel of sugar and tiny pitcher of cream.

Sophie instantly went to help Darlene, with the beverages. She handed a nice steamy hot cup of black coffee to Kyle. He was so pleased how her service skills had come along, and he watched as she went back and made herself a cup of tea. Maybe with a little caffeine they could speed up the meeting, he could forget about his father, and finish his vacation with Sophie, buried deep inside of her for the rest of the trip.

After waiting for Daniel to start talking, Kyle became a little impatient. "As much as I would love to sit here for the rest of the day hashing out shit with you, I've got more important things to do. Please get on with the rest of your story."

"I understand you're bitter. God knows you have the right to be, but I did it out of love for all of you."

"How did I know you were going to say that? Isn't that the line of every lying, cheating man? Am I right or wrong?"

"You only know half of the facts, the half that I wanted people to find, I hid a lot from the world to protect you, your brother, sister and especially your mother. After, I was contacted, by the mafia looking for their paybacks, I had nowhere to turn to, no one to turn to for help. I couldn't talk any sense into Michael about turning over the uncooked up books. Instead, things began to build up and build up.

I got paid a second visit from the mafia, and if you thought the first meeting was bad, the second one was even worse. They started with threats on how they were going to start taking out different important people that were involved in the scandals around the business. At first, I wasn't sure what that meant until I got a phone call from one of the accountants' wives, saying that her husband had committed suicide because of his work at Zellar & Styles.

My first thought after hearing such sadness was the guy was stressed. His wife had just had a baby, and they were having financial problems, it wasn't until I had my third encounter with the Mafia, they asked if I liked their calling card. I wasn't sure what they were talking about at first, but then it hit me they were talking about killing Charlie.

I started noticing little things, Michael was no longer coming to the office, and he was never available. I even went by his house unannounced. Still I couldn't find him. That's when I was contacted by US Custom's, about some illegal activity concerning Zellar & Styles. After several long interrogation sessions with them I knew Michael had fucked up badly. I started making my exit plans immediately.

I went to your grandfather and borrowed money. I told him that I was setting up another company but didn't have a backer, and he agreed to loan me the money. I started Hendricks Association with that money. I never told your grandfather the ins and outs but he somehow knew what was happening.

I pushed your mother away slowly. I'd stay out late, wouldn't come home for days at a time, then I started traveling more and more. I had to make it look like Zellar & Styles was still thriving. It was about a month after I returned from Europe that I knew I only had a limited time left before something drastic happened. By this point, your mother wanted nothing to do with me. She accused me of running around on her.

I tried everything in my power to prove to her that wasn't the case. She didn't want any shame brought down on the family. Several weeks later, Michael, Gloria, Bradley and Meagan Styles bodies were found floating in Loch Raven Reservoir leaving me with a hell of a mess. I knew at that point the mafia was serious about making their threats a reality.

I know you probably don't understand, but it was a hard decision in my life that I had to make. I did what was best for you guys." Kyle felt Sophie shift on the sofa. Trying not to notice too much, he put his hand on her left knee. She settled instantly down.

"Tell me something, this whole time, did you ever give a damn about any of us?"

"Every day I had no contact with any of you, I knew you were safe. A part of my heart was left behind knowing that I would never have contact with any of you. As the years went by, it got easier and easier to cope with my decision. I knew the statute of limitations on a missing person was seven years, and knowing your mother like I did, I knew she would file for a divorce. That's why I never came back. I was sure if I came back that would only put the radar back on all of you. I made sure no one could trace my whereabouts when I left. Kyle, believe me when I say I knew nothing about what Michael had gotten us into until it was too late."

"Why didn't you seek out help from the FBI, or even someone in the state department? I know you were well connected with political figures back then."

"You're right. I was, but they were all corrupt and on the payroll of the mafia. I had no one to turn to. So I took matters into my own hands. My only problem was knowing that I had no one to turn to for help."

"What about your new life you've made for yourself here? I guess once you left us behind, you really didn't give a shit how Julia was going to be able to raise three young children by herself."

"That's not true, Kyle. I knew your grandparents would assume the role that I left open. Your grandfather had enough land and money to support you guys comfortably. He assured me that if something ever happened to me he would always be there for all of you. I left certain things behind for each of you that meant something to me.

Your grandfather was in charge of seeing that each of you each were given those items. I know you got yours on your graduation from high school. You're wearing the watch I left for you."

Kyle took his hand and ran it over the watch facing, not trying to cover it up. He needed to feel the way he did on his graduation. He had been given the watch by his grandfather who handed him a note from his father. He never opened the note but his heart told him to wear the watch.

Even when he was overseas fighting in the military he wore the watch, many nights when alone in a bunker during his watch he would listen to the tick tock of the clock. As long as he heard that sound, he was able to go on. During different low points in his life, Kyle never took off the watch.

Hearing the ring of the telephone snapped Kyle out of his thoughts and back to the present... Sitting in his father's office hearing about how much danger they were in, all due to a bad business decision from his greedy partner. He heard Daniel say, "Ok Darlene, just give me a minute I will come out and get her."

Then he continued speaking to his son. "What you need to know Kyle, is that it took almost a year to plan and set everything up so that no one got suspicious. Every day I died just a little bit inside my heart knowing that I would be leaving you. At some point, I left a clue about what I had been planning. Carmela found a folder with my new identity.

She came to me asking what I had gotten myself involved in. At first, I tried to push her away, but as she figured out everything. I had to confide in someone and that someone was Carmela. I couldn't tell your mother because she already thought I was fooling around with someone. Keeping up with the act so she didn't become suspicious and blow my cover, was extremely hard. Carmela became my pawn, she helped set up things in London, and then a few years later here in Puerto Rico. She used her family connections with the local Mafia, to find out about anything and everything that happened back in the US.

The day I left was the worst day of my life. I felt like I was dead. Worse, I had to make myself believe you too were dead, even though I knew you were all safe at the time. Carmela, watched over you guys for the first year.

She made sure that everyone adjusted to the changes. When Julia decided to let Carmela go, it was a total shocker to Carmela and me. Being told her services were no longer needed, and then only given a two week severance check was the biggest slap in the face, considering Carmela had given almost fifteen years of service to our family."

"Wait… just a minute. Julia told us that she could no longer afford to pay for Carmela and that's why she had to let her go. She said you wiped out all the accounts before high tailing it out of Baltimore leaving her penniless, and if it weren't for your parents who provided shelter, food and warm beds at night for all of us, we would have been out on the streets. So don't give me that bullshit about how letting Carmela go was my mother's fault because it wasn't. It was one hundred percent yours. You were looking out for just yourself. No sane man would have picked up and left his family. Instead, he would have thrown himself to the wolves, but no, you ran like a coward in my book."

"Kyle, I know you don't believe me, but I wasn't taking the easy way out. Living everyday locked away from my family, has been like I was locked up in a jail. Living this way has been no picnic, I can assure you. I tried everything possible to get out of the mess Michael put us all in, but talking to the Mafia was liking talking to that trashcan.

All they wanted was their money and I didn't have it, and had no way of ever getting it for them. I stalled for as long as I could, but after they killed Michael and his family,

I knew we were next, and I wasn't going to let that happen to all of you.

Carmela told me how close they came to you guys, but when they finally believed that I was no longer in the picture they stopped snooping around. After Carmela got fired, she realized she had nowhere to go. She showed up on my doorstep in London. I couldn't throw her out, since she had helped me escape and protected you guys while I couldn't. I felt like I owed her, so I took her in.

I keep her out of the spotlight. I knew she kept her connection back in Baltimore, and she had them watch and protect all of you, and in return I was assured that no harm would come to any of you as long as I never showed back up. So instead of having no one, I had Carmela on my side. I made a deal with Carmela's family, as long as they keep all of you safe, I'd fund as many of their endeavors as necessary and take care of Carmela forever."

"You keep telling me what you lost. How about us, what do you think we lost?"

"I know what you lost, Kyle. You lost me."

"No you're wrong, I lost the man who I looked up to as my hero, the man who wasn't there when I needed to learn how to drive. The man who wasn't there when I had questions about my first love. The man who wasn't present at my high school graduation. The man who wasn't there when I enlisted in the military to serve my country and family. The man who wasn't there when I got my psychology degree. The man who wasn't there when I started my practice or my first business.

Do I need to tell you how you weren't there for Derek or Piper, or for the rest of the family? So, while you sit there telling me how much you ache and moan about what you lost, did you ever consider what we lost?" Kyle waited for his father to answer his question, but deep down in his heart he knew that there was no comparison to what he had gone through growing up.

"You're correct. I did miss out on so many important milestones in your life. I was forced to, but what you choose not to admit is that I instilled in you as a young child right from wrong. I gave you the foundation of life, which you use every day to be the man you are. You're true to yourself and everybody that surrounds you. You take on challenges that seem to be overcoming at times but you always prevail.

Your business sense is a gift that I always knew you had deep down inside your heart, even at the age of ten, I saw it when you were with your friends. You'd seek power from the youths around you. You became the ultimate leader, just as I did at a young age. I imprinted these things on your heart.

I had a feeling that someday you'd seek me out from my hiding, and that day was today. I know you hate me, and that I will have to live knowing for the rest of my life."

Taking a deep breath in Kyle had listened to his father's words. He did feel like they were piercing his soul. He knew if he ever found his father that most likely some kind of danger lurked behind why his father left. Hearing his father's voice finally give him the reason why was the closure Kyle needed.

Desperately, Kyle struggled to fully understand the logic behind getting into bed with one Mafia family to protect what he once loved, but if that's what his father did and said, and did it with compassion, it must be true. The big question that burned inside of Kyle's head was what would become of his relationship with his father now that he knew what his father did for them?

It had been years since he last saw his father or Carmela. Even though his father had aged he still looked rather fit and healthy. He wondered if the same was true about Carmela. Knowing what he knew now about how Carmela was fired by his mother, and then looked after all of their safety did lighten up Kyle's heart towards her. It was his father he was angry and bitter towards, having this kind of emotions towards someone Kyle knew that it was unhealthy to say the least. The big question still remained unanswered now that he knew his father was alive, remarried, and had children. What was he going to tell his family back in Baltimore?

"Did you ever think for just a moment what would happen if and when we found you? How do I to go about living my life knowing that you live here in Puerto Rico, under a different name, with a new family? What do I tell Derek, Piper and Mom when I get back?"

"I always had that fear deep in the back of my mind that one of you would be smart enough to figure it out. Had I ever considered what would happen? No. What are you planning on telling your brother and sister?"

"The only person that knows your possible existence is Derek. We felt that telling Piper would just send her into another fit of acting out. So all she knows is that I took Sophie on vacation to get away from her concerning issues surrounding her gang member attack."

"Mind filling me in on Sophie's problem? Maybe our connections can help deter any further attacks."

"Sophie was shot five weeks ago by a local gang member because his family member died after Sophie tried to save his life. The surgery she performed wasn't successful, so they took out retribution on her and her friend. Luckily I had CCTV in place at her apartment and was able to have them picked up from the police. Hopefully everything's over."

"Kyle, that's what you think, but I know firsthand knowledge from having to deal with gangs, the mafia, and government officials that once you're on their radar, you'll never be truly free."

"I got this. Sophie will always have me to protect her. Thanks for your input." Kyle really didn't need his father trying to help in his situation, he needed to take care of his own business first. He still didn't have an answer to his question about whether to tell Derek about their father, though. He still had some time to think this shit storm through, though. Thank goodness, he could wrap up this meeting with his father. He wasn't here to rebuild a relationship with him, he was just here to confront him, and now that he had done just that, he could go on with the rest of his life. It helped knowing that it wasn't something they had done to cause his father's disappearance; it was his greedy business partner.

"I'm guessing that Carmela is waiting outside with your secretary?"

"Yes she is. When you set up the meeting, Carmela was filling in for Darlene, which she does from time to time. You were actually speaking to her on the phone. Carmela likes to help where she is needed. She was excited to meet the two of you, and she was going to tag along during our trip to the factory. She takes pride and joy with showing how well the factory runs with all of our workers. So she agreed to join us after our initial meeting in the office. Kyle be kind to her. She has saved me from doing the unthinkable. She really does have a heart of gold. She was my rock throughout these years."

Sophie tried not to show her emotions this whole time, Kyle knew she was torn by the look she had plastered across her face. "Soph, are you ok?"

"I'm good. Would you like a few minutes with just you, your dad, and Carmela? I know it's been a long time since you've seen her. I could go out with Jake and wait."

"No Sophie, I want you by my side. You're my family now and I wouldn't have it any other way." Kyle reached over and stroked her cheek. Hearing her sigh was like music to his ears.

"Ok, whatever you want, I'm here for you."

"How about I go out and get Carmela and the four of us sit and talk?" Kyle nodded his head in agreement with his father's plan.

"That's fine with us." It had been almost twenty-one years since Carmela had been Kyle's nanny. The last time he saw her, she had given him a lapel pin that said Zellar & Styles. Kyle never wore the pin but ever so often he would pull it out and just stare at it, thinking someday it would tell him the stories that had been locked away.

He had never put two and two together about her and his father. He secretly thought about his father being attracted to Carmela but when Kyle thought those things he knew his father was loyal to his mother. Finding out now that his father never crossed that line with Carmela had eased an ache that Kyle felt.

As Carmela walked through the office door, Kyle took one look at her and ran into her arms. He always felt a sense of worth, and being alive when he was under her grasp. She had a way of making him feel protected, and he was glad he still felt that way towards her after all these years. If it had been anyone other than Carmela who had helped his father, he probably wouldn't have believed his father's story. However, since Carmela was a huge part of the plot, he had to forgive both of them for what they had done to him and his family.

"Kyle, I can't believe it's really you standing in front of me."

"It's really me, Carmela."

"You're all grown up. I'm so happy you found us after all these years"

"I had no idea that by finding Daniel, I would find you too."

"I had to help your father Kyle. Please forgive me. He had no one else to turn to. Your father was so lost for a few years or so after he left you guys. I was worried he was going to do something to jeopardize everything that was set up for him. That's why I had to help him."

"Carmela I hold no ill feelings against you at all. Even though I don't fully understand, I'm willing to try to forgive." Kyle's terms of endearment towards Carmela had just come out of his mouth without second guessing himself. He looked over to Sophie who still sat on the sofa, and she had tears running down her cheeks. He saw the love in her expression on her face.

"Carmela, I'd like to introduce Dr. Sophie Spencer to you. She's the love of my life. She's the one who gets me going in the morning, the one that pushes me through the day and the one I say my last good night to before I close my eyes. She happens to be my world. She reminds me of you; she has the same kind heart as you do. She loves everyone that she comes in contact with, no matter who or where you come from, Sophie loves unconditionally. Just like you."

Kyle held on to Carmela for dear life, and motioned over to Sophie to join him in greeting her. As soon as Sophie approached the two, Carmela broke from her hug with Kyle and immediately took Sophie in her arms. She kissed her on her cheek. Kyle felt an instant release of all the anger he had built up inside him for twenty-two years against his father. Seeing Carmela made him realize that fact. His father had been taken care of the same way he had been taken care of by Carmela. She gave unconditional love because that is what she was really made up of.

After getting reacquainted with Carmela and Daniel, Carmela asked if Sophie and Kyle would care to join them back at their house for dinner. She also told them about his half brother and sister. Even thought they were very young, they were smart for their ages. Carmela felt that it would be better if the children were told that they were out of town guests coming to visit, and not that they were actual family.

Kyle agreed that bringing in children at this point was not very wise, just as he was only going to tell Derek of his findings. They would wait to tell Piper when she was more stable in her life. .

Chapter Twenty-One

Two days had gone by since Kyle had been reconnected to part of his past with his father and now his new stepmother Carmela. Sophie realized that tomorrow they would be heading back to Baltimore. So much had transpired in the short time. She still hadn't said a word to Kyle about her future plans for the boys' home. She wasn't even sure if it was right time to bring it up; she was running out of time because when they returned to Baltimore she hoped that her father would have almost everything ready to move forward.

Sophie called back home, spoke to her father and he assured her everything was up and running smoothly. Seeing that Kyle had professed his love to her on several occasions, and since he even met with his father without her or Carmela, she knew that anything she had to say to him he would love.

Basking in the warm sun of Puerto Rico allowed Sophie to focus on relaxing and writing the letter that her new therapist Lisa had instructed her to do. At first, Sophie pondered whether or not she could really be honest enough to write the letter to her mother, but once words started to appear on paper, they flowed without any hesitation. Nine pages later, Sophie felt a huge weight lifted off her chest.

She didn't necessarily blame her mother for her specific issues, but more or less wanted to rebuild a relationship with her mother that she hadn't had as a child. She wanted a mother-daughter friendship, someone Sophie could call up and ask advice from, or get direction when needing to be guided.

Sophie realized that not all of her problems were centered on her mother; Sophie too would share the blame. She had been the one who had isolated herself. It's funny, Sophie had never let herself relax before, but being in paradise unlocked some of her pent up unhappiness. She felt a sense of worth, not for the surgical skills but for the Sophie skills. She couldn't wait to get back to Baltimore to finish planning Kyle's birthday party with the rest of the girls. She had so much to look forward to, and most of all she had Kyle to share her ups and downs with.

Rosa had prepared a barbecue cookout feast for dinner. Everyone sat under a large cabana on the beach. Kyle had invited Daniel, Carmela and their two kids for dinner. She wasn't sure when the next time Kyle would be able come back and visit them, so she asked if he could have them over one last time before they returned back home.

Watching the Hendricks children play along the shore, sent a spark through Sophie's soul. She knew not every child was fortunate enough to be raised by loving parents; this only emphasized the importance of her future boys' home. Before the Hendrick's left for the evening, Sophie pulled Kyle aside asking him if he would mind having his picture taken with his newfound family. Carmela had come to her earlier in the evening asking Sophie if she could persuade Kyle, and if she could, Carmela would be forever grateful.

Convincing Kyle to do this for Carmela was easy as pie. He didn't have any hard feelings against her, he just wished that his father would have made different choices, that's all.

She hoped that in time, Kyle could truly forgive his father. Sophie knew that was way down the road.

Once everyone was gone, Sophie had Rosa clean up everything under the cabana, while she and Kyle took their final nightly stroll on the beach. She felt closer to Kyle than she ever had. Their vacation had its ups and downs, but most of all she was finally with the man she wanted to spend the rest of her life with. She still had issues to overcome but knowing that Kyle was beside her, she could accomplish anything.

Halfway down the beach, Sophie slipped her hand inside of Kyle's shorts pocket. She loved holding onto him this way. It was now or never for her to spill her guts. She was experiencing the come to Jesus talk and it was now. "Master, I need to tell you something." Kyle stopped walking and slowly sat down on the sand, pulling Sophie down on his lap. "Go ahead, you have my full attention."

"Ok, before I tell you what I need to tell you, can you kiss me?"

"Baby whatever you need, or want, all you have to do is ask. You know that I love kissing you, so if you need a kiss, I'm your man. Bring those beautiful voluptuous lips to mine. She felt Kyle cup her head, stroking his finger through her hair as their lips met.

Kyle could win an award for being the best kisser in the world, and she was glad his lips belonged only to her and no one else. She needed that little reinforcement knowing that he loved her; he was her wind beneath her wings.

Separating their mouths left Sophie's heart pounding. "I love you, Kyle Zellar. You've opened up my heart, my eyes, and my desires to everything around me."

She saw Kyle stare back at her with a puzzled look. He pulled her even closer to him.

"When we get back to Baltimore, I'm dropping the charges against Devon Webster. Deep down in my heart I feel he deserves a second chance at life. After knowing what

I know about his upbringing, or lack of upbringing I can't see him rotting in some cell for the rest of his life for doing something someone else told him to do.

You probably think I've gone crazy, but I assure you I haven't yet. I don't know what will happen in the future but today I'm perfectly sane. There's a second part to this. When Carl died, he left me a shit ton of money and I mean a lot. He also left me his shares in Volkov Construction, and a beautiful house that I haven't set foot in since Carl died. I plan on changing that. When we get home, I'm meeting with a decorator who plans to furnish the house with everything that will support and house, up to ten boys who are wards of the state, hopefully my first resident will be Devon Webster. I plan on giving them every opportunity that they need to make something for themselves.

I met with my dad before we came here; he's been handling all the legal aspects of getting the permits, making sure it's zoned properly, even down to getting local support. I might not ever go back to being a surgeon, and I've come to grips with that. But what I realized is I can still practice medicine by teaching at either Maryland's School of Medicine, or at Johns Hopkins. I'm going to give it my all with rehab and hopefully I will be able to go back to work at the hospital, but if I can't I will fill my heart with other things that causes happiness.

Now for my last confession of the night… I talked to Lisa about my nightmares that I've been having since the shooting. They started out with Carl and me in the car the night he had the accident. At first I didn't put two and two together, but after having it more and more, it finally was like I was watching a rerun on TV. I think I was a target way back then. The last words Carl said to me were, 'No brakes, baby. Brace yourself!' Those words didn't register until I started having the same dream, but instead of Carl driving the car, you were driving the car. Not only did it startle me, but it jogged my memory of before the accident. I started getting threats then.

Most likely I was the target back then, but unfortunately Carl drove my car that night. I know in time that Lisa is going to work with me about some of my fears and insecurities and I want you by my side. I'm not doing all these things to be the best but instead I'm doing them out of love. It's one thing to do all this without the support from the person you love.

Which brings me to my next problem. I need my independence back. That's one of the things I remember you telling me that you loved about me. You wanted and needed a woman to love you back and I do love you unconditionally, but most importantly, you needed your woman to be able to take care of your property, which is me. I want to be that person again.

I know me wanting independence sounds horrible, but at some point I'll need to start driving myself again. You know I love Jake but him babysitting me is not going to work forever. I have no problem with having a security person with me when I go out, but I don't want to feel trapped. Hopefully my feeling will come back in time and I can regain the full use of my arm. So now that I dropped the bomb on you what do you think?"

"First off, I love you Sophie Spencer, and nothing that you say to me will ever change that. Secondly, not pressing charges against Devon Webster is definitely your choice. In a way I see where you're coming from. Take a bad situation and turn it into a positive. Maybe by doing this act of kindness the potential gang threat will be lifted and you can go and come without being scared.

We take risks every day when we step out of the house. Today it's the gang members and tomorrow it could be a greedy business partner, but that doesn't mean we should lock ourselves away from the world. What I'm trying to say is that we've got to be aware, possible threats do exist.

As for you having dreams and remembering what happened, I think is a positive step in your recovery. Not only did you remember an important part of the accident but it also made you realize that no matter where or when, danger could come knocking on your door. You replaced Carl by adding me into your dream, which essentially means you have the same need to protect me that you had for Carl. That to me is more touching than anything that has ever been done for me.

Your independence is all up to you. Every day you've been taking back that part of you; I see it and so does everyone around you. I love that I can provide that part of security for you. As your Master, part of my Mastering is protecting you. I thrive off of knowing that I can control how, who, and what protects you. As we go forward that can be a workable decision we both strive to achieve together. We'll learn how to protect each other. When we get home, I want your gun in a safe, next to your bed at night. Not in your purse in the kitchen left at night until the next day. If you're serious about protecting me and you, your gun will only work when it's near you."

"How did you know about the gun? Wait did Jake tell you?"

"No baby. Jake didn't say a word."

"Then who?"

"Your dad called me once you left the range. He felt it was best that I knew. Even though you tried to shoot the thing, you still didn't have the strength or accuracy yet."

"I'm going to kill him for telling you."

"Now, now. There'll be no killing of any fathers this week."

Sophie let out an obnoxious laugh, "Are you serious about that?"

"As bad as I hate what my father did to us by leaving, I still don't think I could kill him, and I know the same goes for your father. You'd never do anything to hurt your dad."

"God, how did you get to be so smart?"

"We both had great a support team.

Which brings us to your boys' home. I think starting a boys' home is a wonderful idea. If I can suggest a few things I would like for you to hear me out.

Candy would be a wonderful person to run the entire facility. You know her background about growing up on the streets. She doesn't have formal training, so send her to school to finish up her degree as a program director.

Secondly, you need a licensed child psychologist. Kora Phillips would be perfect. She only works at Lisa's place when Lisa works with a child's parent, which isn't that often. If Kora needs help, I will be her back up. I happen to be trained in both adult and child psychology.

Thirdly, furnishing the place I'll leave to you and your decorator, but as a tribute to Carl, Volkov Security will foot the bill. Sky's the limit."

"Do you really mean it?"

"Yes baby, I really do mean it."

Sophie stared up into his eyes, and her heart began to ache from the things he just told her. She couldn't believe that Kyle was going to support her one hundred percent with her plans. Nothing could be any better than making love on the beach under the stars and the moon with her Master. She didn't want to make the first move so she began to tease him by licking her lips together. She had become a great tease when she wanted sex. Tonight was no different than the rest of the time.

Saying goodbye to Puerto Rico was kind of hard for the both of them. For Kyle knowing that half of his other family now lived here, keeping their secret safe was all Kyle could do at this point. He did made a promise to Sophie that they would return in the future. She was at peace when he told her they would return.

Chapter Twenty-Two

The last eight days had passed by so fast, since Sophie and Kyle had returned from their trip from Puerto Rico. She had been extremely busy and her days and night were beginning to be a big blur. Sophie had checked, double-checked, and even triple-checked making sure everything was set and ready to go for Kyles surprise birthday party.

She made sure Kyle had his morning breakfast before even getting out of bed. She loved when he devoured her body like a starving man who was about to take his last bite of food. He lapped up her juices as they poured from her cunt. Making sure he had his fill of her breasts while in their shower together, Sophie knew that it would be a good two to three weeks before she had any type of play with her nipples after tonight.

Keeping up with her daily rehab and therapy was no different today. George made sure that Sophie felt the burn and soreness in her arm down to her fingers. She was slowly getting some of the feeling back in her pinky, both of them hoped with the extra push in her work out, she would soon start getting feeling elsewhere in her hand.

Shoving Kyle out the door after lunch to go play a round of golf with his brother Derek, Sophie would have enough time to meet Lexi at the spa for a mani/pedi, have her cooch waxed, and style her hair. Her only errand left to run was to have Kyle's birthday present delivered. The jeweler agreed to meet Sophie at the spa to deliver the finished pieces.

Elated with joy, Sophie took the box from Martin. He had exceeded her expectations with the quality of his craftsmanship. He'd taken her original design and added a few more diamonds. She only hoped that Kyle would feel the same way.

Having just enough time, Sophie had Jake drive her over to the club to check in on the final set up. Justine had several crews throughout out the club, all of whom worked feverishly to finish up their perspective jobs.

Everyone was doing a marvelous job. Justine turned the club into every Dom's dream. Canes lined the walls; spanking benches were situated around the room; and rope hung from the three suspension rigs. Demo areas where set up around the room.

In one of the demo areas, Sophie remembered watching a Dom do fire on his bottom, so she had Justine set up the exact scene with a fire table, fire wand torches, white rain foam and glass cups. Master Don was known for drawing attention when he did a fire scene with Orja.

In the center of the room was an area marked off with a tag: Master Kyle. A portable table with a blue chuck covering the silver tray. Sophie took a deep breath as she walked over to the tray. She fingered the black bow that sat on top of small, brightly, wrapped box. She hoped that she hadn't overstepped her boundaries of being a sub, but most of all she prayed that Kyle would actually do what he had told her he would do eventually.

After walking through the entire club making sure all of the stations were set up, Sophie made her way to the kitchen to find Candy.

Seeing Candy do her thing was like watching the cooking network. She could chop, dice, slice just like any well-trained chefs. When Sophie proposed the idea of Candy running her new boys home, seeing the expression on Candy's face was priceless.

Kyle had employed Candy for many years, but never was she ever offered to go to back to college for free. Finally, Candy would be accomplishing a lifelong dream. Candy danced around the large kitchen like she owned the joint. She gave orders to her helpers without even batting an eye. Yup she was meant to run Sophie's boys home.

Before leaving the club to go meet Kyle for dinner, Sophie made her way to the dressing room where her outfit was hanging up in Sophie's locker. Remembering back to the first time she set foot into this area with Candy, brought back memories of how scared and closed off to the world she'd been. Candy had been her guardian angel throughout her first visit. If it hadn't been for Candy's kind words of encouragement, Sophie would not be standing in the same room getting ready to throw a kick ass party for her Master. A burst of shivers went up and down her spine.

Sophie made her way over to her locker, she was grateful that Lexi and Candy insisted that they dress Sophie for the party.

Hanging in the same locker that Candy had assigned to Sophie on her first night coming to the club, hung a beautiful handmade corset. Sophie had never worn a corset before, Lexi and Candy had the best corset maker, measure, design and hand make a steampunk type of corset for Sophie.

The brown leather of the corset matched the leather vest that Kyle had worn on their first encounter. Long gold chains draped down the sides of the corset, which could be attached to a very small thong that sat in the locker.

Sophie had never dressed so risqué before. When Lexi and Candy told her that she was going to have Kyle drooling all over himself, she figured that they knew best when it came to having their Doms go all bat shit crazy. In a way Sophie liked how the corset pulled her waist to a more slender flattering size. Even though she was a size ten, Sophie was super aware of her size ten hips.

She could still breathe and move around comfortably while wearing the corset. Lexi told her since she would be wearing the corset for a few hours while greeting her guests, she needed to be comfortable. Not wanting to pass out from lack of circulation or oxygen from the corset being tied too tightly, Sophie opted to have the corset made just a tad larger, she didn't need friends of Kyle talking about her if she passed out during the party.

Everyone had pitched in to help Sophie pull off the best party possible and Sophie would be forever grateful. She was amazed how most of the club members had never even met Sophie, but somehow that didn't matter to any of them. She had a new extended family, which consisted of life-stylers, something she had never expected. It felt good to be finally accepted for who she was. A submissive. She couldn't wait to repay the next person who needed her help.

Having dinner at Kyle's mother's house took some of the pressure off Sophie for not having to prepare dinner. Sophie felt her phone vibrate in her pocket.

Lexi: Don't forget to eat. You'll need your energy.

Sophie: Kyle's mother made sure of that.

Lexi: T- 1hr.

Sophie: Thank you. For everything.

As soon as dinner was finished, Julia brought out a delicious strawberry shortcake. Decorated with the largest strawberries Sophie had ever seen. Thirty-five candles lit the top of the cake. Julia began to sing happy birthday, as the rest of the family joined in signing along with Julia.

Sophie felt Kyle reach for her hand as he bent to blow out the candles. Sophie always became sappy at anyone's birthday. She hadn't felt this way in a long time. She was so happy that she was finally able to express her emotions in a good way.

Candy motioned for Sophie that it was time to leave for Justine's baby shower. Sophie made her way over to Julia. "Thank you for allowing me to be part of your family tonight. It means a lot to me that you included me."

"Kyle means the world to me, and you're now a part of my son's life. Kyle told me about the boys' home, I'm hoping my help will be needed. Next week let's get together for lunch. You can fill me in on all your plans. You'd be surprised at all of my resources."

"I can't wait. Next Tuesday, then?"

"Great. Ok you two, Sophie needs to get out of here before she's late." Saying her goodbyes was less stressful; she knew that this was her new family. Sophie whispered into Kyle's ear as he took her in his arms, "See ya soon, Master."

"See ya soon, sub."

Lexi, Candy and Orja met Sophie in the women's dressing room. Each woman had touched Sophie's life in such a different way. Lexi had been her BFF since childhood, Candy had been her guarding angel since the first time she visited the club, and Orja had literally nursed Sophie back to health. All three were submissives who loved serving their Masters. What touched Sophie the most was the way they took Sophie into their club making her feel like one of them.

Orja pulled back Sophie's hair, twisting and turning it in such a way that when she was done, Orja had created a beautiful French twist updo, exposing the soft, sensual, sleek, curves of her slender neck.

Candy pulled out a make-up bag. She started applying foundation first, and then she went to outline her eyes with dark black liquid mascara. When she was finally done, Sophie's eyes looked like Candy had painted on thick cat's eyes. Kyle often referred to Sophie as his kitten, what was more fitting was that she had the eyes to play the part. Bright luscious lips finished off her makeup.

Lexi handed Sophie the tiny leather G-string first, then a pair of rhinestone fishnet stockings. The rhinestones went from the top of the ankle up the back of the thigh in a straight line. Lexi picked up the handcrafted corset, wrapping it around her torso. Sophie felt the leather hug her breasts, three bronze clasps lined the front of the corset, making it much easier for Lexi to lace up the back. She began to tug and pull the strings in the back of the corset.

Sophie watched her waist shrink and shrink as Lexi adjusted the back of the corset. She finished off the back with a bow that sat in the middle of her back. Sophie's breasts were tightly bound and popping out of the top of the corset and she just hoped that one of them didn't fall out as she was greeting her guests.

Standing in front of a mirror, Sophie twisted and turned looking at the creation that each of the girls had a part of putting together. She felt warmth touch her heart and she knew that she could cry at this point except for the fear of messing up her make-up.

"Sophie I have one final thing to add to your outfit. Lexi pulled out a delicate multicolor butterfly hair comb. I was actually saving this for your birthday, but after we picked out your corset I knew you had to wear it tonight."

"Lexi, it's gorgeous. You know me so well, don't you?"

"We're sisters, and sisters have each other's backs."

"Shit, you're going to make me cry, and if I do Candy is going to kick my ass because she'll need to reapply my make up."

"I'll fix your makeup first then kick your ass." Candy said to the girls.

"Laughing and giggling in a corset is not easy."

"Yup, that's why we dressed you up first. You look amazing, Sophie. Now get out of here and go walk around while we get dressed. You never know who'll show up first."

Having the rooms full of Kyle's friends had Sophie lusting for her man. She could hardly wait for him to arrive. She had greeted so many people she was sure she would never remember everyone. Thank goodness Lara, the girl at the front desk, had a list of everyone who had signed in. Next week Sophie would send out thank you notes to everyone who attended.

Sophie recognized several guests who were politicians, local law enforcement, and doctors from the hospital. So many different facets of life walked through the club doors. Sophie was honored to be among them.

Marcus, the parking attendant on duty tonight, called the front desk when Derek and Kyle arrived. Sophie had three minutes to gather all of the guests. She was surprised that no play had started yet. Everyone was waiting until after Kyle arrived.

Taking one final look around the room, everything was set and in place. Even the area which held Kyle's birthday present was ready to go.

Sophie went over to where she knew Kyle had to enter the room. Lexi joined her along with Bryce.

The rest of their guests stood behind her and as Kyle entered the room, everyone yelled, "Surprise!"

Kyle stood shocked and stunned until Sophie made her way over to him. "Surprise, Master. Happy birthday." Sophie took off and leapt into his arms, hugging and kissing him like she hadn't seen him in years.

"Baby girl when did you have time to do all this?"

"I had plenty of help."

"I see. You look amazing as hell."

"Thank you, Sir. I had help with that too. Let's go greet some of your guests."

"I think I'm a little under dressed."

"Your clothes are in your office. I had Derek take care of that for me."

"You did."

"Go change, I've got some socializing to do while you're dressing." Him kissing her on the top of her forehead made Sophie feel cherished. She had accomplished what she had set out to do. She had given him the best birthday party ever.

"Ok, I'll be back in a jiffy."

Loving the way everyone seemed to be having a wonderful time, Lexi told her that it was time for her to shine. Watching different scenes beginning to start, sounds of ecstasy, smells of lust filled the room. The music changed from club style music to a more primal beat.

Excitement built up inside of Sophie's stomach. The time had come, and it was now or never. Kyle returned back to where all of his guests were congregating. He was now dressed in his brown leather pants that hugged his waist and his leather vest which was open and showed off his amazing tan from being in Puerto Rico. She could see the outline of his bulging cock. Around his forearm was a gold band that read Master. Seeing his display of beauty in front of her, had Sophie's heart pounding. He was all hers and no one else's.

Chapter Twenty-Three

Sophie reapplied her red lipstick. Kyle loved the color red on her lips, and he often told her that they reminded him of juicy cherries. Thank goodness her corset had a small little zipper that was small enough to hold her lipstick. After kissing and hugging several of their guests, she had to make sure she looked presentable.

Kyle finally made his way back over to where Sophie was talking to Gail and her sub (who was also her husband). Sophie slid her hand into his as he stood listening to Sophie and Gail talk about the boys' home.

After their conversation was over, Sophie motioned to Gail that she was ready. "Master, I have another surprise for you."

"I'm not sure you can top all this."

"Oh, but I think I can."

"Well how about I surprise you first."

"What do you mean?"

"Follow me baby girl." Hand in hand the two strolled to the center of the room. Kyle had Derek go over to the D.J. To turn down the music. Sophie looked around the room, most of the guests were just standing around talking.

"Can I have your attention please?" As everyone turned and looked at both of them standing in the center of the room, Kyle waited for just a few seconds until he had everyone's attention.

"First, I need to thank all of you for surprising me. I'm so touched by the love each and every one of you have shown me. If anyone would have told me a year ago that I would be standing in front of all of you with the most amazing woman by my side, I would have said that you're crazy. My little submissive has done an outstanding job, but now I have a surprise for her. Kitten, kneel before your Master."

Slowly and gracefully Sophie bent her knees sliding down to a kneeling position in front of her Master, tilting her head towards the floor, and spreading her knees apart as wide as her hips would allow. She placed her hands on top of her thighs with her palms facing upward, just as he had showed her several weeks ago.

"I've never collared a slave in front of anyone one before. It gives me great pleasure to have all of my family, my friends and brothers in leather witness this joyous occasion between me and my slave." Everyone watched as Derek handed Kyle a box.

Tears began to run down Sophie's cheeks. She had no clue that Kyle would be collaring her tonight. She knew someday he would want to collar her, but she had no clue that he planned on doing it tonight.

"Sophie Spencer, by accepting my collar around your neck, you're placing yourself into my care. Trust, Honesty, Patience and Integrity are four important characteristics I expect my slave to have. By giving me the gift of being your Master, I will protect, provide, comfort and love you forever. Once I place this collar around your neck, we will be bound as one. You'll be my MINE forever. I will own your body to do with as I wish. You'll wear my collar as a symbol of my ownership, as a sign of you and I becoming as one. Look at me Sophie," he tipped her chin up, making sure she had direct eye contact with him. Not a sound could be heard throughout the entire dungeon. All eyes were on the two of them. "I need to hear your answer."

"Sir, I accept your collar as a symbol of your ownership. I will proudly display and wear your collar for all of our friends and family to see."

Kyle slowly placed the collar around her neck. Thirty diamonds set atop a large black leather band, two O-rings on both sides of her neck, and a two-carat diamond that hung from a silver chain, laid perfectly in the small crevice in the center of her neck.

After locking the collar around her neck he took Sophie's hand and helped her to a standing position. He slowly slid down to his right knee and pulled out a second box.

"Sophie Spencer, will you marry me?"

Tears of joy were now streaming down Sophie's cheeks. "Yes, Master Kyle Zellar. I will marry you."

As he placed the three-carat diamond ring on her left ring finger, the entire room erupted with cheers, clapping and congratulations being shouted throughout the dungeon.

Sophie, was completely swept off her feet, Kyle held her and she cried on his shoulder.

"You've made me the happiest man in the world. I can't wait to properly take you as MINE."

"Master, would you like to have your birthday present?"

"My birthday present is you accepting my proposal. You've made me that happiest man alive."

"My collar is beautiful, and so is my engagement ring, but I have something for you." Sophie walked Kyle over to the area that had been set up for the two of them. She made eye contact with Lexi, Gail and Candy.

The three women, came over to assist Sophie with her birthday present to Kyle. Slowly the women began to undress Sophie in front of her Master. Lexi, slowly took the corset off, Candy bent down and removed Sophie's heels.

Sophie took her hands and slid them down inside of her fish net stockings, and now she was standing in front of her Master in only the small G-string.

Kyle stopped Sophie before she had a chance to remove it. Taking out his knife he cut the small piece of leather away from her hips watching the fabric drop to the floor. "You're beautiful, baby."

Standing in front of him with only the butterfly hair clip in her hair, collar around her neck, and the engagement ring on her finger Sophie stood before her Master completely nude.

Candy picked up the small box from the table and handed it to Sophie, slowly she knelt down in front of her Master presenting him the box. "Master, you told me while I was healing what you wanted to do with my breasts. I present to you the gift of piercing my nipples as a sign of your possession."

Inside the box held two beautifully designed silver hoop nipple rings that held two dangling diamonds. In between the diamonds was a small silver disk that read "Owned." Kyle looked over at Gail, she nodded, agreeing with Sophie's decision.

"Climb up on the table, baby girl. I need to clean off your nipples. You know once I pierce these babies, I'm going to take you in front of everyone."

Sophie already was headed into subspace just by Kyle's words. "My body, is yours Master to do with as it pleases you."

Kyle cleaned off both of her nipples. He was surprised that Sophie had reached out for Gail's hand.

"Mistress Gail, I'm indebted to you forever, for saving my life. Thank you."

"Sophie as long as you make your Master proud and happy that is all I need from you. Now you need to stay still so that you're Master doesn't end up making your piercing lop sided."

Sophie held out her right arm signaling for Lexi to come hold her hand. "Thank you, Lexi, without you I wouldn't be here today. I love you with all my heart."

"Sophie, I need you to be real still. I'm going to apply the clamps to each of your nipples. At first you're going to feel a lot of pinching. I'm going to have Gail hold the clamps for me while I take the 16-gauge needle and pierce your right nipple first, then I'm going to do the same thing to your left nipple. Once the needles are in place I'll replace the needles with the jewelry. You ready?"

"Yes, Master."

Sophie felt the bite of the clamps. She let out a scream, squeezing Lexi's hand. Kyle swiftly fed the needle into her right breast. She felt him do exactly the same thing to her left breast.

"Baby the hard part's over. The needles are in place. All I need to do is replace it with the rings. He could tell the endorphins were kicking in. Both of her pupils were dilated and she was on her way to floating on a huge cloud. Within five minutes Kyle had both of her nipples pierced, cleaned and bandaged up.

Sophie was defiantly in subspace. Lexi and Gail slowly left Sophie's side. Kyle was ready to take what was his. He slowly spread her legs, took his hand and caressed her hips, making his way down to her bare exposed pussy. Sophie began to grind, her pelvis up against his hand. Slowly Kyle lowered his mouth over her pussy. He could smell her essence seeping from her pussy.

"My girl smells like honey." With more swift movement from her hips and pelvis she grinded even harder against his mouth. Kyle slid two fingers inside her pussy and fingered her. With him pulling his fingers in and out of her slowly, she muffled a word from her mouth. Not giving her a chance to collect herself, he knew she had fully given her body over to him, accepting everything Kyle did to her.

She surrendered herself to him. Sophie reared her head back into the pillow as he pushed a third finger into her, giving him full access to what now belonged to him.

Loving the feeling of totally being full sent Sophie yelling out her permission to come.

"Please Master, I can't take much more." She felt his fingers curl upwards until he found her little bundle of nerves. He began massaging her G-spot. Stroking it with his fingers.

"Yes, Sir, Oh My God...feels so good."

"No Pet, you don't have my permission to come yet. If you do, you'll be punished instead of being rewarded."

Her pussy was spread wide open, all juicy, pink and swollen looking at him. Seeing her on display for him made him even harder. He would have this picture forever branded into his mind. His cock was bulging up against the zipper in his leathers. Kyle felt loved when she cried out his name. He gave her two more strokes before pulling his now soaking wet fingers from her swollen pussy. "Clean my fingers like a good girl," he said as he slowly placed his fingers in her mouth and she sucked her own juices off of him.

Sophie had never been on display before, but she was so far gone into subspace that no one existed besides her and Kyle. Just her and her Master, and low beating of drums. Suddenly, feeling empty, Sophie struggled to sit up, all of her muscles ached, and her heart was pounding to the beat of drums.

"Sir, why did you stop," she asked in a raspy voice?"

"Just looking at my beautiful pussy, but I realized something was missing. I need to see my marks on your bronze ass. You have a nice tan from our vacation, but I'm feeling a little sadistic tonight. I want you to feel my possessiveness for the next few days when you sit down, you'll already feel your nipples every time they brush up against your shirt. Knowing that my hands caused that feeling will feed my desires every time I see you squirm."

Taking her legs, looping them up on his shoulders, he gave her ass a nice thwack, leaving a perfectly shaped large handprint, and Sophie screamed out in awe. He slid down in between her legs, and having her ass in the air, he took his hand and thwacked her other ass cheek.

"Oh, yes, Master Kyle."

He loved it when she cried out his name. Giving her two more fast thwacks on her ass again, he slowly lowered his mouth to her pussy and began eating her like she was his favorite dessert. Peach cobbler filled with a lot of cream was what he envisioned when he ate Sophie's pussy.

He licked from the top of her clit all the way down to the crack of her ass, moving his tongue over every sensitive area. When he got back to her pussy, he shoved his tongue into her opening, tongue fucking her until she began grinding up against his mouth.

"My baby girl loves it when her Master eats her pussy, doesn't she?"

"Oh God, Yeeessss, I love everything about my Master."

"Your Master loves everything about his slave. Starting tomorrow we begin preparing your ass to take my big fat cock. I've taken you in every hole except your ass, and I won't be denied that pleasure."

Sophie loved when Kyle talked all dirty and sexy to her. It made her even hotter and wetter for him. He slowly went back to tongue fucking her pussy.

"Oh God, I'm not sure how much more I can take, Sir."

"That's the beauty Sophie, you'll take everything I give you and more, all to please your Master. I have a need to dominate, but my Pet needs to be dominated. The two of us together, we're a perfect match. You're my yin, and I'm your yang."

His words sank deep down into Sophie's once broken heart, touching her in a way no other man had ever done before. He began to lick, bite and stroke her tiny little pearl, hitting her G-spot with the tip of his fingers.

"You are beautiful, slave. I've loved you from the first time I laid eyes on you. I knew then you were mine."

He felt her entire body begin to tremor, Kyle knew that was her sign that she was ready to orgasm.

Not wanting her to fail in front of everyone, he pulled his mouth away from her clit, but continued to stroke her now very swollen G-spot. It had swollen three times the normal size. As her legs started to tremble even more, he softly said to her "Baby, come for me. Let everyone see my beautiful pussy and the shower your about to give my hand."

Deep in subspace, from having her nipples pierced, having her pussy licked, stroked, and finger fucked. To having her ass spanked. She felt Kyle continue to stroke her from inside her pussy. He then went directly to her clit and rubbed it.

Feeling the first burst of her orgasm take her into orbit, Sophie felt the gush of her ejaculation coming from deep down in her pussy. Submitting this deeply, Sophie squirted more freely than anyone Kyle had every been with before and this level of trust touched Kyle's soul. She no longer felt ashamed or embarrassed when she squirted.

Knowing that he could not stand another moment without being inside his woman, he slowly unzipped his leathers, pulled out his very swollen cock and began feeding it into Sophie's swollen wet pussy.

Hearing her moan out, "Please, Master, fuck me hard. I need to have you deep inside of me."

Matching his thrust against hers, Kyle wasn't going to last very long, and he knew it. Hitting up against her cervix, Kyle knew neither was Sophie, "Come with me."

As his words left his mouth he felt Sophie's body shake and release all of her pent energy that had built up inside of her. His seed filled the void that she had once had. Warmth spread across her entire body, slowly floating, feeling free and weightless for what went on for minutes until Sophie felt at peace.

Kyle slowly pulled out of her pussy, looking down at the most amazing woman lying before him. Surrendering her mind, body, and soul to him one hundred percent, he knew by giving her a second chance, they would be soul mates until the end of time.

Grabbing a blanket that had been left for him, he slowly picked up his now sleeping beauty, wrapped her naked body up in his arms, and walked over to one of the nearby empty couches. He held her in his arms, staring at this beautiful person who lay in his arms fast asleep. She finally started to stir, "Master I love you."

"Pet, I love you too."

Sophie never thought that she would ever love again after the death of her first husband, but opening herself up to a whole new lifestyle was just what Sophie needed to make her life complete. She was fortunate to have found the man of her fairy tale dreams.

Kyle filled her life with happiness, peace, and joy. Not knowing what the future held in store for the two of them, Sophie knew that as long as Kyle is by her side she can face everything that is put before her. He was now her protector, lover, Master, and future husband. She could stand up to her fears.

And it was all because he was willing to give her a SECOND CHANCE.

The End

I hope you loved the story between Kyle and Sophie. Next up in the Heart Series, the journey continues with the wedding of Kyle and Sophie and the love between Candy and Derek.

Candy, Sophie's newest friend has had a tough upbringing. Her past fears are suddenly brought back to the surface after helping her friend open a boys' home for abandoned and troubled boys. She is now faced with her own fears of abandonment stemming from her childhood. Life can be challenging when you try to hide from your fears, she bottled up so much of her past and now she is forced to seek help before she can move on with her journey of submission.

Derek Zellar has watched Candy struggle with her issues for the past several years. He watched over Candy after she was brutally beaten up after a being in a bad D/s relationship. Seeing her struggle more and more each day, he knows that he must step in and try to help her with her journey. He too has some of the same fears of abandonment from childhood when his father up and left the family.

Book 3 in the Heart Series: Always and Forever.
Coming winter of 2015.

About the Author

Abigail Lee Justice writes emotional, erotic, romantic suspense that includes a BDSM theme. She creates strong characters who seem real but are flawed in some ways; some couples Happily Ever After will be a work in process. Some characters' problems are just too steamy to fix in one book.

Born and raised in Baltimore City by two wonderful, supportive, loving parents, as a child Abigail made up vivid stories in her head. Until one day a friend told her instead of keeping her stories locked in her head she needed to put them on paper and that's exactly what she did.

Abigail met her husband 29 years ago on a blind date (thanks Dan C.) while working a part time job to put herself through college. She fell madly in love with her Prince Charming and has been since the first day they met.

By day, Abigail practices medicine in a busy Cardiologist practice. By evening she switches her white coat for more relaxed comfortable clothing. She has two wonderful adult sons and a very spoiled chocolate lab. In the wee hours of the night, she writes BDSM romances.

In her spare time when not working or writing, Abigail enjoys reading, concocting vegetarian dishes, exotic vacations, scuba diving, high adventure activities, living in the lifestyle she writes about, and doing lots and lots of research making sure her characters get it just right.

If you'd like to become part of Abigail's street team or become a beta reader for future books, drop Abigail a message on FB @ abigailleejustice or
Visit her website @ www.abigailleejustice.com

58436285R00170

Made in the USA
Charleston, SC
10 July 2016